Dragon PRINCE

THE BRIDE HUNT BOOK 6

CHARLENE HARTNADY

Published by Charlene Hartnady
PO BOX 456, Melrose Arch,
Johannesburg, South Africa, 2176
charlene.hartnady@gmail.com

First Paperback Edition 2017

DEDICATION

To darling sis. Stay as wonderful as you are. Love you always.

CHAPTER 1

S hifters were highly competitive. Tide was a prince for scale's sake, so that made him more competitive than most. He accepted that, thrived off of it even. Pushing down harder on the accelerator, he smiled at the sound of the purr of the engine. At this rate, he'd make it to the bar in no time. It was the speed of the car aided by the fact that he had taken an alternate route. By his careful calculations, he'd get there well ahead of the rest. Call it a mini hunt because he was most definitely on the prowl for a female. A human female. Soft, tasty and so fucking feminine that his mouth watered just thinking about the night ahead.

It had been months since he'd been with one. Far too fucking long. It was one of the hardships that came with being a dragon shifter. Tide could feel his beast, restless beneath his skin. Scales rubbing. A growl lodged deep in his throat, and he had to suppress the urge to push the accelerator down further. All the way to the floor. Thing was, he was on human territory and therefore had to obey their rules.

Fuck it!

He increased the pressure on the pedal, and the sleek SUV obeyed instantly. Tide turned up the radio. Some pop song was playing. Mexican with an English chorus. It was catchy, so he drummed his fingers on the steering wheel. Just a few more minutes and he'd turn off towards town.

What the…? Tide eased off of the gas. His night vision kicked in. Further up the road, he could see a vehicle on the shoulder. Its hazards were flashing. Someone was on their haunches next to the back wheel. As he neared, he eased off the gas. *Fuck!* It was a female, and she looked like she was struggling to loosen the lug nuts. She was putting every ounce of strength she had into the task and… nothing. *Double fuck!*

The female wiped a hand across her forehead, turning to look in his direction. She must have heard his engine as he approached. Her eyes widened as they caught sight of his headlights. They were beautiful, which was rare for a human. Their eyes were usually pretty dull compared to dragon shifters.' His own baby blues had gotten him laid more times than his physique, which was saying something since females loved all the shifters' muscles.

Her green orbs widened, and a look of hope took residence on her face. She pulled in a deep breath, which she held… again, in hope. Hope that he would stop, hope that he would help her.

No! No! No!

This was the last thing he wanted. He planned to rut a damsel, not to rescue one. He wasn't the knight in shining armor, he was the *dragon*. Destroyed plans or not, there was no way he could leave her stranded. Forget that idea, because he could tell by the black smears on her face that she'd been at it for a while. This particular road didn't get much traffic. It wasn't called an alternate route for nothing. It was late and already dark. No place for a human female.

Tide groaned as he pulled in behind her car. So much for making it to the bar before the others. So much for having the first pick of the humans. He'd quickly change her tire and head back out. Even if the female he wanted was already on the arm of another male, he'd win her over, for sure. It wasn't a big-ass ego talking either.

He hopped out of his vehicle and headed over to her.

The human stood up, a big smile on her face. "Thank you so much for stopping." Then her eyes widened, and she swallowed thickly.

"I'm Tide, and it's my pleasure." He hooked his thumbs in his jeans and hunched his shoulders, giving her his best half-smile. This baby had been known to melt the panties right off of the humans. Since it didn't seem to be working on this particular female at the moment, he'd settle for her calming the fuck down. Her heart raced, and he could scent adrenaline. "Can I help change your tire?" He pointed towards the rear of her vehicle. He was a huge motherfucker. Bigger than most dragon shifters, which was saying something. It wasn't a surprise she was intimidated by him. Definitely a little afraid. They were on the outskirts of town on a quiet, dark road so he couldn't blame her.

"Um… sure." She held onto the wrench as if her life

depended on it.

The scent of her fear was peppery in his nostrils. Tide averted his gaze, focusing on the flat. He walked over to where she was standing at the rear of the vehicle and the female moved out of his way. Moved as far away as she seemed to think she could get without giving away the fact that she was terrified of him. He had to give her kudos, although her heart galloped, she looked pretty darned calm on the outside.

He crouched next to the vehicle and held his hand out. When she didn't react, he glanced her way. Those beautiful green eyes of hers were still really wide. Tide cleared his throat and smiled again. "I'm going to need that wrench." He narrowed his eyes on the tool in her hands.

She didn't react for a few seconds and then she smiled back, nodding her head. "Oh, of course you do. Apologies." She handed the tool to him, holding onto the thing for a second or two after his own fingers closed over it, before reluctantly letting go. "I followed all of the steps." She pointed to an open book on the ground next to him.

"That's great." Tide nodded and went to work on the lugs.

"I found a safe location by pulling over onto the shoulder." She gestured around them, a nervous giggle escaped her. "I turned on my hazards, as you can see. In case you were wondering, the parking brake has been applied, so you're safe."

He stifled a grin. Safe. Of course, he was safe. "Good

to know." He handed the wrench back to her since she seemed to feel better holding it. And… yep… her heart-rate slowed within seconds of grabbing hold of the tool. "Where's your jack?"

"It's here." She hurried to the rear of the vehicle and dug in the trunk, then returned with the jack. "I didn't have wheel wedges, so I used some rocks instead. I hope that's not going to be a problem?"

Tide shook his head. "I think we'll be okay."

She huffed out a breath as he placed the jack beneath the vehicle and began to pump. Nothing. *What?* He pumped harder. *Fuck!* It wasn't working. Her jack was stuck or something. The car stayed just where it was. He groaned.

"What's wrong? Is everything okay?" the female leaned in next to him.

"I'll try one more time." He pumped on the handle and low and be-fucking-hold, up went the car. He'd been about to go and fetch the one from his vehicle even though he could hold a car up using his pinkie finger. Thing was, he didn't want her to know he was a non-human, they were here in town on the low-down, pretending to be MMA fighters at a convention. Since dragon shifters only went into one of the small towns every six months, they could get away with whatever story they made up. Sometimes they were football players and other times it was bodybuilders or even wrestlers. No one knew dragon shifters existed and they were more than happy with the situation. If the rest of the shifters and the vampires – don't forget the elves – were happy living alongside the humans, well, that was their business. Dragons didn't want humans sniffing around. *Not a fuck!* They'd almost been wiped out a couple of centuries ago. Not again. Not ever again. Until they were free from their affliction to silver, they were far too susceptible to risk it. Although they were making significant strides, they were far from a cure.

"It looks like the jack is working fine now." He glanced her way.

"Oh good." There was relief in her voice. "Can I help with anything?"

"Hold out your hand." She did as he said. He noticed that her nails were color-free and cut short. Very different to the females who frequented the bar. His back had been ripped open by nails of every color of the rainbow. This was new. Then he realized that she was waiting for him. He removed the lugs and put them in her hand, carefully pulling the wheel free of the hub and placing it on the ground next to him.

"Wait a sec," the female said, he could hear that she was moving to the rear of the vehicle where she dug around in the trunk again.

"Do you need help?" He frowned. What was she doing?

"I'm good." There was strain in her voice.

"You sure?"

"Absolutely." She glanced around the open trunk, smiling at him.

At least she'd started to relax. Tide smiled back. Those black smears on her face were pretty bad, she'd really done a number on herself. The streaks only served to highlight her eyes and the smattering of freckles across her nose. The freckles spilled over onto her cheekbones.

Tide stood up and walked around the vehicle. "Let me do that."

"Oh, thank you," she said as he took the tire from her. "I'm Meghan, by the way." She smiled and held out her hand.

Tide maneuvered the tire into one hand and gripped her much smaller one. "Good to meet you." Despite the smell of grease, she had a delicious scent. Berries and vanilla ice-cream. Her hand was really soft, her handshake firm. She let go almost immediately and turned back to the vehicle. There was no swooning or blushing. No giggling to speak of.

Interesting.

He put the spare tire onto the hub. "I'm going to need those lugs."

Meghan nodded. "Of course." She walked over, placing them in his outstretched hand. Her shoes were flat, black leather with very little detail. She wore plain black pants and a white blouse. All very functional. Tide had to suppress a smile when he caught sight of a big black smear of grease on the side of her top. Her outfit was ruined. He suspected a female like this would hate being so dirty.

He lined up the rim with the lug nuts, tightening each one by hand. He had just started on the third when the jack gave out. There was a popping sound, and the vehicle dropped. On reflex, he grabbed the car – and only with one hand. The remaining lugs were in his other hand. It took him a second or two to realize his mistake. Tide half-dropped half-lowered the vehicle. He turned to the human, hoping she hadn't noticed.

Meghan's mouth hung open, and her eyes were wide. She pointed in his general direction. "How did you do that?"

Tide shrugged. "I'm a big guy." Hopefully, she would buy his lame excuse.

"No way!" She shook her head. "You held up," she paused and lifted her eyes in thought, "at least a ton and a half of solid vehicle with just one hand."

"As I said, I'm really powerful." He flexed his bicep.

Her eyes widened some more as her gaze landed on his arm. She quickly locked her eyes back with his. Meghan pursed her lips for a second. "You held it there without so much as breaking a sweat or flinching. No way." She shook her head. "That's not normal."

"Okay." He breathed out through his nose. "You have me." *Fuck!* How the hell did he get out of this? "I'm not human, but…"

"I knew it. You're a vampire or one of those wolf shifters. You're far from home though." She raised her brows.

"A wolf shifter… yeah." He nodded, trying to stay cool. "I'm a shifter," he affirmed, too quickly but she didn't seem to notice.

"You could've said something, you know." She laughed in a quick burst.

"I didn't want to scare you. You were very nervous earlier."

"Yeah, I guess you're right." She smiled. "So you don't

even need a jack then?"

He lifted the vehicle using just one finger.

"Wow!" She laughed. "That's very impressive."

Tide grinned, letting the vehicle back down. "How's about we get this tire back on. I'm sure you want to get home and on with your plans for the night."

"Um…" She licked her lips. "No plans, but a shower would be really fantastic." Meghan looked down at her clothes, frowning. "I'm filthy."

Just as he suspected, she hated all the muck. Tide thought she looked pretty cute covered in all that grease. Then her words sunk in. "No plans? Really?" It was his turn to frown. "It's Saturday night."

"Yeah, no… not tonight, I was on my way back home from work. It's been a long day."

"Oh, I see."

"I've got to go back tomorrow morning. I'm working on a project. You see, I'm a geneticist. My project details the genetic contributions in asthma but also in other… Oh…" She held up a hand. "Sorry! I didn't mean to rattle on." Her cheeks turned red, for the first time since meeting her.

"Nah, no worries! I get it. I also have to work weekends and all hours. You do what you have to in order to get the job done."

Her smile brightened, and her eyes glinted. Beneath all the dirt and grime was a plain, understated, yet surprisingly pretty female. "I'm glad you understand. Anyway, I'm sure you have somewhere to be… you're all dressed up." For the first time, her eyes moved to his chest, but they quickly flitted back up to his face. "Here, let me find the…" She looked around her on the ground, her eyes landing on the wrench. She bent over to pick it up and… *Holy hotness.* Her ass was a thing of beauty.

"Got it." Meghan turned back and handed it to him. Underneath those baggy, dowdy clothes was a whole lot more going on than what met the eye. He was so used to primped and preened females. Females who wore tiny little outfits, clothing that left nothing to the imagination. This was new to him. Only, she seemed to want to get rid of him even though she didn't have any immediate plans. That was new to him too. Females wanted him. At least, they normally did. This one confused him.

Meghan watched as he lifted her car with one hand. One. Hand. His bicep bulged beneath the soft cotton of his button-down shirt. *Do not stare! It's rude!*

He used the other hand to screw on the rest of the lugs. Once they were on, he picked up the wrench at his feet and began to tighten the lugs. It was so hot. Probably one of the hottest things she'd ever seen. Not just what he was doing was hot, but he was hot too, obscenely hot. Bleached blond hair, the bluest eyes she had ever seen and not to mention the size of him. Incredibly tall with muscle she never thought possible. Yet, he wasn't too big for his frame and somehow managed to carry himself with both masculinity and grace. *Don't stare!*

He was being so nice by helping her, and here she was ogling him like he was a piece of prime steak. But oh was he prime. As prime as they came. More prime than she had ever seen in her life. Forget the not staring part, she had to keep herself from drooling at this point.

He tightened the last lug, eliciting a soft grunt which was just as hot as the rest of him.

"The hubcap is to your right." Meghan pointed. "I'm sure I can manage from here though. I've taken up far too much of your time."

The sex-on-legs, most alpha male she had ever laid eyes on turned to her, a panty-wetting smile on his lips, which were sinful. Meghan had read enough red-hot romance novels to be able to describe this guy, in minute detail. He held her gaze for a moment before shaking his head, slowly. "I always finish what I start."

Do not react! He didn't mean it like that. "Okay, well, in that case, have at it."

He frowned as he reached for the hubcap, quickly putting it into place with a light tap.

Meghan began gathering the various items like the maintenance book and the wrench. The shifter, whose name she couldn't remember on account of being too darned nervous when he introduced himself, raised up to his full height. *Oh lord! Tall.* So gorgeous. She swallowed thickly. He bent over, picking up the damaged tire. His ass was meaty glute heaven. His dark blue shirt pulled tight across his broad back. *Wow! Look away, Meghan. Look away right now, dammit!*

Turning, she got to work packing the items away where they belonged. He was just closing the trunk when she finished. "Well…" She wiped her hands on her thighs.

Her clothes were headed for the trash anyway. "That's that then."

He walked over to her. "All done." He smiled, breaking out a couple of dimples. This guy was too much.

"I can't thank you enough. I'm not sure what I would've done if you hadn't come along just then. Those darned lugs were so tight. I knew what to do, I just…" *Stop! Shut up!* She was babbling again. "I really appreciate it."

He smiled. "No problem! None whatsoever, I assure you." He tipped his head, his eyes glinting with… was he flirting with her? *No way. Not possible.* Guys like this didn't flirt with girls like her. She'd always been the nerd, and he was a jock-type. The jocks dated the cheerleaders, always the slim and trim popular girls. Never her.

"Well, I have to thank you profusely anyway, even if…" She noticed a smear of grime on his shirt. "Oh flip, your shirt…" Without thinking, she rubbed the tiny smudge, making it worse. "Oh no!" She covered her mouth with her hand for a second. "I'm so sorry. I can't believe I did that."

He chuckled. A rich, sexy sound. It wasn't fair that even his voice was delicious. A treat for the ears. "Don't worry about it."

"No, really. I'm sorry. Crikey, you were on your way out and now, not only have I waylaid you, but I've dirtied your clothing as well."

"It doesn't matter. It's just a shirt." He shrugged.

The funny thing was, he looked even better with the smudge on his chest. And oh what a chest. She needed to stop this. Needed to get home. He was reminding her how long it had been since she'd had sex. Over a year. A long lonely year since her and Gus had broken up. She was still a little hurt over how the whole thing had gone down. She wasn't thinking about that right now. "If only I had some soda, I would try to get that stain out. My house is just around the corner—" She widened her eyes. Why was she inviting him over? It was fine because there was no way he would accept. "Come to think of it… I'm sorry, but I can't remember your name." She frowned, feeling like an idiot.

His intense blue eyes flared with shock. "Oh, quite frankly I'm hurt." He put a hand to his chest.

"It's just when you came towards me, so huge and all that muscle." She shook her head. "For a second there I thought you might throw me over your shoulder and… and well…" What was she saying? *Shut up, Meghan!* "Never mind."

The shifter's eyes crinkled around the edges, and his mouth twitched. He folded his arms across his broad chest. "No, I think I'd like to hear what it is you thought I might do."

She swallowed thickly, feeling confused. Was he teasing her or flirting with her or both?

"Um, well…" she widened her eyes. Her cheeks felt hot. Her whole body felt hot.

He chuckled. "It's Tide. My name is Tide, and I don't make a habit of throwing females over my shoulder. At least, not so soon after meeting them." He winked at her. At. Her. Maybe he *was* flirting.

"Thankfully not." She laughed, sounding reasonably calm considering. "Um…" She was terrible at this. "Like I was saying, I live just around the corner. I would be happy to tackle that stain and… I could feed you. I have leftovers. Or I could just take care of that stain, and you could be on your way." She was babbling like an idiot. This wasn't her. She always held her shit together no matter what. It didn't matter the workload or the responsibility. Who was she kidding? She'd never been in this situation. A gorgeous shifter flirting with her.

Tide kept his eyes on hers. Why the hell had she asked him over? He was going to turn her down flat. If he ended up agreeing, it would be for the food and the stain removal. It would not be… for that. For sex. Her body reacted to the word. Her nipples pulled tight beneath the tight confines of her bra and her clit… *Oh boy.* Her clit decided it was all in, along with the rest of her girl parts.

His nostrils flared for a second. Even that was hot. His very pale blue eyes seemed to darken up, and he frowned.

Meghan waved a hand. "No pressure though, I'm sure you have somewhere you—"

"I'd appreciate it. I could do with a meal." He rubbed his abs, and she had to work not to follow the movement of his hand.

Then she realized what he had said and sucked in a breath, sounding shocked. *Don't get excited.* She reminded herself. He wanted food and for his shirt cleaned. Twenty minutes and he'd be on the road. *Stop acting like a sex-starved cat in heat.* The only problem was that she *was* sex-starved and Tide was just about the best looking guy she had ever laid eyes on.

"I'll follow you," he said – and it wasn't a question.

She nodded once. "Perfect." Her voice sounded calm. Much calmer than she felt. Her heart raced as she headed for her car and got in.

"Oh boy," she mumbled as she put her key in the ignition. The 'leftovers,' as she'd put it, were a tiny scraping of lasagna she should've just thrown away. Not enough for her and certainly, not nearly sufficient for a big man like Tide. She didn't have any bread. Maybe there was something in the freezer, but she doubted it. Meghan had planned on ordering take-out. Thing was, she'd asked Tide to come over on a whim. She hadn't really expected him to take her up on her offer and now he would be expecting food. What would he think when he found out she had none to give? He might think she had some ulterior motive.

CHAPTER 2

Tide followed the red taillights of Meghan's vehicle, and within a few minutes, they pulled into a long driveway. It was gravel but smoothed out flat. Trees lined each side of the drive. Her house was beautiful. It had big windows and a wrap-around porch. It overlooked large grassy fields with the mountains as a backdrop.

She parked in a big red barn to the side of the house, and he pulled in behind her. She got out of the vehicle, her back straight, glancing his way. Meghan was an interesting female. This was indeed an unexpected turn of events. She was attracted to him. Her scent had given that away a time or two and yet, he wasn't sure if she had really invited him for the food or something more. Tide sure as fuck hoped it was for more.

He climbed out of his vehicle, and they headed to the front door. "Your place is amazing."

She smiled. "Thank you. I love it. It's just a pity that I don't get to spend as much time here as I would like."

"Oh?" He raised his brows.

Meghan nodded as she unlocked the door. "I work

crazy hours, sometimes seven days a week, so," she shrugged, "I'm not here as often as I would like." She switched on the light, continuing into the living room.

Somehow he'd expected something more sterile. Not this. 'Country chic,' as he'd read in a magazine once. Florals, soft tones with more modern finishes. It was warm and inviting.

"Come on in." The keys clanged as she set them in a bowl on the middle of the dining room table. "Let's put some stain remover on that shirt and then I'm going to take a really quick shower if... Oh!" She managed her shock well. Her eyes widened as they landed on his naked torso before shooting back to lock with his. "You didn't have to take off your shirt," she shook her head, "but... um..."

Flustered! Awesome! She definitely wasn't immune to him. "I thought it would be easier this way." He handed the garment to her.

"Right, let me sort this out." She turned away from him. Again, this was different. Typically, females would eyeball the fuck out of him. Their eyes would turn all greedy. Their breathing would become louder, so much choppier. Aside from a slightly elevated heart-rate... nothing.

"Can I help you with that?" He sidled in next to her. Watching as she smeared some or other chemical on the stain.

"That's okay." She shook her head. "I've got it." Using a clean cloth, she rubbed on the mark for a few seconds before hanging the shirt carefully over a chair. She was either avoiding looking at him, or he really didn't do it for her. Such mixed signals. He had no idea what she was thinking. It intrigued him. "Right, that needs a few minutes to work its magic." She touched his shirt, glancing at him. "I'm going to order us some pizzas. I'll jump in the shower while we wait. I won't be ten minutes and…"

Tide frowned. "I thought you had leftovers." He clenched his jaw to stop himself from grinning.

"Yeah," she nodded, "I do, but take-out might be better. We don't have to get pizza, we could get Chinese or Thai or a couple of burgers." She bit down on her lip like she was trying to keep herself from saying anything else. And what a plump lip it was. "On me of course. I wouldn't expect you to pay after you changed my tire and I ruined your shirt."

Maybe he really was just here because she felt bad about the stupid shirt. There was only one way to find out. "I'd really like to try your leftovers. Is it food you cooked yourself?"

She nodded. "Yes, but I think that—"

"Sounds really good to me." He headed for the refrigerator. "Is it in here?"

"Well, um… yes but…"

He opened the door, and a laugh burst out of him. He turned back to her. "How do you even stay alive?" The fridge was empty. Okay, aside from milk and a few bottles of condiments, it was empty. There was a single Tupperware on the middle shelf.

"I eat breakfast at home and most other meals at work, so—"

Tide reached for the container, taking it out.

"I don't think that..." Meghan let the sentence die as he pulled up the lid.

Tide looked over at her. "I take it that these are the leftovers that you promised me?"

Meghan blushed, and she blushed hard. It was evident even under all the grease. "That's why I suggested getting a—"

"We don't need takeout." Tide put the Tupperware back in the fridge and slammed the door.

"Why not? I thought you were hungry?"

"I'm not hungry." He shook his head, taking a step towards her. Meghan took a small step back. Fuck, but this female intrigued him. Her pupils dilated, and he scented both nervousness and excitement on her.

"You're not?" She frowned, her voice had a breathless edge. *Finally!*

"No, and you didn't invite me here for leftovers."

He watched her throat work. "I guess I didn't. I mostly invited you here to clean your shirt."

He choked out a laugh. It was deep and husky. Totally giving away his level of attraction to her. So fucking sweet and lush. "Forget the damned shirt. I know you don't give a shit about my shirt either."

"Of course I do," she blurted.

He raised his brows.

"I do... I really do, but," she swallowed hard again, "it's also not the reason I invited you here."

"Why did you invite me then?" He took another step towards her and this time she stood her ground.

"I don't know, I guess..." She cleared her throat. "Why

did you come? You said it wasn't for the food and I know you don't mind the stain. You said so yourself, so why are *you* here?"

"Oh, I came for you, Meghan… only for you."

She gasped, and her mouth fell open for a second or two. "Oh! Oh, I see."

"I have this thing about not touching a female unless she asks me to." He shoved his hands into his jeans pockets to prove a point and stepped right into her space, looking down at her.

Her eyes were wide. Her face had gone from full blush to pale in an instant. He knew he hadn't misread this whole thing, but Meghan wasn't his usual stag run type of female. A one-night stand might not be for her. It wasn't for everyone.

"Also, you need to know that I'm just passing through, so…"

"I'm not looking for a relationship." She shook her head, her gaze moving to his chest. At long fucking last her eyes turned a whole lot greedy.

"How would you feel about one night?"

Her gaze lifted back to his face. "One night I could do," her voice was timid. "I would really like it if you touched me." Her chest rose and fell in quick succession.

"Good because I would like nothing more…" He touched the side of her arm just to test the waters. A female would normally be all over him by now. Not this one and he loved the hell out of it.

She pulled away. *What the fuck?* Shook her head. *What the all-ever-loving…?* "I really must shower, I'm—"

"Don't worry about that. I think you look sexy as fuck."
He hooked an arm around her middle and pulled her
against him.

"I really should…" Then she registered what it was he
had said. "Oh, you do?"

"Yes, most definitely and I'm going to dirty you up a
whole hell of a lot more so there's no need for a shower."

"Oh, I see." She was struggling to catch her breath.

"And you're going to put so many damned stains all
over me, I may never get them out." He maneuvered her
so that her back was against the refrigerator.

"That would be bad."

He chuckled as he nuzzled into her neck, tasting a bit
of grease but also a whole lot of female, and she was
fucking delectable. She gave a startled yelp when he
nipped her flesh. Right where her collarbone and her neck
met. It quickly turned into a moan that sent a shock of
need straight to his cock. "I'm going to make you feel so
good," he mumbled against her skin.

"You will?" Her voice was filled with awe.

"Yes, you'd better believe it." He cupped one of her
breasts and just as he expected, it was plump as fuck. She
moaned again as he brushed his thumb over her tightening
nipple. Receptive and needy. His favorite combination.

Then he captured her lips. Human females loved to
kiss, and Meghan was no exception. She dove straight in,
her arms threaded around his neck. Her lips smacked, and
her tongue dueled with his. Her little fingers dug into the
tops of his shoulders, and her hips rocked. Tide doubted
she knew she was even doing it. His cock loved the

attention, the rub of her body against his.

He slipped a hand between her legs and cupped her sex through her pants. Meghan's eyes sprung open, and she moaned. The scent of her arousal tripled. She broke the kiss though, and he pulled his hand back.

"I really should shower and shave and stuff. I'm not…" She shook her head.

"You're perfect." He kissed her again, gently cupping her again. Using his thumb, he rubbed over the area where he knew her clit would be.

She pushed out a deep groan that had desperation written all over it.

Keeping his touch really soft, he continued to rub on her clit through the layers of clothing. He broke the kiss. "I'm going to undo your pants."

"Okay." She was full on panting at this point.

"And your top." He was feeling a bit desperate himself. He couldn't wait to get his hands on her tits. *Fuck!*

"Yeah, okay." Her eyes were glassy. *Rub, rub, rub.* He kept stroking her through the material. Her hips rocked.

She was something alright. Tide had seriously lucked out. Thank fuck he'd taken the alternate route. If he were to take a guess, he'd say she hadn't had sex in a really long time. He planned on making good on his promise. Meghan was about to have the best night of her life. Tide kissed her again. She tasted just as good as she felt. The little noises she made had his groin tightening.

This wasn't happening!

Yes, it was.

Oh, good god, this was happening. Please let this not be a dream. She had a feeling that this was about to become the best night of her life.

Tide tugged on her top, parting the material. She hadn't even felt him undo the buttons. Then he pulled back mid-kiss, his gaze on her chest. "Fucking stunning," he mumbled. It sounded like he meant it. His eyes shone a brighter blue as he tugged one of her bra cups. Her boob spilled right out. "Incredible," he mumbled some more, his voice deep and husky sounding.

He seemed to really like her boobs. Like, make that love. She'd always been a bit self-conscious. They were huge and well, gravity was a thing, and mass played a significant role and Newton had this law… She moaned when he sucked on her nipple. It wasn't gentle or playful. It was serious. He was serious. A zing of pleasure mingled with a hint of pain had her crying out.

It sounded like he said 'So receptive' against her flesh before sucking on her nipple some more.

There was the sound of a zipper going down and a tugging on her pants. *Flip, oh, flip!* They were her pants, her zipper. She hadn't noticed him undoing them.

She squeezed her eyes shut, wishing for the hundredth time that she'd trimmed her bush. Wishing even harder that she'd worn sexy underwear.

"You okay?"

She'd been so busy worrying about… stuff down there… that she hadn't noticed him stop.

"Yes," she squeaked. "I just really need a trim… down

there, that is."

His eyes flared with understanding and then narrowed into hers. "Listen to me, you are one hell of a sexy female. I'm seriously fucking turned on by you, and I don't care about a few smears of grease or a bit of fur. Do you understand?"

"Yes," a whisper.

"Good. I'm going to make you come now."

Oh shit! Oh Hell! "Okay," she squeaked again.

She held onto his biceps. They were huge and firm like the rest of him. The refrigerator felt cool at her back. Tide kept his beautiful blue eyes on hers as he slipped her pants down to about halfway down her hips, leaving her underwear in place. His gaze softened. "You look frightened."

"I'm not. It's just that…" She moaned when he slipped a hand into her suit pants, rubbing her through her underwear. It was like he could sense her nervousness.

"Relax," he murmured. Tide brushed his lips over hers. Then brushed a kiss on her jawline, moving to her earlobe. All the while, he rubbed right over her clit with his finger. Really softly and yet firm enough to have her squirming. Enough to make her want to shove her pants right down and hook a leg around him.

More.

More.

More.

She moaned when he sucked on her earlobe. Then he was pushing her panties to the side and the very tip of his finger connected with her clit. *Thank god!* Skin to skin. She both sighed and mewled as her hips shot forward.

More.

It felt so darned good as the pad of his thumb slid over the very sensitive bundle of nerves. She was horrified to find that she was rocking against his hand. The word 'more' still on the tip of her tongue. It reverberated around her brain like an overzealous ping pong ball.

By now her hips were rocking like mad, and she was making silly little noises. "Sorry," she whispered, all breathless. "It's been a while." She choked out a sob. "A long while." Her words were strained.

"Don't apologize." His voice sounded even deeper than before. All the huskier. "Make as much noise as you want. In fact, I insist." He slid a finger inside her, curling the tip so that… Meghan cried out. "That's it," his voice gravelly. So sexy.

Tide fingered her again and again, it felt amazing. It was like he knew exactly where to touch her for the most impact. The pad of his thumb was firmly on her clit. While his finger… make that fingers – plural… did amazing things to her. Deep inside her. Meghan was panting at this point, her eyes were wide open. She continued to rock her hips. Continued to mewl and groan, or to all-out yell, with every slip and slide of his finger. Right now, she didn't care about anything but the pleasure he was bringing her. She gripped his biceps all the tighter, feeling the build in the pit of her stomach. A coiling that seemed to take hold of her entire body. Her skin felt tight. She felt hot all over.

"Oh, my… oh…" she groaned, gritting her teeth. If she came now, it would be too soon. She'd come across as needy and desperate. Had to try and hold on. *Hold. On.*

"Come for me," he whispered, his words tickled her ear. "Let go." His chest rumbled. "You're so damned wet, so tight…" His dirty words sent her tumbling over the edge with a loud yell that seemed to echo around the otherwise quiet room.

Her hips jerked as pleasure rushed through her. He kept fingering, kept rubbing while she fell apart. The yell turned into a deep moan. Tide knew precisely when to ease off. Slower, softer, even slower until he was barely moving.

She had buried her head against her chest. Was struggling to catch her breath. He stopped and pulled her underwear back into place. Thankfully, he had an arm hooked around her waist, or she might have crumpled into a heap on the floor.

"Are you okay?" he asked. His voice still impossibly deep.

"Yeah," she managed to push out. *Shit!* Her suit pants were around her ankles. *When did that happen?* That meant that she was just in her undies. They were the full set of cotton briefs. Not very flattering.

"Let's get you out of these." He lifted her, stepping on the pants so that they stayed behind, a pool of black material on the floor. "Put your legs around me."

"I'm too heavy, I—"

"Do it now!" he growled. The sound sending shivers racing up and down her spine. She did as he said.

"Oh shit." Her voice was a bit croaky after all that moaning. "I don't have any condoms in the house." It wasn't like she had a boyfriend. She didn't normally do things like this either so…

Tide chuckled. "Don't worry. I have a couple in my wallet."

A couple.

More than one.

"That's good news." What a lame thing to say. She was feeling relieved though. Big time. The thought of not getting to have sex with this beautiful man… shifter, didn't sit right with her. This wasn't her typical MO, but she was damned if she was missing out on a night like this.

Tide walked straight to her bedroom, which was weird since she lived in a four-bedroom house and her room wasn't the first one down the hall. "How did you know this one was mine?" she asked as he turned on the light with the sweep of the hand.

"Shifters have a great sense of smell." He nuzzled her neck and sniffed her. Kind of like a dog, only for some strange reason it was a turn on. He kept walking towards her bed.

Then she remembered that she'd last showered this morning. That she was covered in grease and grime. He sniffed her again, his nose against her skin. "I wouldn't do that if I were you. I'm in desperate need of a—"

"You smell delicious. I might just eat you all up."

Then she was weightless for a few moments before landing on the soft mattress. She bounced once or twice. Meghan watched as Tide toed off his boots, one and then the other. He bent down and removed his socks. His jeans stayed on though. She could see a large, make that – she swallowed thickly – enormous, bulge in his pants.

Flip!

The bed dipped as he put a knee down, his gaze firmly fixed on her. He was taking her in, his intense blue stare raked over her. Slightly embarrassed, she glanced down. Her shirt gaped open… oh gosh… boobs were still spilling out over the cups of her bra. Then there were those god-awful panties. Full briefs. To make matters worse, they were off-white from all the washing. *Arghhh!* It wasn't like she could have guessed this would happen to her. Not in a million years.

Meghan looked back up at him. His chest was amazing, so smooth and masculine even although there was not a single hair to speak of. Not to mention his abs, ripped to perfection. She wanted to run her tongue across them and suck on his pecks. In short, he was spectacular.

Tide licked his lips. "I think I'll start with your pussy."

"W-what?" She sounded like a blithering idiot. *Just because you died and went to hunk heaven does not mean you get to lose your faculties, Meghan.*

He cocked his head, his gaze turning feral. "I said, I'm going to eat you up, and I think I'll start with that piece of heaven nestled between your legs."

Meghan bit down on her lower lip to keep from groaning. His words were so filthy. She loved it.

"Take off the panties," he ordered.

"Um… okay…" She felt her cheeks heat as she hooked her fingers in the elastic band. It was a mess down there. An utter war-zone. "I must warn you—"

Tide shook his head. He looked angry. "Don't say it,"

he rasped. "The only words I want to hear coming out of those lips are 'fuck me' and 'harder.' I might accept 'deeper,' and you're more than welcome to scream my name, but that's it. Are we clear?" As he spoke, he lifted her legs – which were still closed – over one shoulder and gently peeled her panties off. Slipping them up her thighs and over her feet.

He ran his hands up and down her legs. Try as she might, her knees stayed locked together. She felt mortified about what he would think when he got a proper look down there. It didn't deter him however. Tide leaned down and licked her slit. Her legs were together, straight up in the air. His tongue was long and very warm. He licked her again and again. Meghan moaned and moaned some more. *Good. So good. Oh so very good.* Especially considering she had just come.

Somehow or other – she wasn't sure when or how – her legs ended up over his shoulders and spread so wide that the insides of her thighs burned. She didn't care though because she was well on her way to another orgasm. Tide was suckling on her clit. It was a sensation she'd never experienced before. It was mind-blowing. His hot mouth was closed over her flesh, and every so often his tongue would flick across her clit, mid-suck. She made a weird noise, sounding a little like a dying animal, but she didn't give a rat's ass. Meghan was so far beyond giving a damn that it was obscene. It had never felt this good before. His tongue, his mouth, his hands, him.

Oh.

Oh.

Yes.

Both of her hands were buried deep in his hair, which she was pulling. Meghan couldn't make herself stop. She was thrusting her hips. Pretty much fucking the poor guy's face. She couldn't stop that either. *Nearly, so very nearly…*

Tide pulled away. She may have removed a chunk of his hair trying to stop him. "No! More…" She was panting hard.

"'Fuck me,' 'harder,' 'deeper' or my name," Tide growled, but she wasn't sure what he was on about. Her brain was a fog of need. "But I'll accept 'more.'" He pulled down his zipper and the biggest cock she had ever seen before jutted forward. It was thick as well as long. The head was shiny; it leaked pre-come.

Her mouth fell open. "Crikey," she whispered.

Tide moaned. "Don't look at me like that… like you want to eat me all up."

"I do," she blurted. She'd never been so brazen before. It felt good.

His Adam's apple bobbed. He stroked himself once and shook his head, his eyes were on her mouth. "Don't tempt me, female." He stood and pulled his jeans all the way off, stepping out of them one leg at a time. His sacs were heavy between his legs. His thighs thick with muscle and his hips narrow. He even had that whole V-thing going on.

Good lord!

"Take those off." He gestured with his eyes to her top and bra. "I want you naked."

His eyes were feral and hungry – for her. It looked like

he really wanted her. She nodded and with fumbling hands somehow managed to pull the blouse from her shoulders. Next, she reached back and unhooked her bra, pulling that from her shoulders as well.

Tide tore a condom foil with his teeth but stopped mid-motion. "You're gorgeous." His gaze moved from between her legs, which were still wide open, to her boobs and then to her face. "Very sexy," he added. He finished tearing open the condom. "It's been a while for me too." His eyes were bright, almost as if they were glowing.

A zing of need coursed through Meghan as he fisted his cock, running it down his length as he sheathed his member. Then he was back between her legs, his mouth suckling on her clit, his fingers deep inside her. It didn't take more than what felt like a few seconds to have her moaning again. Just as she was getting close – her skin tightening, her yells becoming louder – Tide flipped her over onto all fours. He gripped her hips, pulling her ass into the air. "I'm going to take you now." His voice was a deep rasp. One hand slid around her belly, his deft fingers finding her clit. "I'll go easy but I can't be gentle."

Rub, rub, rub. His ministrations were turning her mind to mush. At this point, she was desperate for release. So close but not there yet. She was panting like a wild thing. The sound of her breathing filled the room.

He put his tip at her opening. There was pressure but not enough to breach. All the while, he kept up that rub on her clit. Soft and easy. Enough to destroy every brain cell but not enough to tip her over the edge. She felt something drip down her leg.

Oh god! She was just that wet. She'd never been this turned on, this desperate. "Please!" It came out as a half moan, half plea.

Tide chuckled, it sounded strained. "That's not one of the magic words."

"What magic words?" she moaned as he circled her clit with his finger. Round and around now instead of side to side.

"Oh god!"

"That's not my name." He circled the other way. Lazy and slow. His cock right there. So hard.

She tried to push back with her ass.

"Ah… no," he tutted. "Tell me what you want?" The pressure increased and eased and increased and eased. His finger danced around her clit, barely touching her. She glanced back. *Oh good god!* Tide was making small thrusting motions with his hips even though he hadn't breached her yet. His eyes were glowing, his jaw tight. So darned sexy that it almost had her coming.

He stopped moving his finger. Meghan was going to die if he didn't take her now. She tried to recall the words he'd told her to use. "Fuck me," she sobbed, feeling so darned naughty. She'd never said anything like it before. Not ever. It was empowering. Especially when his eyes darkened up, when his jaw tightened. She could see how turned on he was.

"It would be my pleasure." Tide thrust into her. It hurt but at the same time it felt amazing.

Meghan cried out, her fingers gripping the comforter so hard that she was sure she broke a nail. Her back bowed as his dick slid all the way in. As his hips hit her ass. As he bottomed out inside her.

"Fucking tight," he growled, sounding more animal than man.

He pulled out and then thrust back into her with a hard grunt. "Amazing," he muttered. His fingers dug into her hips as he thrust again and again. Her boobs were mashed against the bed. The light stinging feeling slowly subsided, making way for even more pleasure.

Her eyes rolled back in her skull, she ground her teeth, groaning deeply with every hard, even thrust. This was precisely what she needed. The bed shook harder as he picked up the pace, grunting with every stroke. She could hear the sucking noises her body was making. Could hear the slap of his balls against her ass. Meghan had never been taken like this before. The men in her past had always been so gentle and considerate. This was animalistic. It was… incredible.

"Oh god!" she yelled, as the coiling sensation took hold. As her belly tightened up all over again. As her skin tightened.

Meghan felt a sharp sting on her ass. "It's Tide," he growled.

"W-what?" she managed to sob. Her ass felt warm where he had slapped her. More wetness dripped between her legs. She'd actually liked that he had smacked her. What was wrong with her? Ordinary people didn't enjoy being spanked… or did they?

He rubbed a hand over the stinging flesh of her ass and she groaned. Apparently, they did enjoy it. She did, at any rate.

The bed shook and rocked so hard that she thought it might break. "My name," he grunted. "It's Tide." His voice was so deep. He continued to grunt. Not letting up an inch.

"Oh," she moaned. "Oooooooh…" Everything was tightening. She couldn't catch her breath and didn't want to.

Tide reached around her, caging her with his massive body. His hard chest against her back. She couldn't move. Good thing Meghan was right where she wanted to be.

Rub.

Rub.

More frantic this time. The tip of Tide's finger slid over her clit. She clenched her jaw and squeezed her eyes shut. Then everything let go. Meghan screamed his name as her orgasm belted through her.

Tide groaned and tightened his grip on her. His hips jerked, his thrusts became deeper and more insistent. Her fingers dug into the comforter. Her whole body was being pinned down by him. Her orgasm continued to rush through her with each hard drive. Tide kept pushing into her, slower this time. Her jaw turned slack, her deep groan turning into a softer moan.

Then he was undulating his hips in what felt like little circles, drawing the last bit of pleasure out of her. Tide finally slumped over her. She could feel his chest expand and contract rapidly, could hear his heavy breathing. He wasn't crushing her, so he must be taking some of the weight on himself. "You feel amazing," Tide finally whispered. "So damned good… I might never want to leave." He gave a tiny thrust.

Meghan whimpered. She was still shaking. Still struggling to breathe after that life-changing orgasm. How did she go back to getting herself off? What would be the point?

"Are you okay?" He pulled out and she actually felt empty. It was, of course, because he was just so darned big. That was all. It had nothing to do with this talk of him not wanting to leave.

Meghan realized, in that moment, that she was lonely. She really did need to work on getting a life. Outside of work anyway. Tide lay down next to her and gently tugged her so that she was facing him. He cupped her chin. "Are you alright?"

"I'm good." She smiled. "Better than good. Thank you for that. I appreciate it. You don't have to stay, by the way," she blurted. "I'm not sure how one-night stands work, but…"

"We're not done." Tide narrowed his eyes. "Not nearly. I'm just giving you a break before round two."

"Round two?" She could feel herself frown. Could feel how her cheeks heated. Make that, how her whole body heated. She felt his words between her legs. Meghan was appalled to find that she wanted more. Much more. She frowned, not sure if she was happy with this newly awakened sex kitten side of her. She had always enjoyed sex but she'd never craved it before.

CHAPTER 3

Tide watched Meghan frown. She looked like she was deep in thought. Looked like she didn't like the idea of a second round of rutting.

What the hell?

Females begged him to stay and not the other way around.

"I'm just going to take care of this." He gestured to the filled condom on his cock and slid from the bed. His mind racing. Surely she'd enjoyed the sex. By the way she had squeezed the hell out of him, and the scent of her, she'd come. Twice — and both times had been hard. By the noises she had made, she'd loved every minute of it and yet she wanted him gone.

Why?

"Unless you would prefer it if I left," he asked as he returned to the room after disposing of the rubber.

"No!" Her voice was high-pitched. "You're welcome to stay. I just... wasn't sure what to expect."

"I like you and I enjoyed being inside you. I want to make you come again. At least once or twice more, if that's okay?"

Meghan widened her eyes in what looked like shock and then smiled. "Are shifters always this forward?"

Tide nodded. "Yes, it's better to be forward and direct about what you want. Did you enjoy that?"

She swallowed hard. "Yes, very much."

"Do you want more?"

She nodded, her eyes glinted. "Yes, I do. Just give me a minute to catch my breath."

Tide chuckled. He felt relieved. For a second there he thought that he had read it all wrong. "No problem. You mentioned you were working tomorrow?"

She nodded once.

"You might need to call it off. Is that going to be a problem?"

Her eyes took on a worried look. "Yes, it would be. I need to get to work. We're so close to a breakthrough. My research…" She pursed her lips. "I won't bore you with all the details but I need to be there. It doesn't matter that it's Sunday."

"I'll go easy on you then." He couldn't help but grin.

"You'll go easy?" Her eyes widened.

Tide brushed his lips against hers. "Nothing to worry about. Tell me more about your work. Why did you choose," he had to think about what it was that she did, "genetics?"

"I guess I'm a geek. I always wondered why one person had brown hair and another blond. You're a shifter right?" She moved onto her stomach, lifting herself onto her elbows. Tide had to work to keep his eyes on her face instead of gaping at her breasts. They were full, her nipples dark like ripe cherries. Despite his recent orgasm, his dick twitched. He wanted her under him. *Slow down, Tide!* The human needed to catch her breath. Especially if she was going to need her faculties come morning.

"That's right, I'm a shifter," he quickly answered, realizing she was waiting.

"Exactly, your genetics make you who you are. They give you your better sense of smell. They allow you the ability to shift into your wolf form. I'm sure if I were to take your blood and explore your genetic footprint, I would find canine DNA mixed in with your human DNA. You see, I find it all quite fascinating."

Tide nodded. There would be no canine DNA, but she didn't need to know that. He worked at keeping his facial expression neutral. *Fuck.* He hated lying. There was nothing he could do about it though.

"Having said all of that," she looked thoughtful for a few seconds, "there is more to it. My sister has asthma and she nearly died as a kid."

He frowned. "Excuse my ignorance. Shifters don't have human illnesses. What is asthma?"

She smiled and pulled a face. "The short answer, and in layman's terms, it's a chronic disease that inflames and narrows the airways in the lungs. It causes wheezing, shortness of breath and chest tightness. There are many causes, like pollen, dust mites or even a bit of exercise can trigger an attack."

Tide nodded. "Sounds terrible."

"It is. Asthma affects an estimated three hundred

million people worldwide, with a quarter of a million deaths attributed to the illness thus far. My aunt is also a sufferer and my sister's little boy has the illness as well." She shook her head, her eyes turning up in thought. "I can still remember that day like it happened yesterday. It was Saturday morning, we were playing ball out front and my little sis started breathing funny. It was nothing new. She got regular attacks. We went inside and she rustled up her pump but it didn't work. Her spare pump wasn't in the drawer where it usually was. Our mom had just stepped out to go to the store and left us alone. I was thirteen and Carly was eleven, so we weren't babies anymore. Anyway, the attack was bad and Carly deteriorated quickly. Her lungs literally closed right before my eyes and there was nothing I could do to stop it." She clenched her hand tightly as she talked about her sister's lungs closing. "I called an ambulance but she was barely breathing by the time they got there. Her lips were blue. I'll never forget the petrified look on her face while I held her hand and prayed for the emergency services to get there. I kept telling her over and over that she was going to be just fine, but I was completely helpless." She exhaled loudly. "I decided back then that I wanted to help people like Carly, my aunt and nephew... It's also why finding a cure for asthma is so important to me. I believe it needs to happen at base level, with the building blocks of our bodies, with our genes, but..." She widened her eyes. "I'll stop there. Once I start talking nucleotides you're done for. Your ears will bleed." She smiled. There were still a couple of grease marks on her face. It wasn't as bad as earlier though. Very cute and very sweet. He enjoyed listening to her talk. Enjoyed the passion he could see reflecting in her eyes.

"No, I'm finding it very interesting," he said. "My ears feel fine."

She looked down at the comforter for a few seconds before locking eyes with him once again. "You're just being nice." Her cheeks flushed red.

"No really, we non-humans suffer from an… allergy," he used her word, "to silver. It greatly affects us and can kill us. I understand how you would want to help your family and other sufferers. We feel the same." He was saying too much. Needed to keep his trap shut.

"Yeah, I had heard something about that."

"What have you heard?" He narrowed his eyes, his voice turned serious. *Shit!*

She frowned, her eyes darting to the side and back to his face. "Just that it's your one weakness, your kryptonite." She shrugged.

For a moment he thought she was talking specifically about dragons and the research they were doing on their affliction but that was crazy thinking. He smiled, trying to defuse the situation. "Exactly. So you see, I get it. You do need time off though, or do you make a habit of working seven days a week?"

She sighed. "You said it earlier, we do what we have to do. Funds are limited. I'm always trying to raise money for research, but at the same time, I need to show some actual results. It's a fine line between obtaining the funding and actually doing sufficient research to keep the investors happy. Thing is, fund-raising can be time-consuming."

She stopped talking, clapped her mouth shut for a moment. "There I go again, off on a tangent."

Tide laughed. "I told you that I'm enjoying our conversation. I swear."

She smiled back. "You're just being nice. So, what brings you into town? You guys live out in the mountains somewhere don't you?"

He nodded and made a sound of affirmation. *Shit!* What should he tell her? That he was here on a convention? That didn't seem right. "Sex," he blurted. There'd been enough lying for one night.

She choked out a laugh. "Are you serious?"

Tide shrugged. He'd stick as close to the truth as he could. "Yes. We don't have many female shifters. In fact, there are just a handful of unmated females where I come from. I'm a male in my prime and well…" He widened his eyes.

"You have needs."

"Exactly. So, I blow into town on occasion to… take care of them."

She was grinning. "You come into town specifically to have sex?"

Tide nodded. "Sad, but true."

"And you ended up with me." Her eyes clouded. "You didn't have to come back to my place, you know?"

"I know that. I wanted to or I wouldn't be here. You're," he grabbed a handful of her ass, "delectable." It came out as a deep rumble.

Meghan didn't look convinced. "I'm sure that I'm nothing like the other women you hang out with."

"You're right, you're nothing like them."

Her eyes clouded even more and she folded her arms to cover her chest.

"You're better." He rubbed his hand over her back. "So much more real. There's no pretense. You don't try too hard and yet you're fucking sexy. So damned lush."

"Lush? Really? Lush is another word for chubby." The glint was back in her eyes, but there was also a vulnerability.

"Lush is another word for curvy and you are plenty curvy." He let his gaze track her ample side-boob and then down to her plump ass and thighs. He wished he could get an eyeful of the rest of her but she was still lying on her stomach. "Shifters love the hell out of curves. Something to hold onto. Besides, there should be plenty of bouncing during a hard rutting."

He could scent her arousal. "I have no problem with my curves. I've always just found that guys like you—"

"Woah! What do you mean guys like me?"

"Sorry! That didn't come out right." She sighed. "You're good-looking – seriously gorgeous. Guys like you don't normally look at girls like me."

"Human males are blind then. You're really beautiful." He ran a thumb down the side of her cheek. "Grease smudges and all."

"You should have let me shower first. It's your own fault."

"I'm not complaining. You need to stop being so hard on yourself."

"I have plenty of great attributes, my eyes, my smile and

I have a higher than average IQ. Look, like I said, I don't have a problem with my curves, although I wouldn't mind if my boobs were a tad smaller, they—"

"Bullshit!" he all but snarled. "You have amazing breasts. Don't ever say anything like that again."

She laughed. "Finding bras in my size is not always easy and," she turned to the side, looking around them for a few seconds before lifting a bra up, "look at this. When I do find one, it's plain and boring. It's like manufacturers expect large breasted women not to want to feel sexy." It was very plain and an off-white color. Now that he looked at it, he had to agree that it wasn't very flattering. He knew that some of the human coverings were lacy and silky. They came in many colors. It didn't matter though.

"You don't need a bra." He tugged it out of her hand and threw it to the other side of the room. "You're perfect just like that."

Meghan laughed. "Trust me, I do need a bra. I can't leave the house without one. Might start an earthquake."

"Yeah, from all the males who would be clambering behind you to catch a glimpse of your amazing rack."

She rolled her eyes. "It wouldn't do any of them any good. I'm too busy for a relationship. My ex-boyfriend ended up breaking up with me via email because I kept canceling our plans." She looked shocked at her own admission and then shrugged it off. "It took me three days to finally getting around to reading it."

"What a dick!"

"No, he really did try hard to see me in person to do it. It wasn't his fault. I really should have made more time for him." She looked thoughtful for a few seconds. "It's why he broke up with me in the end. We hardly ever saw one another."

"So you weren't that into him then?"

"We'd been dating for eight months and it was going well." She pulled a face. "Except for not seeing each other enough."

"I think if you really want to be with someone, you'll make the time. You didn't make the time to be with him."

He could see her mulling it over. "You're probably right. So, those women shifters… are none of them your type then? Why is a guy like you still single?"

"A guy like me?" He raised his brows. "There you go again."

Her cheeks flushed. "Sorry! I really didn't mean it like that. It's just… I'm sure you would have no trouble attracting the opposite sex, no matter how limited they are. That's what I meant."

He shrugged. "It's complicated."

"Not really." She shook her head. "Boy meets girl, boy likes girl. Boy spends time with girl and they end up together. See, easy."

"It doesn't work like that with our kind. The unmated shifter females enjoy being single. There are so few of them that they have their pick of the males."

"What about human women? I had read an article about how compatible shifters and humans are. That there have been shifter/human pairings. How does it work then?" Her eyes were filled with sweet innocence.

"You're right, shifters and humans are compatible,

but…" He couldn't exactly tell her about the hunt, now could he? Not when she was talking about regular shifters and not dragons. "As I said, it's complicated. Now," he lifted her, Meghan squealed as he slid her on top of him, "it's time for round number two. Straddle me."

She did as he said. Meghan squealed again as he flipped her over so that she was under him. She was so damned soft. "Put your legs over my shoulders."

"W-what?" She swallowed thickly. "I'm not sure I can get them up there."

Tide chuckled. "Of course you can."

She pulled her legs higher up his body. Tide hooked his arms around her thighs until her legs were indeed, over his shoulders. "Oh my god, I'm a pretzel," she moaned. "Whatever you do, don't hurt me. You're a really big guy." Her eyes were wide.

Tide nuzzled into her neck. His cock was hard and throbbing. All he wanted was to sink into her heat. "Hurt you? No way. I'm going to do the exact opposite."

"Are you really going to make me come again? That would make three times. I don't think I've ever come three times in one night."

He grabbed his wallet and pulled out another condom, ripping it open and sheathing himself with it. "No, sweet Meghan." He swiped a wisp of hair from her forehead. "Not three times." He shook his head once.

Tide slid his hand between their bodies and began rubbing on her clit, using a slow easy motion. Her eyes widened and her breath came quicker. "That's okay," her voice sounded strained, "I wouldn't mind if it doesn't happen again, I—"

Tide chuckled. "I'm going to make you come more than just three times." He put his cock at her opening. Still slippery. He was in for another treat.

"Oh," she moaned as he began to ease into her. "Okay." Meghan was panting, her eyes on his. She clenched her jaw and he found himself doing the same. She felt so damned good.

"It's going to be more than just okay." It was his turn to grunt as his hips hit her ass. She was so damned snug. She felt amazing. So damned good. He undulated his hips, circling into her. *Fuck! Oh so…*

Her legs tightened around his shoulders and her pussy clamped tight. Meghan's jaw was slack, her eyes wide. She groaned deeply, her fingers digging into his shoulders. Her sex spasmed hard and he had to work not to come with her. *Oops!* Maybe he'd gotten a bit carried away rubbing on her clit. *Oh well!* He'd just have to bring her there again. The night was but a whelp.

"You good?" he asked as her hold on him eased. His skin felt taut. His teeth threatened to erupt.

Meghan was panting so hard that she couldn't string any words together. She nodded. He eased right off of her clit, moving to his knees. Her legs were still over his shoulders. "I can't," she groaned.

Tide chuckled as he gently thrust into her welcoming flesh. "Oh, but you will." He'd have to prove her wrong. This female was one of the most receptive he had ever encountered. She was utterly spectacular.

CHAPTER 4

Meghan cracked opened her eyelids. First the one and then the other. It took her a few seconds to focus on the white ceiling above her bed. Even though the ceiling fan was one she had looked at many times, it still took her another moment or two to realize where she was. In bed. Her bed. The room was flooded with light. That's why everything looked so different. She never slept in. Not ever. She was too busy for such luxuries. Why was she still at home? Why hadn't her alarm gone off?

Meghan sat upright, moving too quickly. She groaned, wincing as the sheet pooled around her hips. Her muscles hurt. Her... girl parts... hurt. It wasn't an entirely unpleasant pain. It was the kind of pain that told a woman she'd had one hell of a good night. With a soft gasp, she turned her head to the other side of the bed. Empty. The sheets were rumpled, the pillow dented but of the shifter there was no sign.

There was a big black smear on the edge of the sheet. When she looked closer, there were more of such smears on the comforter. Grease. From her car. Images of Tide flowed through her mind. Images of the two of them. Of him. How his jaw tightened and his eyes grew stern just as he was about to come. How he'd grunted when he was inside of her. All the compliments he'd paid her. How sexy he'd made her feel. They'd had sex, a ton of times. No wonder she was tender. She tried to hold back a grin and failed. It had been good. Better than good.

Bright light.

Late.

She was late. *Shit!* She scrambled from the bed, her legs giving out. She landed on her ass. Her head felt fuzzy from lack of sleep and her body felt slow and used up. Meghan laughed, despite being late. He'd really worked her over, and this had been him going easy. Another laugh bubbled inside her but she stifled it with her hand. Maybe he was still there. She didn't want him to hear her laughing like a mad woman. He'd think she was a loon, laughing to herself after falling on her ass. Her heart beat faster at the prospect of him still being in her house. Maybe they could have breakfast together before he left. *No!* She needed to get to work. There was no sign of his jeans or shoes. Maybe he had already left. She didn't like the idea. For whatever reason she wanted to spend a bit more time with him. She had enjoyed their conversations as much as she had the sex.

Meghan sucked in a couple of deep breaths and carefully rose to her feet. Her legs shook. Her throat felt raw. There was a tenderness between her legs. Her arms felt like she'd been lifting weights. She walked over to the closet and carefully pulled a robe over her shoulders, fastening the tie. Then she slowly made her way to the living room. There was no sign of him. "Tide?" She felt stupid calling his name.

Meghan walked into the kitchen. And peered through the window. His car was gone. Tide was gone. She clenched her teeth. He'd come into town for sex. Now that he had what he wanted, he was gone.

Typical.

What an asshole.

The least he could've done was said goodbye to her. Meghan huffed out a breath. She was being silly. He hadn't promised her anything. No, that wasn't true. He'd promised her a night filled with orgasms. He'd promised to make her feel good and he'd delivered in spades. She couldn't blame her own loneliness on him. Tide had been nothing but helpful and sweet. If only he wasn't just passing through. She might be tempted to make time for a guy like him and it wasn't just that he was gorgeous or the size of his member. It was him.

Then she spotted his shirt. The one with the grease stain. It was still slung over the chair where she'd left it to soak last night. She picked up the garment and inhaled. It still carried his scent. Woodsy, masculine, clean.

Oh well, it was time to put the night behind her and to get on with her life, her research. There was a cure and she would find it.

CHAPTER 5

Three weeks later . . .

M eghan felt like she was in a daze. Her brain both raced and felt bogged down. She slumped into her office chair and put her face in her hands.

"What's gotten you so rattled?" George asked from the other side of the lab.

"Don't ask." Her words were muffled behind her hands and she felt her eyes well with tears. Just as quickly, anger rose up in her, drying up the tears before they had a chance to form properly. She pushed back on her chair and stood up. "It's not fair." She shook her head, her hands curling into fists.

"Oh no!" George widened his eyes and put down the beaker he was holding, placing his hands on his hips. "I've never seen you like this. Not when what's-his-name broke up with you. Not when the IRS sent you that letter requesting a crap ton of money. Not even when that rude asshole rammed into your car at the grocery store last month and blamed you."

"That was nothing," she mumbled. The CCTV footage had cleared up that little spat. Even if it hadn't been resolved, it was just a car. This was different. It had been a very long time since Meghan had felt like this. Helpless. At a loss. At her wits' end. "We were so close." She wiped her hand across her desk and papers went flying.

"Don't do that. Trashing the place won't help." George took a step towards her. "What the hell is going on?"

Shit! Tears began to gather in her eyes once more.

"Oh, honey." George shook his head once before rushing around her desk, careful not to step on any of the papers littering the floor. "Speak to Georgy. Tell me what's going on?" he asked as he enveloped her in his arms.

"You don't want to know." She sniffed, trying hard not to cry and failing as the first tears fell.

He pulled back, cocking his head and looking her in the eyes. "It can't be that bad. You'll feel so much better once it's out. Guaranteed."

She wiped her eyes. "ARJ Packaging are no longer funding our research." Even as she said it, she still couldn't believe it. The packaging company had been their biggest supporters. They paid Meghan and George's salaries. Without which they were finished.

George clutched his heart, sitting on her desk with a bang. "That *is* bad. It's freaking terrible. What the hell happened? Why? I don't understand." He shook his head. "Our research is so close to Alex Jackson's heart." Her lab assistant looked bewildered. "I would never have expected this. Not from him."

"One of ARJ's biggest clients is Aztec

Pharmaceuticals."

George frowned. "So what. What does that have to do with anything? Alex lost his daughter to asthma. How could he withdraw the funding? Especially now when we're so close."

"Aztec has ARJ by the proverbial short and curlies. They're one of ARJ's biggest clients and are threatening to cancel their contract if ARJ Packaging doesn't stop funding us."

"That's got to be fucking illegal." George jumped to his feet. "How did Aztec find out about the funding in the first place?"

Meghan shrugged. "Who knows. It doesn't matter in the end who told them. Ultimately, ARJ can't afford to lose that contract. Alex was gutted at having to stop funding our research but what can he do?" She sighed. "He's the CEO and has shareholders to contend with; bottom line, losing a contract like Aztec would mean having to lay off staff members." She pursed her lips for a few seconds. "People's lives are at stake. He didn't have a choice."

"Shit!" George rolled his eyes. He scrubbed a hand over his face. "This sucks. I don't want to have to go back to Dalton Springs Gen. It's a fucking hellhole. Maggie Jacobs is the devil." He was referring to the head of department.

"It's not that bad," Meghan said. "More like you'd die of boredom." George could be a prima donna.

"I doubt she'd take me back anyways," he added. "I didn't write the nicest letter of resignation."

"I told you not to burn your bridges."

"Yeah, yeah. You were right." George pulled a face.

"You could always take up stripping. I heard that Up the Jackson's on Fifth is looking for a new drag queen to take over from Miss Sally-Ann who recently retired."

"Please! I don't think so." George laughed. "I'll do the gig with pleasure but there is no money in it. Dancers get two drinks and dinner on the house and that's it. Up the Jackson's is an institution, not a business."

"Oh flip, so you're well and truly screwed then." Meghan felt her smile falter, felt her lip quiver. She wasn't a crier for goodness sake. "I'll think of something, George." She sniffed. "I'll redouble my efforts to find more funding. I'll…"

"What about that email you received last week. That might—"

"It was a hoax. I'll go door-to-door if I have to. There must—"

"Do you still have the email?" George looked animated, his big brown eyes were wide.

"No! It's utter garbage. There is no way in hell any company – local or otherwise – is going to pay that kind of money. Forget about it. It's a scam."

George walked around her desk and gave her mouse a shake. "I'm sure it's in your trash file. Come on, missy… what's your password?"

Meghan rolled her eyes. "Like you don't know my password."

George grinned, he looked at her from under his lashes. "We've been working together too long. It's C. H. O. C. O. L. A. T. E. C. R. U. S. H." He said each letter as he typed them. "Your favorite." He bobbed his brows. "No other crushes for you since your vag never gets any action." He stuck his tongue out at her.

"Hey!" She laughed, feeling a little bad. George was technically her employee, although you would never say it. First and foremost, they were really good friends. She hadn't said anything to him about Tide. Hadn't told a soul. No one needed to know about it. It wasn't like she would ever see the shifter again or anything. "Chocolate is my one guilty pleasure," she admitted as her home screen appeared.

"And it's a tragedy. You're still young and you're attractive for a total geek with no dress sense." He looked her up and down.

"I'm thirty-two, hardly that young anymore."

"It is still young, trust me!" He raised his brows.

"You're only a year older than I am, George." Meghan had to laugh. "Stop being such a drama queen."

"Don't remind me. Anyway, maybe this would be your chance to get out more. Meet new people." George worked the mouse, opening her mail. "Right. Let's check in your trash file." He clicked a couple more times, scrolling down. Within a half a minute his eyes lit up and he smiled. "Here it is." Another click of the mouse. This time with flourish. "Right," his whole face was animated, "they're extending a request for you to apply for a position. They need a geneticist with your kinds of specializations." He continued, "The assignment would be abroad with an opportunity to return home for one weekend every month."

"Who is this *they* the email refers to?"

"*They,*" he smiled, "don't specify. There is mention that

it's classified."

Meghan shook her head. "Exactly. There's no company logo. No type of identification."

"Look at what just happened with ARJ Packaging and Aztec. It might be that whoever this is, doesn't want one of the pharmaceutical companies to catch wind."

Meghan felt her frown deepen. She wasn't buying it. "You said it's a remote location. Do they specify where?"

George shook his head. "That's all they say about it."

Meghan snorted. "More secrecy."

"The package they're offering is phenomenal. Everything else might be vague but they're fully transparent when it comes to the money." He raised his brows and whistled low, turning the screen to her. "Take a look at the number of zeros."

"That's just it. There's no darned way that's for real." She pointed in the general direction of the computer.

"How do you know? There aren't many scientists who do what you do." His hands made a flourish. "You're worth your weight in gold, lady. You just don't seem to realize it."

"Worth my weight in gold, hey?" She laughed. "Well, in that case, maybe the zeros are accurate."

"Stop that. There are plenty of guys who are all about the tits and ass. You have those in spades."

His comment made her think of Tide. She felt her cheeks heat. Lush and delectable were the words he'd used to describe her. The way he looked at her had made her feel plenty desirable.

George smiled at her. "It also helps that you're pretty

cute as well. No paper bag necessary in your case."

Meghan choked out a laugh. "You didn't just say that!"

"What?" he shrugged. "It's true. You know me, I say it like it is and if it wasn't for the fact that I happen to like my dick with a side of balls, I'd be all over you."

She laughed some more. "You were right," she paused, "I do feel much better after talking this out. I'll find a way to fix it."

George took her hand and squeezed. "I know you will and I'm here to help. This isn't all on you."

Meghan nodded. "Thank you, but I think you should start applying for—"

"I have some money saved, so I'll survive for a while." George looked her head-on for a few moments. "Promise me you'll reply to this email."

"It's nothing but a dumb hoax." Meghan sat down at her desk. "I'll prove it." She typed a quick replying stating that she was interested and requesting further information. "I'm willing to bet you they ask for money or personal details so that they can phish my account or something."

"You never know, maybe it is for real and then…" George's eyes widened as a beep sounded. It was an incoming email alert.

It couldn't be. No way.

Using the mouse, she opened the message. "It's a meeting request for next Tuesday. It's for the entire day." She rolled her eyes. "Someone called Bianca Evans. This can't be for real. What the hell do I have to lose though?" She clicked that she accepted the request and George jumped up and down a few times clapping his hands. Her friend was short and slim. Even though he was a lab technician, there was nothing nerdy about him. He always wore the latest fashion. With his big, brown eyes and perfectly coifed hair, he was very good-looking.

"They'll be asking for my banking details next. Just you wait."

"You are so damned negative. Stop it already."

She huffed out a breath and folded her arms. "I don't want to get my hopes up, George. That's all. I don't like living on hopes and dreams. Life doesn't work that way. We need to formulate a plan of action. Let's start with our current sponsors, then I'll approach companies that haven't funded our project in…"

Another alert sounded. There was another mail. Her heart beat a little faster. She wanted so badly for George to be right but she feared the worst.

"What are you waiting for?" George asked.

"I'm too scared to open it. It's from her… from Bianca Evans."

George pulled a face. "I'll do it then." With a flick of the wrist he opened the email. "Shit!"

"What is it?"

"It's a ticket… a plane ticket. You're going to New York. Bianca works for one of the top recruitment firms in the country. You leave first thing on Tuesday. The return flight is on the same day. Pack your bags, baby, you're going to the Big Apple."

"No way!" She shook her head.

"Yes, way! This is legit," George squealed. "I told you

so. I damn well told you so. You're brilliant and it turns out that someone wants you on their team."

Excited now, Meghan opened the original email, scanning the contents and actually taking note this time. "It says that I would need to sign a contract for a minimum of a year. There's a big bonus if I extend it to two. Oh my word." She clapped a hand over her mouth.

"It's huge money," George spoke from over her shoulder.

"Even after a year abroad, there'd be enough to continue our research for a long time. No more begging and pleading. No more looking for funds. We can do this ourselves. We can find a cure ourselves." It cost big money to keep even a small lab operational. The equipment, the rent, things like lights and water. It all added up quickly.

"You've got this," George said. "And I'll be waiting to pick up where we left off when you get back."

Meghan shook her head. "No! They take us both as a team or not at all."

George frowned. "They want you, not me. And from how quickly that ticket came through, I'd say they want you badly."

"We're a package deal. If they want me so badly, they can take both of us."

"Once you have an offer on the table you can negotiate. This might not even be something you want."

"This is scary," she groaned.

"It's exciting." George clapped his hands. "Everything is going to work out just fine, I can feel it."

CHAPTER 6

Two weeks later . . .

Tide knocked once and entered.

Blaze and his brother, Torrent were bent over the desk, staring at the computer screen. Blaze looked up, he gestured for him to move closer. "We're just finalizing who to take on board for our new project." This had nothing to do with Tide. Why had he been called to this meeting? He had a feeling he wasn't going to like the answer to that particular question.

His brother gave a nod of the head in greeting. "Why don't we take the other healer then?" Torrent asked.

"You said you wanted the best, well this female is the best." Blaze shrugged. "Truth be told, I would prefer it if you settled on the male doctor. A male would cause much less trouble."

"That's sexist," Torrent snorted. "You can be thankful my mate is not around to hear you." His brother looked around the room. The male actually looked fearful. "What would Roxanne have to say about you talking like that?"

Blaze looked sheepish at the mention of his own mate. The most feared of the non-humans, king of all four dragon kingdoms, bowed his head. It was pitiful and laughable. The male sucked in a deep breath. "You are right. That's why we have contracts in the first place, to lower the risk to both our males and any humans within our territory. Unfortunately, it is a simple fact that females are more vulnerable."

Torrent stood up to his full height. "You are right, and that's my point exactly. We should take on the best possible person for the job rather than look at the gender of the person. There is a lot at stake." His voice turned deep and his hands fisted at his sides. Torrent probably didn't even realize he was doing it.

"That's why I called this meeting in the first place." Blaze frowned. "The recruitment specialist, Bianca Evans, has informed me that the female doctor we selected is refusing to sign the contract."

"What is she demanding now?" Tide folded his arms. Torrent had brought him up to speed earlier when he requested that Tide attend, on Blaze's instruction. So far, the healer had insisted that they hire her male assistant and at fifty percent more than his current salary. She'd stated that he was her right hand and that she couldn't work without him. They'd reluctantly agreed, and so the contracts had been drawn up. Now she wouldn't sign. This female must be good if she was this full of shit.

"Look," Torrent looked from Tide to Blaze and back again, "it's a negotiation. The human is permitted to come with demands. How bad can it be?"

"That's just it," Blaze sighed. "Doctor Roberts is pissed and I'm afraid I can't blame her."

"What is she pissed about? Those contracts were pretty standard. If she's refusing to sign the non-disclosure—"

"She's happy to sign the non-disclosure, that's not the problem."

Torrent frowned. "What is it then?"

"It can't be the money," Tide blurted. "She'll make more in a month than she did in a year. If she's demanding to go home more than the once a month," he shook his head, "she can forget that."

"That's not it either. She's pretty much married to her work." He paused. "It's the non-fraternization policy. Miss Evans mentioned more than once how angry the doctor became over that particular clause."

"We can't have a human female on our territory unless she signs the contract, including that policy." His brother's eyes were wide. "It's for her own protection and for our sanity. For the sanity of every male in my kingdom. If she's out of bounds there can be no temptation."

Blaze closed the laptop, his jaw was tense, his eyes blazed. "I hear you and I agree. The problem is that the law firm that draws up our contracts fucked up and I'm afraid it hasn't left us with even half a leg to stand on. They omitted to include the same policy in the male's contract. Her laboratory technician, and subordinate, received a contract without the clause. Doctor Roberts is refusing to sign her own contract unless the clause is removed as well."

"That's ridiculous," Tide couldn't help blurting. "We're

a kingdom full of unmated males. A female with freedom to rut whomever she chooses puts herself at great risk. She puts us all at great risk as a direct result. What if something were to happen to her? What if she were to become with child? A human male, on the other hand, is of no interest to our females. There is no need for a male to sign such a clause."

"So what difference would it have made if he did," Blaze snarled. "None! Those contracts should have been the same. Equal rights." He turned to Torrent. "You are right, if Roxy had heard my earlier statement she would have had my balls. As it turns out, she's not impressed with this oversight. Two colleagues, and yet, only the female has a non-fraternization policy in her contract." He scrubbed a hand over his face. "It's a fucking farce. You need to tell me if you want this female in your employ, because she has made this one particular demand a deal-breaker."

Tide exhaled sharply. "When you put it like that, I can understand her frustration."

"I can't blame her for being upset and we can't turn back the clock." Blaze looked back at Torrent. It was his call after all.

His brother looked thoughtful for a few moments. "You're sure she's the right person for the job?"

Blaze frowned. "Her credentials are as long as my arm. The male doctor is probably half as qualified. There is another female with similar credentials but she is mated and has young. She's unwilling to leave her family for an extended period."

"That's just it." Torrent's voice was deep, his eyes blazed. "I'm not willing to risk Sky and her unborn child. There's so much more at stake." He sighed. "We need the best and if Doctor Roberts is the best, then we will work around the policy being omitted."

"I thought you would say that. That's why I included Tide in this meeting. You will need to keep a close eye on this female." Blaze turned back to him. "And it needs to be someone we trust."

And there it was. "What? Why me?" Tide growled. "I'm sorry, it's just that I'm swamped at the moment. I have a trip to the mines planned. There are—"

"Cancel it," Blaze ordered.

"It's not as simple as that, I'm overseeing—"

"I will assign another male to the task." Blaze folded his arms. "One of the Earth dragons can go in your place…" The male lifted his eyes in contemplation for a second or two. "Shale will go in your place."

All of his hard work. His project. His baby. *Fuck!* "That's not a great idea. Shale is a jokester. He is not fit to oversee the sinking of a new shaft."

"Yes, he does like to pull pranks and does take things a little too far at times but he is ultimately a hard worker. Set up a meeting with him and hand the project over to him."

Not a fuck! He'd been working on this for months. All of his research and for what? So that he could hand it all over to that idiot, Shale. Tide swallowed hard, he shook his head. "Please don't make me do this, my lord."

"I'm sorry, Tide," Blaze apologized but remained resolute. "Look, according to the recruitment specialist,

Doctor Roberts is very fixated on her work. So much so that she doesn't have time for relationships. She hasn't been in one for over a year and isn't interested in being tied down anytime soon." The male walked over to him. "You are the only person I trust to watch this female. Storm is still very young, he isn't responsible enough. None of your subordinates will take a task like this seriously. This female is pivotal to the continuation of our work. Nothing can happen to her."

"There has to be someone else. A mated male would be a better choice. What about Lake?"

"That wouldn't work," Torrent said, frowning. "His focus is on his family. His female."

Blaze and Torrent exchanged looks. What was going on? Blaze stepped forward but stopped and glanced back at Torrent. "Can I tell him?"

Torrent nodded. "It's not public knowledge yet, but it will be soon," he turned to Tide, "Candy is expecting. You're going to be an uncle... again."

"What?" Tide couldn't hide his delight. "Candy *and* Sky are with child?"

Torrent nodded. "Yes."

"That's fantastic news. Congratulations." He hugged Torrent, who was grinning broadly.

"We are very excited." His expression soon turned serious. "Both Candy and Sky are part of the experiment. I'm sure you'll understand that Lake is nervous, just as worried as I am. That's what I meant earlier when I said that there was so much at stake. We're talking about my son and heir. My Candy." He looked distraught, his voice thick with emotion.

"Sky and Candy are the only two royal pregnant females at this time." Blaze was animated. "We're making big strides with the silver desensitization. This new program could completely change the face of our affliction. Our future generations could be completely cured of it. It isn't without risk however."

"Major risk." For the first time, Tide noticed how tired his brother looked. How worried.

"Watch this female. Make sure the males stay away from her. Tide doesn't need the added stress right now. Keep a close eye on her. If she is as focused on her work as she says she is, you can step away and eventually go back to the mine. I know how much work you've put into the sinking of the new shaft. I understand your frustration."

Tide ran a hand through his hair, trying hard not to sigh. "You're asking me to babysit a human indefinitely."

"Yes." It was his brother who spoke. "Keep her safe! The males need to know that she is off limits. On top of that, any humans on our territory are a major security risk. Even though we are assigning the male a guard of his own, we want you to keep an eye on both of them. This healer holds the lives of my Candy and our unborn whelp in her hands."

How did he say no to that? He didn't, that was how. Tide squeezed the back of his neck.

"Doctor Roberts is going to play a major role in finding a cure for our silver affliction. Doctor Parry, Granite's mate, made great strides in desensitizing the Earth males but it is a time-consuming process. Another healer has since taken her place. So far it has improved the reactions the males have, but has not been successful in totally eradicating the affliction. Doctor Parry stated that the only way forward is to bring in a specialist, someone who looks specifically at the cause. This healer will look at the building blocks, at the DNA, firstly with an eye to curing our future generations. And secondly with a hope of not just improving but completely eradicating our affliction."

"Can you imagine," his brother's eyes were wide, "if my son, our heir, was born completely free of this burden? Think of how wonderful that would be. A future where there is no more skulking. No hiding. It would be the same for all of our offspring. For all of our future generations." Torrent quickly added, glancing in Blaze's direction, careful to be politically correct.

"It sounds amazing," Tide had to admit. One of the major problems the mine faced was to stay unnoticed. Unrecognizable from the air. Especially considering how many unmarked aircraft had been seen in their airspace of late. It was restricted airspace but that didn't seem to make any difference. They were being actively sought out. Actively hunted. A shiver ran up his spine. "Now that I understand the bigger picture, I think that this new assignment is more important than the sinking of the new mine."

His brother breathed out, his shoulders seemed to slump for a few seconds. "Thank you, brother. You have no idea how much this means to me."

"I think I have an inkling," Tide smiled; he clapped

Torrent on the back before looking Blaze's way. "I only wish you would reconsider Shale as being the right choice. There has to be someone else."

Blaze shook his head. "I'm afraid not. It is important that all four kingdoms are represented when it comes to our shared interests in the mines. Know that I will keep an eye on things."

"If the human hunters were to catch wind of the location of the mine…" Tide shook his head, unwilling to finish the sentence. *Disaster, it would spell disaster.*

"He will do a good job. You will see." Blaze looked Tide in the eyes.

Tide finally nodded. "Very well, I will hand the project over to him."

"Like I said," Blaze went on, "if the human is as focused on her work as she claims to be, I will assign a regular guard in due course and you can resume your duties at the mine."

"Let us hope it happens sooner rather than later," Tide said.

CHAPTER 7

"Oh my god!" Meghan had a hand over her mouth. She could feel that her eyes were wide. "That is the most beautiful thing I have ever seen. Wow!" she added, her eyes tracking the sight before her.

"I completely agree," George mumbled.

She turned towards him, noticing that he wasn't looking at the view like she was. His gaze wasn't tacked to the mountains and valleys as far as the eye could see on one side, and to the deep blue oceans and harsh white cliffs on the other. Or to the sun, as it painted the sky in ribbons of pinks and yellows as it set.

Nope, George had his eyes firmly on a group of men. Big, burly, very naked men. "Oh," Meghan yelped as she looked away. She felt her cheeks heat. They reminded her so much of Tide. Tall and so well built... everywhere. She guessed that all non-humans had big builds in common. She'd found herself stealing glances at each of the guys' faces, real quick, just to be sure that none of them was him. Of course they weren't.

It was stupid of her. "I still can't believe it," she sighed.

"Dragons," a breathy whisper. "They actually exist and are not just a myth."

"Me neither," George sighed. "They're gorgeous. I'm so glad you managed to get us out of that non-fraternization policy. The tattoos are just too much."

"Yeah, what's with that?"

"I don't know, but I likey likey." He was grinning from ear to ear. His eyes were darting from one guy to the next like he couldn't get enough.

"Stop," she whispered, taking a step towards him. "We are here to work, not to mess around."

"All work and no play makes George a dull boy."

"One of those guys would snap you in two," she whispered some more.

"I sure as shit hope so." George made a groaning noise that drew the attention of one of the men.

"Stop it!" she whispered behind her hand. "You're going to get us fired before we even get started."

"You're overreacting."

"Hello," one of the guys greeted as he approached. "I'm River."

"Good to meet you, I'm George and this is Megh—"

"I'm Doctor Roberts." Meghan held out her hand and the guy took it and shook once. He had a hefty grip.

"Please follow me," River announced. Thank god he was wearing pants. They were thin cotton. He wasn't wearing anything else. Not even shoes.

"You don't have to ask me twice." George winked at River, who grinned.

Meghan elbowed her friend as soon as the shifter

turned his back. "Don't make me regret bringing you on board. Don't forget, I hired you, I can just as quickly fire you and don't think I won't. Our future research depends on this."

"Okay, okay," George whispered. He put up his hands as they walked. "We're on the clock, so it's all business, but what I do on my own time is my business."

"As long as you don't do anything stupid."

"Deal." They shook hands.

"Just don't cause any trouble," she added.

"Fine." George rolled his eyes as they gave another quick handshake.

After that, they didn't talk, they gaped at everything around them. The passageways were voluminous. The floors gleamed and were made of what looked like polished volcanic rock. The doors were made of large oak panels and were mostly double volume and ornately carved. The furniture definitely wasn't store bought. It looked hand-carved and from heavy wood. It was all quite simple and yet very impressive.

It wasn't long before they arrived at one of the sets of double doors. To Meghan, the doorknob looked like it was made of copper or brass. It was encrusted with what appeared to be jewels. Rubies, emeralds and diamonds. Excellent fakes, that was for sure.

George widened his eyes at her as they entered the room. It was very spacious and had an open plan with an office area, a long conference table and chairs, as well as a lounge area. There were several crystal chandeliers that seemed to be made from the same metal as the doorknob.

They were so pretty, with hanging fish, seahorses and starfish. All sparkling with the same fake jewels. Only this time in all the colors of the rainbow. It was the view though that took Meghan's breath away all over again. By now, the sunset was rich with deep burgundies. The sun was huge and golden, hanging over a vast deep blue ocean.

George elbowed her and cleared his throat.

When Meghan turned back, she almost walked into a massive man with vivid green eyes. "Oh, so sorry!" She pointed to the window.

The guy smiled. He was handsome. "Spectacular view isn't it."

"Definitely." He wore a pair of black pants, chest bare and oh what a chest. He had the same tattoo as all the others, except his was golden instead of silver. "I'm Meghan… um… Doctor Roberts and this is my colleague, George."

"Your right-hand man." The guy raised his brows.

"Yes, most definitely." *Stop saying definitely, Meghan.* "Couldn't do without him," she added, sounding a little too animated. *Just shut up, Meghan.* Then again, she was entitled to being a bit rattled. This was all too much for a person to take in.

"Let me be the first to welcome you to our lands." He opened his arms and gestured around them. "I am Blaze, king of the Fire dragons and of the four kingdoms."

Oh wow, a king.

"Good to meet you, and thank you," George said. "We're delighted to be here. You could not have hired a better geneticist or a better lab tech, for that matter." He smiled broadly, looking completely unfazed by the intimidating man.

Blaze oozed authority. "Oh, I know. MFA Staffing Solutions highly rec—"

The door opened and the sound of voices carried into the room ahead of the men who entered. Meghan turned her head as they did. *What? Wait. No! Surely not!* She felt like rubbing her eyes and doing a double-take because Tide walked in. He stopped in his tracks as he caught sight of her, his mouth fell open, just as hers had.

"Meghan?" He shook his head like he was trying to shake out of a haze.

"Tide?" Her voice was just as shock-filled. Her eyes flitted from his chest to his face and back again. He too was sporting a big golden tattoo on his chest, as was the guy next to him. It hadn't been there when she had last seen him. She would have noticed, for sure. Tide and the other guy looked like they were related. They had the same build… freaking huge. They both had the same eye and hair color, only Tide's hair was cut shorter.

"You know each other?" someone asked.

Meghan couldn't take her eyes off of Tide long enough to find out who it had been. His eyes seemed to darken as they narrowed in on her and his brow creased. He even put his hands on his hips. "What the hell are you doing here?" His voice was a gruff rasp.

She felt her own brow crease, although hers was with confusion where he looked angry. "I should ask you the same. I thought you said you were a wolf shifter?"

"*You* said I was a wolf shifter and I didn't correct you."

"Okay." There was hesitancy in her voice. Where was he going with this and why were his cheeks turning red?

"You two know each other?" The other guy stepped forward, almost between them, he was also frowning heavily. "Explain quickly, Tide."

"Who are you and what are you doing here?" Tide ignored the other guy. He took a couple of big strides in her direction. Meghan forced herself to stand her ground, he looked that menacing.

"What do you mean? You know who I am." This was starting to irritate her. His whole attitude was uncalled for. "Why didn't you have that tattoo on your chest the last time I saw you?"

"How did you find out about us? What type of intel do you have?" Tide kept on advancing.

She had to crane her neck as he got closer. "Hey!" she yelled as he grabbed her wrists. His hold was firm. Meghan tried to pull free. "Let me go," she finally said, when it didn't work.

"Stop that!" one of the men shouted. His voice deep and menacing. "Let her go."

Tide took no notice, his eyes stayed locked with hers. "You'd better start talking." He walked forward, forcing her to step back. He didn't let up his hold on her.

"Meghan!" George yelled, sounding worried.

"What the hell do you think—?" She yelped as he turned her around, twisting one arm behind her back. It didn't hurt, but it angered her how he had her completely under his control. He kept walking and she was helpless but to let him lead her.

"Tide," Blaze growled. At least, she was pretty sure it was him. It was deep and scary sounding. "Unhand the healer!"

"Listen to your king," the other guy shouted from somewhere behind them. George kept screaming her name followed by 'oh no.' She could hear that his hand was over his mouth and that he was becoming frantic. Thankfully, he didn't try to intervene. Tide would squish him if he did.

"This female obviously knows something," Tide growled, he kept marching her forwards until they reached the wall. He pushed her against it. Again, he didn't hurt her, even though her face was pushed up against the smooth painted surface. "Speak up. Who sent you?" He had her completely trapped. His big body caged her in from behind. Pure muscle. Pure strength. Strangely enough, she wasn't afraid. Meghan didn't think he was going to hurt her. Maybe it was because she was too pissed off to feel fear. *What a jerk! Who did he think he was?*

"You've lost your ever-loving mind!" she yelled, trying to turn back so that she could look him in the face.

"You staged that flat tire. You staged the whole thing," he rasped, his mouth right by her ear. Then his hands were on her, moving over her flesh.

"Hey!" she hollered, trying in vain to break free. "No! Stop that!"

Both of the shifter men behind them screamed Tide's name. They may have said more to try to stop him but there was blood was rushing in her ears. Meghan didn't hear a thing, she only felt his big, warm hands as they moved over her body.

Over her ribs, across her belly. Up and down her legs... *Oh hell!* Up her inner thighs. She tried to keep her legs together but he used his thigh to shove them open. His fingers brushing against her. She moaned, and even though it was out of pure frustration, it still aggravated her even more. "Stop this. I didn't know who you were. I still have no idea. This is a total misunderstanding."

"Why are you here then?" Tide questioned, his mouth even closer to her ear than it had been before. His grip had eased somewhat. Not enough for her to escape.

"I don't know." Frustration was etched into every word. "You tell me. It must be a coincidence."

"I don't believe in coincidences." He shoved his hand between her breasts and then over the tops of them before cupping the undersides. Still looking for a mystery weapon. It was all business though, he wasn't trying to cop a feel.

Her blood boiled nonetheless. "You asshole," she growled. Unable to believe that this was happening.

Both men were yelling behind them with George still shouting her name somewhere in the background. Tide finally let her go. He stepped back. Instant silence befell the room.

Meghan turned. Her face felt hot. Blood pumped through her veins. Her hands were clenched at her sides. "Did you enjoy that?" she spat. "Maybe you should start by telling me who the hell *you* are?"

"What has gotten into you, Tide? There had better be a damned good explanation for this," Blaze demanded.

"Get yourself under control."

"How is it that you know this female?" the other guy asked, directing his question at Tide.

George, face pale, jogged up to her. He flung his arms around her. "You poor baby." His eyes were glistening. Poor thing looked like he had been crying. "You animal!" he shouted in Tide's direction.

"We met at my last stag run," Tide answered, his eyes still on her.

"Oh," Blaze said.

"I see." The other guy nodded his head.

"What does that mean?" George pulled back, eyes wide.

"No, you don't see," Tide insisted. "Her car had conveniently broken down on the side of the road that I just happened to be driving on."

"I was doing perfectly fine on my own. You didn't even need to stop," she blurted.

"Bullshit! You would never have unfastened those lugs on your own. A damsel in distress, covered in grease, you knew I would stop. It was staged."

"Staged!" she yelled. "Are you even hearing yourself?"

"You must have known, somehow, that I was going to drive that way. Why don't you just admit it."

What was wrong with this guy? "Paranoid much! I staged the whole thing on a quiet side road? Really? On a route not many people take. A route that just happens to be on the way to my house. That was clever of me, especially considering I had no idea who you were or where you even came from."

Tide sighed, his jaw tightened. "Okay, I will admit, there was no way you could've known I was going to be on that road." He shook his head. "I only decided to go that route at the last minute. I didn't tell anyone."

"Hah!" She pointed at him. "See. What did I tell you?"

Blaze raised his eyes to the high ceiling for a few moments as if he was trying to compose himself. He finally turned to Tide. "This is our new healer. Doctor Roberts is a highly qualified geneticist, she specializes in hereditary allergies. This is her laboratory assistant, George Norton." Blaze was frowning heavily. "This has to be some kind of misunderstanding, Tide."

"I am Torrent." The other guy stepped forward. "Tide's my brother. He is normally level-headed and rational, that's why we didn't intervene but we should have. I am deeply ashamed and must apologize on—"

"Hold up just a second, before you apologize." Tide's eyes were still intense and still focused solely on her. "I'll buy that our initial meeting wasn't a set-up, but I'm not buying that your being here is a coincidence. Forget that! How did you discover my identity? How did you know where and how to find me? Especially considering I wore a concealer to cover my chest marking." He said the last to himself.

"Wait a minute!" Meghan's eyes felt huge in her head, which she shook in utter disbelief. "Are you accusing me of stalking you?"

George snorted. "As if."

"My phone." Tide lifted his eyes in thought. "Did you look through it? Did you obtain my personal information by snooping?"

"I told you to put a password on that device," Tide's brother muttered through clenched teeth.

"I didn't go through his damned phone." There was frustration laced in every word.

"Meghan would never." George clutched his chest. "Never in a million years. How do you even know this... person?"

Tide cocked his head. "Admit that you're here because of me. This has nothing to do with finding a cure for our silver affliction. You planned this in the hopes that we could pick up where we left off. That's why you insisted on the non-fraternization policy being removed."

"Oh my gosh!" Meghan pushed out a hard breath, trying to keep calm. "You're too much, do you know that? Get off of your high horse. Go and find a safe place to deflate that head of yours." She massaged her temples for a few seconds. "I can't actually believe what I'm hearing." *What a dick! What a jerk!* Her blood boiled at the audacity of his accusations.

"There is no other explanation." Tide kept his eyes on her, searching for a sign that she was lying. A change in her voice. A flicker in her eyes. A quickening of her heartbeat. Something. This was not some big coincidence. *No damned way!*

"How about I accepted a position to work here. I had no idea you would be here. How's that for a reason. It was *you* guys who contacted *me*. Not the other way around."

The little human glared at him. "How do I know that you didn't orchestrate this whole thing? Maybe *you're* the stalker." She pointed at him.

Absurd! He didn't speak out loud though. Blaze scratched his chin. "It's true, we did reach out to Doctor Roberts. It wasn't the other way around and you'll remember all the rounds of negotiations. Getting Doctor Roberts on board was no easy task. The only reason she objected to the non-fraternization policy was because it wasn't in the male's contract. Only hers."

"It was the principle of the matter and not for any other reason." Meghan nodded her head. "I told you it was a coincidence, didn't I?"

"How convenient. You used it as an excuse so that you didn't have to sign." It had to be. Lonely human females could be desperate. He hadn't seen Meghan in that light but maybe he was wrong.

"No, I didn't. I was very upset that you have different criteria for men and women. Last time I checked, this wasn't the dark ages." She scowled at him.

His brother stepped forward, putting himself almost between them. "You had a copy of all of the files of the candidates. Including Doctor Robert's file." Torrent frowned. "There is a picture of her tacked in the front, first page. Her name is in bold on the front cover."

"What do you have to say to that?" Meghan asked, her eyes on him.

Fuck! He didn't buy that this was a coincidence. He didn't. What then?

"Exactly," Meghan said when he didn't say anything

back. She folded her arms as well and there was a smug grin on her face. "Don't try to turn this around on me, bucko."

"I didn't even open that file," Tide retorted. "I didn't open any of them. No reason to. As far as I was concerned, I was going to be sinking…" And now he'd almost blurted out confidential information. He needed to get a damn grip. He sucked in a deep breath. "I was on another assignment. I didn't think it was necessary to go through the files. You," he looked at his brother, "and Blaze had it fully under control."

She snorted. "Yeah right! Tell us another one. My name was in bold on the front cover. You didn't have to open that file to know I was one of the candidates."

"I only knew your first name." He had to work not to shout. "You didn't tell me your surname. I had no idea that Doctor Meghan Roberts was the same person I spent the night with."

"You could easily have seen a piece of mail while you were at my place… something with my full name on it." Her eyes widened and she sucked in a breath. "How do I know you didn't search my house that night, rifle through my drawers while I was sleeping?"

"Why was he at your house while you were sleeping?" The human male piped up, but they all ignored him.

"I would never," Tide denied in a low growl that had the tiny human male flinching. *Good!*

"How do I know you didn't go through *my* phone?" Her eyes twinkled. "*My* phone, *my* personal belongings. You could have found out everything about me. Even where I worked. I think *you* stalked *me* and now you're trying to cover your tracks by putting the blame on me. You may as well admit it." She gave him a self-satisfied smile.

She was jerking him around. Tide rolled his eyes. "You know I didn't… I wouldn't…"

"Oh, but I think you did." Meghan was grinning. Loving every minute of this.

"Okay fine!" he sighed. "You got me. This must be a coincidence." He worked hard at relaxing his stance, at keeping his voice even.

"What was that?" She cupped a hand around her ear.

Tide rolled his eyes. "You heard me."

"Yes, I did. It's a coincidence. Plain and simple. I'll take my apology now." She widened her eyes at him.

"A big part of my job is security. I won't apologize for my actions. They were in the best interest of my people. I *won't* apologize for doing my job. Ever!"

The male elbowed Meghan, his eyes bright. "He spent the night with you?"

"Not now, George," Meghan whispered in the direction of her staff member.

"You were quite heavy-handed with the healer just then," Torrent said.

"You manhandled her," the human, George, said. It was strange because he seemed oddly excited by the fact. "Put your hands all over Doctor Roberts and you seemed to enjoy it too."

"Bullshit!" he snarled and the human shrank back. Not Meghan however, she put her hands on her hips and stepped in between them. "I won't hurt the tiny male," he quickly assured her, frowning. "It would be an unfair fight," he added. The female finally stepped out of the way. "I don't rut human females twice. I was merely checking for weapons."

"Rut?" The male frowned. Then his eyes widened. "Oh… rut." The human laughed and clapped his hands with glee. It was bizarre to see. Humans could be funny creatures. Tide had never spent much time in the company of the males of the species. He had never paid them much attention to them in the past. No wonder human females preferred non-humans.

"Stop. It." Meghan spoke through clenched teeth, her gaze firmly on George. "We will talk about this later."

"Yes, we most certainly will," the male said, eyes still shining with… excitement. His reaction didn't make any sense to Tide.

"This changes things," Torrent muttered, frowning heavily.

"Yes, you are right." Blaze nodded.

"I'm not sure that it would be wise to give you this assignment in light of the new development." His brother looked deep in thought.

Yes!

This was great. He could head to the mine and oversee the sinking of the new shaft just as he planned all along. Shale had been completely serious during their meeting and had even surprised him by asking relevant questions. One or two had been angles he hadn't considered himself. The male had seemed competent to do the job, and yet, all those months of prep. All those months of work. *His* work. This was his project, dammit.

"Maybe we should stick to our original plan," Blaze spoke to Torrent.

"Keep them on their original assignments?" Torrent nodded.

"What plan? What assignments?" Shale sauntered into Torrent's office. "My lords." He nodded to Blaze and then Torrent in turn.

"To send Tide on his original assignment and to give you this one. It turns out that Doctor Roberts and Tide have had previous dealings."

"Oh, is that right?" The male raised his brows, a stupid grin on his face. His eyes had this glint that Tide didn't like. Now this was the Shale he knew well. The male who was full of shit. "How is it that the two of you know one another?" Shale asked, looking from the healer to him and back again.

"It's not important," Meghan blurted.

"They met at a stag run," Blaze said, at the same time.

"Oh, I see. How interesting." Shale's gaze moved to the female, whose face was flaming red. His eyes dipped down to her chest for a second, two before moving back to her face. He was checking her out. *What the fuck!* The male was checking her out. Even worse, he seemed interested. "I would be happy to keep an eye on the lovely Doctor Roberts."

"I told you, I don't need a babysitter." Meghan shook her head.

"It's not something that's up for discussion, Doctor,"

Torrent paused. "All humans on dragon territory are guarded. It's just as much… it's for your own safety," he blurted.

"In that case, I'd rather that he," she gestured to Shale, "was my guard then. I don't want Tide anywhere near me." She glanced at him, her eyes narrowed and her jaw tightened.

"Then it's settled." Shale's grin turned into a big-ass smirk.

"No, it's not." Tide shook his head. "I will guard the female," he announced. *What the hell had he just said? Fuck!* Then again, he knew why. Shale was a dick. The male planned on taking advantage of the female. For whatever reason, the male had been serious about the tasks at the mine, but he wasn't serious about this. There was so much at stake. The healer was very important. Finding a proper cure for their affliction was essential for the species' continuation. Shale could screw this up. Put a sexy female in front of a male like Shale and watch him lose his sense of reason. Good thing Tide didn't suffer from the same problem.

Blaze shook his head. "I don't think it's a good idea."

Torrent stepped forward. "I agree with Blaze. You and Doctor Roberts have a history. It wouldn't be wise to—"

"I'm the perfect male for the job. Even more so than before. I never rut a human female twice. You know that, Torrent."

The female put a hand over her mouth as she gasped. "What happened that night is private. How dare you."

Tide ignored her. "I'm the best male for the job because

there will be no temptation. I've already had her."

"Oh my… Tell everyone everything, why don't you?" Meghan was breathing heavily. He wasn't sure what the problem was. He was simply stating facts. "You are a horrible person." She bit down on her lip and shook her head. Looking both sad and angry. Tide wasn't sure why.

"Tide is right," Torrent acknowledged. "I've never known him to bed the same human female twice."

Meghan made a squeaking noise and started counting. *Weird!*

"You're sure?" Blaze asked, eyes on Torrent. His brother nodded.

"I don't want him as my guard. I refuse." The human folded her arms. "I'll take anyone else."

"You've had your way throughout this entire negation," Tide hesitated. He needed to tread carefully. "I'm sorry I accused you of wrongdoings. I'm sorry I patted you down in that manner and for accusing you of stalking me, but this is non-negotiable. I will be your guard for the foreseeable future." He glanced Blaze's way. The male inclined his head to show his approval.

"No, I…" Meghan stopped talking when the human male grabbed her hand and squeezed. "You don't expect me to agree to this?" she turned to the male, talking to him.

"We'll talk about it later." George widened his eyes to tell her to keep quiet.

"I'm not happy with this." Meghan pulled her hand free and folded her arms.

"Tide is the best male for the job," Torrent addressed

the female, talking carefully and softly.

"I disagree. Like you said," she addressed Blaze, "there is a history there." Her cheeks were still red.

"In this instance, it does not matter," Blaze said.

"Of course it matters. I don't like him at all and yet he's going to trail me twenty-four-seven."

"Not quite twenty-four-seven. Dragons sleep too," Tide interjected, "but I will choose my reliever very carefully."

The female glanced his way but didn't respond. "Fine, not twenty-four-seven then," she addressed Torrent. "Fact is, I will be expected to spend a ton of time with him. I don't like him at all."

"Meghan," the male, George, interrupted in a sing-song voice. He was trying to get her to cooperate.

"You don't have to like me," Tide said. "It's probably better that you don't like me. I'm not going to be your companion, I'm going to be your guard."

"The point is that I'll have to see you every damn day. I don't like the idea of that."

"Meghan," the human male said, more forcefully this time. "Let it go," he said, under his breath.

"Tough luck, female. Ignore me then. Forget I'm even there." His voice took on a ragged edge.

"Fat chance of ignoring your ugly mug."

His brother laughed. He fucking laughed. *The prick.*

"Have you seen how big you are?" the female went on. "Hard to ignore a big lump like you."

Torrent laughed some more. His brother was loving this. *Fucker!*

"I'm your shadow for the foreseeable future. Get used to the idea." Tide narrowed his eyes on her.

"You had better stay out of my way." Her eyes blazed. "Don't speak to me. I want nothing to do with you." She pointed her finger at him. "I hope that's clear."

"Best you behave then," Tide said.

Her mouth fell open. It didn't take her long to regain her composure. "I'm not some damn child. You can't talk to me like that." She glanced at Torrent. "He can't talk to me like that."

"Things will settle quickly. You will see, Doctor. Ignore my brother. I know that he will be nothing but polite going forward." Torrent gave him a hard stare. "Won't you brother?"

Tide clenched his teeth to keep from responding. Shale chuckled. *The jerk.*

"Won't you, brother?" Torrent asked again. Even more forcefully this time. "Nothing but polite?"

Shale all out laughed.

"Yes," he pushed the word out between gritted teeth. Great, he was already regretting his decision of taking on this assignment. As the healer walked towards the door, Shale's gaze dropped to the female's ass. Meghan might be annoying, but she was important to his people. He'd do his job and he'd make damned certain that she stayed focused on hers. Shale could go to hell. Tide had to bite back a growl.

CHAPTER 8

"Unpack please," George pleaded. "Let me help you." He walked over to her suitcase which was still closed at the foot of the bed.

"No!" She folded her arms. "I'm not staying."

"Megs, babe, you're being unreasonable."

"Do. Not. Megs babe. Me!" She knew she was being a tad unreasonable but she couldn't seem to get herself under control. She'd never been so humiliated in her whole life.

George swallowed hard. He took a seat on the edge of her bed. "I'm sorry."

He did look sorry but she knew he couldn't possibly mean it. "You're not sorry. You think this is hilarious."

"No, I don't." There was a pleading edge to his voice.

"You do too." She stomped to the other side of the room before heading back. "As soon as that door closed," she gestured to the front door, "you laughed so hard you were crying. Real tears and all."

"Some of this *is* pretty funny. Come on!"

"There was nothing funny about being humiliated like

that." She felt her lip wobble.

"Oh, hun… don't cry." George jumped up. "I'm such a cow, I'm sorry. I mean it this time." Sincerity shone in his eyes. "I didn't realize you had taken it so hard. The way you handled that Tide guy, in the end, was brilliant. I'm so darned sorry. Look at you all teary-eyed."

"Teary-eyed my ass." She sniffed. "Don't you worry. I won't be crying over that asshole. We had a one-night stand, that was all. It's over and done with. I cannot believe he said those things." She shook her head.

"He's a big ole ass," George tutted. "At least he's a gorgeous ass though. Did you see his eyes? Oh," his lips twitched, "I'm forgetting, you've seen way more than his eyes." He bobbed his brows.

"Don't. I want to forget that night ever happened. He's an ass, full stop." She said it with venom.

"Was he at least good in bed?" George's eyes brightened and his back straightened. "Please tell me he was good."

"It doesn't matter."

"Of course it matters. He seems like quite the intense type and those normally make the best lovers. It's just that you're not one for casual hook-ups."

George looked at her like he was sizing her up or something. Like maybe he didn't know her as well as he thought he did.

"No." She shook her head. "It wasn't like me to invite him back to my place. I don't normally do things like that… no." She shook her head again. Why did she feel the need to defend herself? "We don't live in the dark ages.

Women can be sexual as well, you know."

"Absolutely! There's nothing wrong with a bit of good, clean fun. Thing is, it's not something you would normally do…?" Again, his eyes narrowed and he seemed to size her up."

She shook her head.

"So, it's a hope it was at least good for you, right?"

She didn't answer. She didn't want to think about Tide or the night they had spent together. She certainly didn't want to be reminded of how good it was. "It doesn't matter," she mumbled. "I don't want to stay anymore, George. We can figure something else out."

"Why? Because your assigned guard is someone from your past? How long ago was your little tryst?"

She sighed. "Going on two months ago."

He raised his brows. "So recent then. Understandable that you might be a bit sensitive about it. You need to think carefully about this, Meghan. You're going to blow this opportunity because you're pissed at Tide. Talk about cutting your nose off to spite your face. You need to do as he says and completely ignore him. Tide is as arrogant as they come, he'll hate it if you do."

Meghan frowned. "Doubtful, since he's the one who suggested it."

"You saw the way he reacted, he couldn't believe your being here was a coincidence. Why? Because the guy has an ego as big as this mountain. Maybe bigger."

"That's for sure." *Asshole!*

"Guys like that expect women to fall at their feet. They expect to be chased. I'm sure he's had it happen before.

The chasing, the stalking, the begging. All of it. It's what he's used to."

Meghan made a snorting noise. "He can forget it. I'm not chasing or stalking him. He's not getting even a glance from me."

"Exactly. Tide isn't used to being ignored," George said. "You saw him – he might be a jerk-off but he's damned hot. Hotter than most." Then he laughed. "Did you see his face when you told him he had an ugly mug?" He laughed some more. "I doubt anyone has said anything like that to him before."

She smiled. "He *was* shocked. I just said the first thing that came into my head. Asshole deserved it."

"Yes he did, and he'll flip if you follow through and ignore the hell out of him."

"I knew he was a bit arrogant when I met him but I didn't realize the extent of that arrogance. Also, even though he was full of himself, he was pretty sweet. I guess I was wrong about that. He just wanted to get into my pants, that's all."

"I hate to break it to you, hun, but a guy like Tide can have almost anyone he wants."

"Oh gee, thanks."

"No, I don't mean it like that. I keep telling you that you're a catch, but you won't listen. What I meant was, I doubt he was just being nice to get into your pants. Maybe deep down under all of that macho man exterior is a half decent guy."

"I highly doubt it," she blurted.

"Mmmmm…" George raised his eyes in thought.

"Then again, maybe you're right. It doesn't matter though, does it? It's not like you actually want to be with him or anything."

"Hell no!" she answered, her voice high-pitched.

"It's not like you're going to let him hop back into bed with you?" George raised his brows, clearly waiting for an answer.

"In his dreams." Her hands actually curled into fists at her side as she said it. Tide could go to hell for all she cared.

CHAPTER 9

Meghan sucked in a deep breath and walked out of her apartment. She could do this. Screw Tide. She was going to focus on the job at hand, and in so doing, she'd earn enough money over the next year or two to fund her asthma research. She relished the idea of not having to search for funding. Of being in control of her own future.

"Good morning," a loud voice sounded from a few meters down the hall.

Meghan just about jumped out of her skin. She made a yelping noise and clutched her chest.

"My apologies!" The big dragon shifter looked sheepish. "I didn't mean to scare you."

"It's fine. Just don't sneak up on me again."

The guy smiled brightly. "I'm Bay. I was standing here the whole time. In fact, I've been here all night."

"Oh, okay. I didn't see you there." She could feel her heart-rate normalizing.

"It looked like you were deep in thought. Don't mind me. Tide assigned me as the backup guard." Bay was smiling broadly. He looked really sweet.

"Good to meet you, I'm Meghan."

"I've been instructed to call you Doctor Roberts, if you don't mind?" He clasped his hands together behind his back.

"Of course." She inclined her head.

"Follow me and I'll take you through to the laboratory." Bay glanced back at Meghan as he strode ahead. They walked down several passages. All of them wide and high ceilinged. After a couple more twists and turns, Bay opened a door and gestured for her to enter.

Meghan walked in, finding George already there. "How awesome is this?" He gestured around them.

Meghan gasped. "We got everything." She swallowed hard. "Every item on our list." At least it looked that way at a glance.

"Oh yes, and all top of the line." He spoke quickly, obviously excited.

"Oh my word. An Electrophoresis System." Meghan gaped at the sleek machine.

"Yep and a Thermal Cycler. It's a scientist's wet dream."

"That's for sure." Meghan walked around the large space. It too had the same high, cave-like ceilings she'd come to expect in the dragon castle. Only, this wasn't like a traditional castle. Not that she'd seen many but heck, she didn't need to have. This one was built into the side of a cliff. The view from the lab was just as spectacular as through any other window. A horse-shoe shaped bay with sheer cliffs. The blue, sparkling ocean and mountains in the backdrop, they went on for as far as the eye could see. She shivered, realizing how distant they were from any kind of civilization. Not that the dragon castle didn't possess all of the modern conveniences. Meghan only had to look around her to know that she lacked for nothing.

"Good morning." Torrent stepped through the door.

"Morning," both she and George said.

"And who is this little princess?" asked George, his eyes on the tiny girl in Torrent's arms. Just then a petite blonde entered the room. With big blue eyes, she was beautiful, reminding Meghan a bit of a Barbie doll.

"This is my mate Candy and our daughter, Rain" The little girl buried her head into her father's chest. She was a carbon copy of her mother. Very pretty with delicate features and blonde hair. The only difference was that her hair was slightly curly where Candy's hair was perfectly straight.

"It's lovely to meet you. I'm Doctor Roberts and this is my assistant, George." He stepped forward and shook the woman's hand. Meghan went on, "I will be taking care of you during your pregnancy. Congratulations, by the way, I believe you only just found out."

Candy smiled. "Thank you. We're very excited. It's good to meet both of you."

"Shall we all take a seat and have a chat about what the coming months will entail?" Meghan grabbed her notepad and a pen off of her desk.

Candy nodded. Torrent put a hand to her back, he gave his wife a look that was filled with such affection.

In a similar fashion to Torrent's office, there was a

lounge area. They made their way there, Torrent and his family made themselves comfortable on a loveseat.

"I'll just take inventory." George pointed to where all the smaller equipment was kept. "I'll be over there if you need me."

Meghan nodded and then turned back to the couple. She opened the notepad and clicked the pen. She still found it hard to believe that they were amongst dragon shifters and Torrent was the king of the Water dragons. It was surreal.

She needed to push those thoughts aside. As well as any lingering notions she had of Tide and what had happened the day before. Maybe he had changed his mind about being her guard. She hoped so. "Right, let's begin. I have a couple of questions and then I'm going to explain how I foresee this going. We need to remain flexible and acknowledge that changes are going to be made as we go along. Nothing quite like this has ever been attempted. Not to this degree anyway."

Both Torrent and Candy nodded.

"Okay then. How long is a normal pregnancy?"

"Six months," Torrent and Candy answered together.

Torrent smiled and gave Candy's thigh a squeeze. "I'll leave you to it. Let me know if you want my input."

Candy nodded and smiled. Her eyes filled with so much love it was sickening, but only because Meghan was a bit jealous. People didn't often find love like that. It was incredibly rare. *Concentrate!* Meghan made a note. "Good. How far along are you?"

"I suspect around three weeks. Give or take a day or

two." She beamed.

Meghan noted that down. "And…"

"Oh," Candy said, "it's important to note that Rain isn't Torrent's biological daughter. We were together when I was pregnant with her and she does have some dragon traits."

Meghan frowned. "I'm not sure if I follow. If she isn't his child, then she shouldn't have any of his traits."

"That's the thing. When humans mate with non-humans, they slowly take on some of their traits. I can only speak for myself here, but I know it's true of all of the other human women mated to dragon shifters as well. The longer we're mated, the more apparent it is. I can hear better, see better… way better." She lifted her shoulders. "It's incredible. I can't breathe underwater, but—"

"Wait just a minute." Meghan held up a hand. She frowned. "Breathe under water?"

"Sorry." Candy sucked in a deep breath. "I keep forgetting that you're not from here. Water dragons can breathe underwater."

"We don't have gills. Not on the surface at least." Torrent gestured to the sides of his neck and moved his head to the left and then to the right in an exaggerated fashion. "We believe that they must be built into our lungs. Or that our lungs have the ability to take oxygen out of the water, but yeah, we can breathe underwater."

"Wow, that's interesting."

"I can stay underwater much longer than before. Much longer than what is considered normal," Candy said. "Seven or eight minutes at a time."

Meghan made a note. "Okay. That's amazing. I'll want to take a look at both your DNA and that of your child." She looked down at Rain who was playing with a stuffed toy. "More specifically, at how it's changed."

Candy nodded.

"Not if it's going to put our unborn child at risk." Torrent sounded gruff.

"This type of test is risk-free. I will simply swab the inside of your mouth. So it's non-evasive."

"Not everything you have planned will be non-evasive though?" His voice was a rough rasp.

Meghan clasped her hands together on her lap. "No, you are right. We will discuss risk shortly," she sighed. "I will say right off the bat that what I'm about to propose is not without risk. We will monitor Candy and Sky carefully." She looked at her watch. "I'm meeting with Sky and Lake after this. I will fill you in on all the details and then you can both decide if this is what you really want to do, given the risks."

Torrent nodded. He was frowning heavily and looked worried. "I'm not sure this is what we should be doing," he spoke to Candy.

"It will be for the benefit of our people. We have to try."

"I don't know." Torrent shook his head. "I don't want to take any risks. Not with you, my love." He turned to look at Meghan. "You need to understand, healer, that most dragon females do not survive miscarriages. The further along a female is, the more chance she has of dying. Candy is a fragile human. She carries a dragon child, a son and my heir. He is strong. Dragons fight to survive no matter their age. Dragon young, even when still in the womb, will hold on. They hold on, to the detriment of their mother, often ripping them apart from the inside. It is normally the blood loss that ends up being fatal. Even to a fully-fledged dragon female. My Candy would not stand a chance."

"I see." She deliberated for a moment. "I propose that we take the least evasive route. I would recommend that any female planning to become pregnant start on my autoimmune therapy as well. It would have been ideal to have had Candy already on the program. Unfortunately, that is not the case."

"Well then, it's probably too great a risk——"

"Like I said, we will take every precaution. Did you order the special hypodermic needles like I requested?"

"Yes, they're in the cupboard with the rest of the supplies."

"Good." She nodded. "The questionnaire you filled out previously was very informative."

Torrent nodded.

"You stated that dragon skin, even when you're in human form, is practically impenetrable due to the fact that you heal at such a rapid rate. That the only time it takes longer to heal is when your immune system is compromised, like when you have been injured by silver or if a female is pregnant. This is particularly true if both circumstances occur together."

"Yes, that's correct." Torrent nodded.

"You also mentioned that the only way to successfully

breach skin is to use silver, but that high dose contact is toxic to a fetus and can kill the mother too. As you pointed out. Even a healthy dragon shifter will become sick with prolonged contact."

"Yes, That's right." Candy looked down at her lap for a few moments.

"Well," Meghan went on. "Has anyone thought to use a stainless-steel silver mix, or have you always just used a pure silver blade or hypodermic needle?"

"Oh," Torrent breathed out the word rather than spoke it. "That's genius," he went on. When he looked her head on, his eyes were bright with excitement. "That's why you had me order an array of needles. Two percent silver, four, eight and so forth."

"Exactly, so, we're not just going to look at contact time but we're going to start with the needles that contain the least amount of silver. The idea is to slowly introduce more and more allergens, thus building up a resistance. I need to meet with Doctor Parry. I believe she is with the Earth dragons."

"That is correct. Doctor Parry is an allergist, she has been treating the males for our allergy affliction and has made some major headway."

Meghan nodded her head. "Yes, I read her files but have some questions for her."

"You may meet with her. Doctor Parry had twins a couple of months ago. Another healer has taken her place."

"I will need to meet with both of them then, if that's okay?"

Torrent nodded. "As far as I'm concerned, you can have whatever you need to do your job and," he frowned heavily, "to keep my Candy safe. Sky too of course. You also have Blaze's blessing, so it won't be a problem."

Just then, the door opened and Tide walked in. He wore a pair of dark blue cotton pants. Otherwise, his chest was bare. Not something she would get used to easily. She quickly looked away. She didn't want him thinking that she was interested in any way. She planned on ignoring the hell out of him just as George had recommended. She pulled in a breath and held it for a few moments before continuing. "The plan is to slowly desensitize you during this pregnancy by exposing you to higher levels of the allergen and by increasing the contact time."

"I'm not allergic," Candy said.

Bay left the room, quietly closing the door behind him and Tide took his place. *Not looking!* "Yes, but according to the reports I have read, children born to non-humans are more like their fathers. In fact, all have been males. It shows that non-human genes are dominant. None of the children, however, have ever been tested for the allergy."

Torrent nodded. "That is correct."

"I need to verify this before we begin, but it stands to reason that they will be affected."

"I'm sure this will be the case," Torrent said gravely.

"Therefore, your child will most likely also be allergic. By going through the motions of desensitizing you, we hope to improve or even to eradicate the allergy in your unborn son."

Torrent nodded. He looked worried.

"Like I said," she went on. "I will take every precaution. We will monitor both Candy and the baby, every step of the way, to ensure that all is well."

"I'm still not sure." He shook his head.

"I typed up a full report. It will give you a good idea of what you can expect over the next few months leading up to your son's birth. It will outline every procedure. Obviously we need to remain flexible, and, I can tell you now, the desensitization program will need to be altered as we go along. I'm hoping that at least one of the children, either yours or Sky's, will be born free of the silver allergy. Obviously, both would be the ideal situation."

"Do you really think it will be possible to create a vaccine from the blood of a dragon baby born without the affliction?"

She nodded. "Yes, it's an involved, complicated process. It's also groundbreaking work but I know it can be done."

"In other words, it's not a tried and tested method."

She shook her head. "No, in fact, there are scientists who don't believe it's possible. I'm not one of them."

"It seems like an awful lot of risk for something that may just be pie in the sky," Torrent's voice had taken on a rasping tone.

"Honey, don't be rude." Candy clasped his arm and the little girl on his lap squirmed. She giggled. Rain was looking at Tide, who pulled another face. The little girl giggled again, trying to get off of her father's lap.

Torrent finally let her go with a sigh. Rain tottered over to Tide, who picked her up. Rain laughed wildly. Torrent turned towards his brother. He must have given him a dirty look because Tide put up a hand. "Sorry, I'll take Rain outside for a few minutes. Leave you to talk." He held her tight with one arm and tickled her with the other. Rain squealed with glee. The door clicked closed, drowning out the noise of the little girl's laughter. She obviously loved her uncle. It was strange to see how good he was with her. *Moving on!*

"Sorry about that," Torrent apologized. "Tide takes his uncle duties very seriously."

She nodded. "I understand. Back to our conversation." She certainly didn't want to think about how cute the little girl had looked in her uncle's arms. Or how good Tide was with her. He was still a jerk. "It's called a prophylactic injection. There has been some success in creating this type of non-infectious vaccine for cancer, as well as with type 1 diabetes. Look, it is new and completely revolutionary but I believe strongly in my research. I'm this close," she held two fingers together, almost touching, "to developing a vaccine against asthma. Not only do I believe it's possible but I'm going to make it happen."

"I know this already," Torrent went on. "It is why you are here. I'm just not convinced."

"I understand your fear. Thing is, I strongly believe it's possible to create a vaccine that will cure you of your allergy to silver. Worst case scenario, through immunotherapy in the pregnant women, in your wife, I believe that we will either eradicate the allergy in the children completely. Or at the very least, significantly decrease their reaction to silver. It's a process though.

Here…" Meghan stood up and reached for her leather sling bag. She removed the file she had prepared. "This outlines and explains everything. I took Doctor Parry's findings and combined them with my research and have come up with a detailed plan. In a nutshell, we will slowly increase the exposure to allergens. In your case, Candy, we will monitor the fetus closely. In the case of Sky, I will monitor both mother and child throughout."

"Thank you for this." Candy held up the file.

Torrent gripped her hand in a firm grasp. "If we decide to proceed with this, you will take every precaution imaginable. I will be here for every session."

"Darling, I—"

"No, my love," his voice turned thick with emotion, "I cannot abide the possibility of anything happening to you."

Meghan felt awkward. She wasn't sure where to look as Torrent cupped his wife's cheek. "Oh, my love," Candy whispered, "I will be fine. You heard the doctor."

"You should let Sky—"

"No!" Candy shook her head. "We will take every precaution. I need to do this, for our people, but most of all I need to do it for him." She stroked her belly. "For our son."

Torrent cupped her other cheek and put his forehead to hers. Meghan looked away. Maybe she should leave the room. There was a sucking noise. She glanced back at the couple, who were kissing at this point. Tongues and all. George busied himself counting and noting down stock.

She looked down at the notepad on her lap and added

some doodles. She couldn't think rationally while the two of them…

The door opened. "Hey, you two," Tide said, putting his head around the jamb.

"Oh," Candy said, as Torrent released her. She rubbed her lips with the tips of her fingers.

Tide grinned, he shook his head and pushed the door all the way open. Rain was still in his arms.

"Mama," she yelled as she caught sight of Candy.

"Hey, baby." Candy smiled. Both she and Torrent stood up. Tide put the squirming girl down.

"We will let you know what we decide," Torrent said.

"Thank you." Candy picked up her daughter and gave the little one a kiss on the top of her head. "We'll be in touch."

"You shouldn't carry heavy things." Torrent took Rain from her mother's arms. "Come to dada." He smiled at the tiny girl.

"I will need to visit the various dragon kingdoms and to test every child, particularly those born to human women. Maybe one of them has a natural immunity, in which case, I can develop a vaccine that way. I'm afraid I'll have to start soon after that. Your pregnancy is much shorter than that of a human to human pairing. So the window of opportunity is a small one."

"Oh, I didn't realize you planned on visiting all the kingdoms. I thought it was just Doctor Parry." Torrent raised his brows.

She shook her head. "No, I need to visit them all and test all the children, whether royals or not. I will also need permission to test Rain."

"That's fine." Candy nodded. "As long as it won't hurt her or make her sick."

"No." Meghan shook her head. "At most, she would have a tiny red mark on the inside of her arm. That's if she is allergic. It would disappear within a few hours. Maybe less. Again, I assure you, I would take every precaution."

They said their goodbyes. Tide kissed the little girl on the forehead. "You be good." He tweaked her little button nose. "Or the tickle monster will come and get you." He proceeded to pretend he was going to tickle her. Rain squealed and laughed, crunching over against her father to protect her mid-section.

"You need one of your own," Torrent said, smiling.

"Maybe one day." Tide gave Rain another soft kiss on the temple and they left. Tide walked out into the hall.

Ignore him! Maybe he was going to stay out in the hall. A girl could hope. Meghan walked over to her desk but before she could sit down, the door opened and Tide entered with another guy. "This is Ice," he announced.

She wanted so badly to ignore him flat out, but that would be rude to the new guy in the room. Meghan nodded. "It's good to meet you." She chose to focus on Ice, still ignoring Tide.

"Good to meet you too, Doctor Roberts. You must be George." He looked towards the back of the lab. George held a test tube tray.

He put down the tray and walked over. "Ice. That's an interesting name." There was a gleam in his eye and a smirk on his face.

Meghan had to work to keep from rolling her eyes. Ice had dark hair and very blue eyes. He, just like the others, was really good-looking. George was having an absolute field day.

Ice's smile grew bigger. "Water dragons are named after anything to do with water. I'm sure you have come to realize that by now. Our chest markings have green threaded through them."

"Why are your makings silver, while some of the others I've seen have been golden?" George asked, his eyes roving all over Ice's chest as he spoke.

"Royals have golden markings. Tide is a prince."

"Interesting." George nudged her with his elbow. "Isn't that interesting, doc?"

She made a noise that showed her disinterest, pretending to look at something in the notepad.

"Ice will be your assigned guard. He will introduce you to his reliever at change of shift," Tide said, speaking to George. "Ice, will you please show George around a bit? There is something I need to discuss with the doctor."

"Actually, George is busy at the moment." She looked up from her notepad and into his eyes. His very blue, very gorgeous eyes. It irritated her how attracted she still was to him. Her body didn't seem to care that he was a grade-A ass.

"I'm sure you can spare him for a few minutes. Ice, if you will?" He gestured to the door.

Asshole!

"I would prefer it if…"

"It's fine," George responded, he widened his eyes at

her, trying to tell her to drop it. "I'll be back shortly. If Ice is going to be my guard, then we need to get acquainted." He winked at Meghan and she battled to keep from snorting.

"Fine, but I need you back here in five. We have a lot to do."

The door closed behind them as they left and the room seemed to close in on her. Suddenly the ceiling wasn't as high. The air seemed to thin as well because it was harder to breathe. Her skin prickled with awareness. She hated how she was reacting to him. Hated. It. "What happened to us ignoring one another?" She looked at him with as much malevolence as she could muster. "That was the deal."

CHAPTER 10

T here was definite venom in her eyes, which were narrowed on him.

"There are a few things I need to say, and then, for the most part, we will ignore one another, if that's really what you want." He shrugged. If it made her feel more comfortable, then so be it. He had thought that maybe she would have calmed down by today, but he was obviously wrong.

"It is." She folded her arms. She really was pissed at him, although he wasn't sure exactly why. Was it his treatment of her when they first saw each other again yesterday or was it his mention of the fact that he didn't rut human females twice? She hadn't liked it when he had said that he was done with her. He got the feeling it was a bit of both. Her feelings had been hurt. Also, it was his experience that human females wanted more from him. Meghan was no different. It couldn't be helped. However, he needed to be clear where things stood between them.

"Fine with me," he said, folding his own arms across his chest.

"What did you want to tell me?" She pursed her full lips. Definitely pissed.

"A couple of things. Firstly, a warning. Shall we sit down?" He gestured towards the couch.

Meghan shook her head, her ponytail bounced. "I'm fine."

"Suit yourself." He suppressed a sigh. *So damned dramatic.* "Right. You need to tread carefully when it comes to this therapy you're prescribing. If anything were to happen to Candy, my brother would kill you…"

"I've made it clear that it's not without risk. I detailed everything in that file. Any patients I test or run therapies on will need to sign an indemnity. I will explain—"

"We are not human."

"I know that." Irritation was laced into every word.

"No, I don't think you do. We are governed more by instinct than by logic, particularly in difficult, emotional situations. If anything were to happen to Candy, Rain or that unborn child, he might very well lash out and literally kill you. As in, end your existence."

Her mouth dropped open and she paled. Good, she'd actually listened to him and had taken him seriously. "I see." Her gaze moved to the floor.

"I hope that you do. Plan your course of action well. Think very carefully before you act. We would like nothing more than to see our people cured of this affliction but not at the cost of the lives of our mates and children."

"That is understandable and I assure you that I have…"

He shook his head. "Don't assure me, Meghan—"

"Doctor Roberts," she narrowed her eyes, "you can call

me Doctor Roberts."

"Really?" Tide blurted. "I spent the night in your bed. I tasted your pussy and felt your g-spot at the end of my dick."

She gasped. "That's inappropriate and I would appreciate it if you never mentioned that night again."

"Why? It happened. Not mentioning it won't make it go away."

"It may have happened, but it's in the past and quite frankly I regret the whole thing."

Tide couldn't help the chuckle that was pulled from him. "Bullshit. It was the best sex you've ever had and there's no way you could scream that loud and say my name so many damn times and have regrets."

"Want to bet?" Her eyes widened when she realized what she'd said. It might be a bet he was willing to take if goaded enough. "For your information, I've had better sex. Way better." She actually looked serious.

He all out laughed. "Yeah right. I don't believe you."

"Believe whatever you want. I don't care. Now if we're done, I would like to go back to ignoring you, please."

"Just because I said I don't have sex with the same human female twice. That's why you're pissed, isn't it? Did I hurt your feelings?"

Meghan snorted. "No, not at all. It was a one-night stand. Nothing more. You are the total opposite of my type."

"Oh really?"

"Yes," she nodded, "really. I know it's hard for you to believe but I prefer brains over brawn."

"Right."

"I can see that, once again, you don't believe me." She rolled her eyes. "You have the biggest ego I've ever encountered. You'll just have to take my word for it."

Meghan... Doctor Roberts... was right, he didn't believe her. Not one bit. "It doesn't matter either way because I won't be fucking you anytime soon."

Meghan began to choke and on nothing. She put a hand to her chest, breathing deeply. "Oh my," she finally said when she got herself under control. "Your ego is even bigger than I suspected. I have a perfectly good working dildo. I don't need you or any man for that matter. Now if we're done, I'd like you to go and stand in that corner and you can stay far out of my way. In fact, I would prefer it if you stood outside of *my* laboratory. You don't need to be in here."

"No!" He shook his head. "I'm staying right here where I can keep a close eye on you."

"What about when I'm in my apartment? Do you plan on showering with me and sleeping in my bed as well?"

He shrugged. "That can be arranged but you wouldn't be able to make use of the merchandise." Tide palmed his cock through his pants. Little fucker liked the idea of being in her bed. Of being inside her. It wasn't going to happen though.

"Stop it already," she growled. Her cheeks were red with anger. "You are too much."

Truth was, he didn't need to be inside the laboratory. He could just as well stand outside the door but she didn't need to know that. He was a dick, but he liked how

flustered she had become. It would be more fun keeping
an eye on things from in here. "I will stay outside the door
of your apartment. I have fantastic hearing, so be very
careful of what you decide to get up to." He paused. "I
will be your shadow at all other times."

"Fine. Are we done?" She huffed, folding her arms and
looking at him like something the cat dragged in.

He shook his head. "Ice mentioned that he finds you
attractive. He specifically mentioned your melons."

"My what?" She turned and walked away, gripping the
base of her ponytail. "I literally can not believe what I am
hearing."

He followed her. "You do have a fantastic body. Ultra
curvy and soft. You're exactly what a dragon would look
for in a bed partner." He kept his voice stern and tried
hard not to remember how her breasts had bounced while
he had fucked her. How gorgeous she had looked as she
had come. Especially that first time on the end of his
fingers. Like she couldn't quite believe it was happening
to her.

She turned so suddenly that he almost walked into her.
"You are disgusting!"

"It wasn't me who said it. He just remarked on your
body. I have heard several males talking about you. You
may not have signed that particular clause within the
contract, but—"

"Which clause?" She narrowed her eyes, frowning hard.

"The non-fraternization policy."

"Oh that." She gave a shake of the head. "What about
it?"

"You may not have signed it, but it still stands. There will be no fucking while on dragon territory. What you do back home on your weekends off is your business. Your focus is to remain on your job at hand while here, and it's my job to protect you. I take my duties very seriously."

"What does that have to do with anything? I told your brother and Blaze that I came here to work not to… mess around."

"I'm glad to hear it. Life will be much easier if it stays that way." There was a gruff edge to his voice. *Good!* She needed to know that he was serious.

She ground her teeth together, looking like she might lose it with him any second. "What I do in my own free time is my business. Do you hear me?"

"You are my business for the foreseeable future. So therefore what you do every second of every day while here on dragon territory is my business."

"Your job is to make sure that I don't do anything to jeopardize your people. That I'm not some spy or terrorist or something. At least that's what Torrent told me."

"My job is also to keep *you* safe." He tried to keep the growl from his voice and failed.

"So how is having sex going to hurt me? We managed just fine."

Yeah they had. More than just fine. It was spectacular. He'd never fit more tightly inside a body so damned soft. His balls gave a clench, remembering what it felt like to unload inside her sweet body. *Fuck!* At this rate, he was going to get hard. Make that, he *was* getting hard. "When every male within the walls of this castle scents another male on you, they'll assume you're available. They'll all come after you. They'll fight, even to the death. What if you were to get caught in the cross-fire?"

"That's crazy talk."

"Is it? You have no fucking idea how much testosterone pumps through these veins." He held up an arm, his veins stood out for her to see. "Even talking about fucking is making me hard."

She gasped, her gaze moving to... "Oh my gosh! You're such a pig. I can't believe you..." She looked away, even putting a hand over her eyes.

"It's nothing you haven't seen before. Or touched, or—"

"Stop it." She put her hands on her hips. "I told you it's in the past and that I don't want to talk about that night. Ever again!"

So much for calming down. His dick was full-on hard by now. "Don't worry," he put up a hand, "I'm not going to touch you. It's not me you have to worry about. It's every other red-blooded male within these walls."

"I don't believe such wonderful, kind, polite men could change so dramatically. That they could become savages over... me..."

"Well believe it. They would fight each other to the death to have at you. Condoms are only handed out at stag night so you would be fucked bareback, which brings about risk of pregnancy. Birth control doesn't always work, not when it comes to non-human seed. Potent as hell. You know how biology works, don't you, doc?"

Her face looked pale and her neck worked as she

swallowed deeply. "That's Doctor Roberts to you."

"I don't have to explain reproduction, do I, Doctor Roberts?"

"Of course not!" she half yelled. "I understand exactly how reproduction works, but if you think I'm going to allow myself to be seduced by some guy you're wrong."

Tide couldn't help the laugh that was pulled from him. There was no humor in it. "Some guy. Not just some guy, a dragon shifter. A male who would know exactly what to say and how to touch you. There would be no saying 'no.'"

"You're crazy if you think I would let—"

Tide wasn't sure what came over him. Maybe it was the need to prove to her that what he was saying was true. Or perhaps it was her scent. Berries and cream. Fucking delicious. The good doctor was turned on by what he was saying. So much so that the smell of her arousal was thick in the air. It made his dick throb and his mouth water. With a low growl, he pushed her onto her desk. She gasped as her ass hit the wooden surface. He swept his hand between her thighs, which fell open. She was wearing a knee-length skirt. It was up in seconds. His fingers brushed her sex right through her panties. Wet and hot. So fucking wet. His cock gave a twitch.

Her eyes widened and her mouth dropped open. Meghan moaned as his fingers brushed against her sex for a second time, zoning in on her clit. Her eyes became glassy as they fluttered closed. Just as he thought. She wanted this, she wanted him. *Good!* He wanted her back in that moment, and so damned badly. All of his focus was directed on the growing damp spot between her lush thighs. Just as Tide was about to shred her underwear, she slapped him. The crack reverberated around the room. His cheek stung a little, but the force of her blow had not been enough to move him.

"Get off of me!" she yelled. "Now!"

Her words, on the other hand, were enough to have him stepping back, in an instant. "Just trying to make a point. Your scent." He sniffed the air. "You're turned on. Very fucking turned on."

"You groped me," she spluttered. "It's no wonder. I'm not interested though. Not at all!"

"You were turned on before that. I'm a dragon, I could scent it, then I could feel it on the tips of my fingers." He put his hand to his nose and sniffed. Fuck if the scent clinging there didn't make his sacs tighten. "You're soaking wet."

She made a noise of disbelief. "You have no right to smell me or to put your hands on me. I'm not interested, okay? You really do need to get that through your thick skull."

Who was she trying to convince here? "Not interested?" He snorted. "Let's just agree to disagree on that one as well. It's not like I was actually going to fuck you or anything. I was just proving a point."

"Stay far away from me." She wagged her finger at him.

"Fine." He put up his hands. "Like I said yesterday, behave and we'll have nothing to talk about. I won't need to prove anything to you again."

"I'm not a child. You can't tell me what to do." Anger flashed in her stunning green eyes.

"They're coming back."

"What?" She shook her head, clearly out of sorts.

"Ice and George are on their way back," he whispered. "You should go and wash up." he opened a nearby window, pushing it as wide as it would go.

"Why do I need…?"

"This whole room smells like pussy." He looked her in the eyes. "*Your* pussy, and as much as I really like the—"

She gasped. "You're disgusting…"

He put a finger in front of his lips and shushed her. "Yeah, yeah, you can tell me how much I disgust you later." He kept his voice low. "Go wash up. I suggest you lose the panties. Throw them away and wash yourself." He looked down at the junction of her thighs. "Use soap." He spied a bottle of sanitizer attached to the wall next to the hospital bed and pumped two squirts into his hands, which he wiped together vigorously. Then he squirted another glop of the stuff, working it over his fingers, especially the ones that had brushed against her pussy.

Meghan opened and closed her mouth. "You can't be serious," she whispered.

"Go now or Ice is going to know just how turned on you are right now."

"I'm not—"

"Save it. Go or…" He chuckled as she ran for the bathroom, shutting the door behind her. The scent of her arousal diminished considerably with her gone. Within seconds, the door opened and George and Ice walked in.

Ice immediately stopped in his tracks and gave the air a sniff. He looked quizzically at Tide. The male would scent

Tide's own arousal. Human pussy would do that to a male every time. So sweet. So delectable. Tide shrugged. "You can't blame a male. Nothing happened."

Ice's face broke out into a grin. "I guess not and I know. You take your assignments seriously."

"Yes I do."

"Did I miss something?" George asked, frowning.

"Nothing at all. If you'll excuse us, Ice and I are going to stand over there in the corner and leave the two of you to get to work."

"Okay."

It took five minutes before Meghan came back into the room. She scented strongly of soap. Her cheeks were bright, flaming red. Tide had to suppress a chuckle at how guilty she looked. He was fucked if he didn't actually like the idea of her not wearing any underwear. Her sweet little pussy was naked beneath that uppity skirt.

Ice sniffed the air and gave him a look. Okay, so maybe she was still interesting to him and maybe Ice could scent that he was becoming turned on all over again. He shrugged. Ice smiled and he shrugged back. There would be no acting on this attraction. Even if her body didn't agree, the curvy doctor didn't seem to want him. It was for the best. There was too much at stake and Torrent would have both his balls if he touched her.

CHAPTER 11

Tide leaned right in. So close she could feel the heat radiating off of his body. So close that she could barely breathe. "You're acting like you've never seen me naked." He whispered the words so softly that she wasn't sure she had actually heard right. Then again, she knew that she had by the glint in his eyes, as he pulled back. It was the first time he had spoken to her since she'd arrived a few minutes ago.

Flip but she had forgotten how sexy he was. Okay, maybe she hadn't forgotten exactly, she had just chosen to try and forget. Selective amnesia at its best. Right now, naked and glorious in the mid-morning light, she couldn't deny what was right in front of her. Tide was incredible. From his long muscled legs to his rock hard abs. Not forgetting his broad shoulders or those thick biceps. To top it all off, he had incredible eyes and a head of thick hair. Tide smirked and out popped his dimples. A little bit of cute dribbled on a whole lot of sexy. It was official, she hated him. Hated him so much!

She snorted as his words sunk in. "Puh-lease, it's not

your nakedness that's affecting me, it's all of them." She pointed to a group of shifters on the other side of the large balcony, forcing herself to let her eyeballs drift all over their naked bodies. "They're pretty yummy." She fanned herself. Her cheeks feeling distinctly hot and not because of that group of shifters. Oh no, that would be too easy. She hated Tide so darned much. Sexy asshole that he was. The only guy she was attracted to, was him. *Why oh why?*

"Who's yummy?" George asked, his gaze firmly on Tide's package.

"Them." Meghan couldn't believe what she was doing when she pointed at the group of guys. Two of them waved at her and she waved back. Tide growled. He actually growled and so loudly that the team snapped to attention. *Was he jealous?*

"Oh yeah... um... them..." George bobbed his eyebrows at her. Her friend knew exactly who Meghan found yummy. Knew it had nothing to do with the group of shifters.

"Enough," Tide said. "We need to leave if we are to make it to the Earth lair on time for your meeting."

Ice arrived, forcing Meghan to stare at the sky. All these naked male parts dangling in the wind. She couldn't take it. The worst thing was that it seemed perfectly natural to all of them. None of them was self-conscious in any way. "Good idea," she mumbled.

"Stand back," Tide instructed. Both she and George took a couple of steps back. Ice moved away from Tide, who breathed in deeply. His muscles bulged beneath his skin. Then there was a roping and popping noise and the two men seemed to fold out. Scales, a tail, wide gossamer wings. It took mere seconds. It left her gaping.

The dragon that was Tide rose up on his hind legs and roared. Meghan realized that she was holding her breath and clutching her chest. He was huge, bigger than a car. At least as tall as a bus. Certainly bigger than any animal she'd ever seen. Her mouth still hung open but she couldn't seem to close it. He was magnificent. They both were. Tide was bigger than Ice though. His chest so golden she almost felt like she might need to shield her eyes if she looked at him head-on for too much longer. The rest of his scales were a radiant green. His eyes were blue and slitted. Tide roared again as he flapped his wings, rising slowly and gracefully from the ground with each hard sweep.

"I think I'm in love," George murmured. "For real this time." He was staring at Ice who had also just taken to the sky.

Before she could reply, Tide shot up, making her yelp. Flip but he could move. Then he was swooping back down, his great big claws stretched out towards her.

Oh no.

No way!

"This is going to be fun." George lifted his arms and Ice – the dragon – picked him up.

"No!" she yelled, running in the direction of the door. Then his talons were wrapping around her middle and her stomach lurched as she was swept off of the ground. She screamed, grabbing at his claws, which were hard and scaly and so huge. One false move and she was dead. "Put me down! I've changed my mind." she yelled as they rose up and up. Slower than before but fast enough that her hair whipped about her face. If she'd known this was going to happen, she would've worn it up.

They'd been unconscious when they'd been taken to the dragon kingdom. Fast asleep. She knew what the mode of transport had been and had been happy to be fast asleep for the actual journey. Why had she thought that the method of transport would be different this time around?

She squeezed her eyes closed and continued to cling to his scaly talons. It took a few minutes to work up the courage to open her eyes. The view was breathtaking and although they were moving at a steady pace, it wasn't ridiculously fast.

She concentrated on breathing in and out. On calming herself down. It wasn't so bad. She was wearing a thick fur coat and fur boots. No wonder Bay had recommended that she change into them this morning before he had taken her to the balcony.

"Here goes nothing." Her words were snapped up by the wind generated by Tide's massive wings. She let go of his claws and quickly pulled the hood of her thick jacket up and over her head. She pushed her hair into the hood and fumbled with the tie until it was firmly secured. Then she checked to make sure that her backpack was still secured on her back. It was. Meghan gripped his talons, holding on for dear life. "Don't drop me!" she yelled. She felt the vibration as Tide gave a deep rumble.

Thankfully, the flight wasn't very long. Twenty minutes at the most, and they were descending towards a mountain. As they drew closer, she noticed the glass windows and balconies. It was the Earth dragon's castle. It was positioned in the heart of the mountains. "Thank god," she whispered as they drew closer and closer.

Oh flip. All of a sudden she wasn't so sure about the landing part. If he landed with her, Tide would surely crush her beneath him. Maybe he planned on dropping her. That might hurt too. At least according to the forces of gravity and Newton's Law. They descended more quickly, going almost vertically at this point. Dropping, dropping.

"Oh boy," she moaned. "Easy." She spoke gently, trying to soothe him. "Too fast!" she yelled. Tide continued to descend quickly though. Surprise, surprise he ignored her flat out. At the last second, he seemed to hover, dropping a little more before letting her go. As in, his claws opened. She held on tight. It was only when Meghan realized how close her feet were to the ground – couldn't be more than a couple of inches – that she let go, landing softly and gently.

"That was amazing!" George shouted. "I loved it." He jumped up and down, waving at Ice who slowly descended a small way further up the balcony. Tide landed next to him and they changed back. It was like they folded in on themselves. Tails and limbs shortening. Scales sinking into their skin.

Then there were two very naked, very buff men standing in front of her. Meghan looked away, trying hard not to blush. She didn't want to give Tide the satisfaction. He'd get a kick out of it.

The side door opened and the most muscular guy she had ever seen walked through it. His head was clean shaven and he was scary looking. He, thankfully, was dressed in a pair of those cotton yoga-style pants that all the dragons wore, when they actually wore anything.

"Mountain," Ice called out in greeting.

The big guy gave a nod of the head. He and Ice clasped wrists. "Long time no see." Mountain had a deep, booming voice. "My lord." He turned towards Tide and looked down at his feet for a second as an apparent show of submission. His chest was silver, so not a royal. She was beginning to get the hang of this.

Then he turned his dark eyes towards them. "Hello, humans, you are safe with me."

"Good to know," George said, smiling.

"Hello, shifter. You are safe with us too," Meghan blurted.

Ice cracked up in a laugh. Mountain smiled. It was feral and violent looking. Meghan didn't want to get on this guy's wrong side.

"Good one," Mountain said, he was serious in an instant. "Please come this way." He walked ahead. Meghan and George followed, with Tide and Ice trailing behind. Meghan pulled the hood off of her head and tried to hand-comb her hair, which must look a disaster. Once they were inside, Ice and Tide helped themselves to some pants which were stored on a chest of drawers right next to the door. There was also a laundry basket with a couple of crumpled pants inside of it.

"Our king and queen are awaiting your presence in their

chamber," Mountain addressed Meghan.

"Thank you. That's great," she replied when he seemed to be waiting for an answer.

He inclined his head. "You may all follow me." He led them through a series of hallways that reminded her of the Water dragon's lair. The only difference was that the Earth dragons they encountered had dark flecks threaded within their chest markings.

Every single shifter they passed stopped and stared. They even passed one or two women. They also wore loose-fitting cotton dresses. Not very flattering. The women stared as well but their focus was on Tide. Meghan felt a twinge of something. It wasn't jealousy, not exactly. She didn't know him well enough to feel jealous, yet, there was definitely something. She'd had sex with the guy, so it was normal... wasn't it?

Topaz winked at him. "See you at lunch?" she asked, grabbing Tide's hand.

Meghan turned back, her eyes narrowed on where Topaz held onto him. Then her head snapped forward and she picked up the pace. She seemed... jealous. Precisely as he suspected, Meghan was like all the rest. Except for that slap. She'd been aroused, and yet she hadn't welcomed his touch. It was safe to say that he didn't understand her.

"See you later?" Topaz repeated.

"Yes, sure," he answered quickly, squeezing her hand before pulling away. "I need to go." He kept his eyes on the retreating group. Without a backward glance, he jogged so that he could catch up.

Mountain knocked on a set of double doors and entered. Tide filed in behind the group, inclining his head at Granite and his healer mate. He took up his position at the wall as was customary of a guard. Ice next to him.

After introductions, Meghan went through the motions explaining what she had planned. She and Louise, Granite's mate, went to town talking in their own healer lingo. Tide saw Granite stifle a yawn on more than one occasion. After a while, even he and Ice were shuffling from one leg to another. Meghan asked Louise some questions and then Louise asked Meghan a couple and so it went. Back and forth for what felt like an age. It was almost impossible to understand what the hell they were saying.

Finally, there was crying from the next room.

"That would be the twins." Louise smiled. She and Granite headed off to fetch them. Returning, each of them held a baby.

"They are beautiful." Tide stepped forward to get a better look. He looked from Louise to Granite and back again.

"Thank you," Granite beamed. "They're a handful, but I wouldn't trade them for the world."

"I'm sure." Meghan had that look all females get when looking at cute little babies. Granite might be an ugly mother, but he'd done a decent job making these children.

"We need to make this quick," Louise advised. "They will want to eat soon and then all hell will break loose."

"No problem." Meghan was rooting around in her bag.

She pulled out a couple of items before placing them on the coffee table. "I'll do the swabs first and then we'll test them for the allergy. I would suggest you have bottles at the ready."

"I'm still breastfeeding," Louise said.

It wasn't his imagination when Granite gave both him and Ice a scathing look. Males could be so possessive over their mates. He'd seen it with his brother and Candy. Hell, his brother had almost lost his mate early on in their relationship because of jealousy. He fought back an eyeroll. *Poor schmucks.* There were definite downsides to the whole relationship thing.

"Let's get started," Meghan announced as she finished laying out the supplies. She picked up a test tube and pulled out a swab. Then she leaned over Granite and swiped the swab inside the baby's mouth. "What's his name?"

"Quake," Granite said.

Meghan grabbed a marker and wrote what he presumed was the child's name on a label on the test tube, which she then sealed.

Meghan did the same with the other baby and wrote Declan on the label. She carefully packed the test tubes away in the backpack and produced a needle out of a black velvet case.

"Woah." Granite's eyes widened up, Tide could see the male bristle. If he was even slightly more agitated, his scales would show and smoke would waft from his nostrils.

"I'm not going to actually stick them with the needle,"

Meghan quickly assured them, obviously noticing the change of atmosphere. "I plan on touching the blunt side to his skin. She turned the needle over, touching the tip of her finger to the blunt edge. "See?" She gave a nervous looking smile. "One quick touch to the inside of Quake's arm. That's it. This is a two percent silver needle. Only two." She held up two fingers. "It might take a few seconds or even a minute for a red mark to appear. If none is apparent, I'll have to use a four percent needle and so on and so forth."

Granite was frowning so hard that his face might crack at any second. Tide couldn't blame the male. Dragons were touchy when it came to what was theirs. The need to protect would be riding him hard. Louise must have sensed the lingering aggression in the air because she touched the side of her mate's arm. "It's okay. They'll be fine."

Some of the tension eased from Granite's frame and he gave a nod.

"I'll start with Declan," Meghan said, moving over to Louise.

Tide felt his lip twitch. Smart female. There were a couple of things he liked about Meghan. That was for sure.

She touched the needle to the inside of the baby's arm and then looked at her watch. The seconds ticked by.

Louise shook her head as she pulled Declan's arm away from his body to check the spot where the needle had touched. "Nothing."

They went through the same process with Quake.

Meghan pulled another needle from the velvet box.

"Let's try four percent."

Louise nodded, holding the babies arm out so that Meghan could touch the needle to his skin. He squirmed and made a yelping noise. Within seconds the little one was crying.

Louise rocked the tiny baby. "He's allergic." She pointed to a red mark on his arm. Half a minute later and the mark had turned into a raised welt.

Tide could hear how Granite ground his teeth. Tide only realized he had moved when he found himself just a few feet behind Meghan. He sucked in a deep breath. It was all good. Louise glanced at her mate. "He'll be fine. This is perfectly normal." She used a soothing voice, continuing to rock little Declan. The baby had already calmed down significantly. "Declan will be fine in no time."

Meghan turned to Granite. "Aside from that red mark, he'll be fine, since none of the silver has entered his bloodstream."

"Look, he's already forgotten all about it," Louise said, looking down at the little boy in her arms.

"I need to test Quake." Meghan didn't move forward.

Granite cradled the little one in his arms. He looked pissed. *Shit!* Looking after the good doctor was going to be fun and fucking games. The Earth king finally relinquished his hold on the baby enough for Meghan to proceed. "Ready?" She looked at Granite, waiting for his approval.

The male finally pulled in a deep breath and nodded his head. "Yes."

"Since they are identical twins, we can expect the same reaction. I must test Quake, just to be sure."

"Go ahead." He held the baby out.

Meghan carefully clasped his little arm and touched the blunt side of the needle to his skin.

Quake screamed blue murder within a second of the needle touching his skin. First, smoke wafted from his nostrils and then flames shot from the baby's mouth. Actual honest to god flames. Orange, twirling and about two feet long. Granite roared. Tide clasped Meghan around the waist and pulled her behind his back, snarling at Granite, fists clenched and ready. It was purely instinctual. He had been tasked with protecting the human and protect her he would.

Both Meghan and Louise screamed. Both females were yelling for them to stop. Louise was more insistent, probably because she knew what dragons were capable of.

Granite was on his feet in a nanosecond. His tiny son still cradled in his arms. His eyes were narrowed and his brow creased. His one free hand was fisted. In short, baby or no baby, the male was ready.

"No! Stop! Quake!" Louise screamed, grabbing her mate by the arm.

"Wait." Tide forced himself to stand down. It went against everything in him. Especially considering the adrenaline that coursed through his veins. "Don't," he spoke softly, still holding Meghan in place behind his back. He spoke to both her — she was trying to move — and to Granite who still looked pissed. "You'll hurt your boy." Tide looked down at the baby in Granite's arms.

"It's over. Quake's fine." There was a pleading edge to Louise's voice.

"I'm sorry," Meghan whispered from behind him, she stuck her head around him.

Granite's gaze softened. He sucked in a deep breath. "I'm sorry. I reacted... make that, I overreacted," he corrected himself.

"What was that?" Tide asked. The events of the last few minutes replaying in his mind. "What the hell just happened?"

"An Earth dragon should not be able to breathe fire." Ice sounded just as shocked.

"It's happened once before," Louise said. "We weren't sure if it was a one-time thing, or..." She let the sentence die.

"What?" Tide shook his head. "Did you report it? Because I sure as hell didn't hear about it," he asked Granite, who shook his head.

"No." The male tapped Quake on the back in a rhythmic fashion. Still trying to soothe the child. "It only happened once. My mate and another female witnessed it. We thought it might be a fluke."

"Well, it's not." Tide's mind raced. "Is this an isolated case? Have any of the others with mixed breed children reported any... strange occurrences?"

Granite shook his head. "I don't know of any others. Thunder had a son a couple of weeks ago. He didn't mention anything the last time we spoke. Blaze hasn't mentioned anything about his or Coal's sons either."

"Okay." Meghan came out from behind him, shaking

off his hand. "I'm going to assume that that's not normal."

"No," Tide said. "Only Fire dragons can breathe fire. May I see his marking. I hear that there is no coloring, only an outline."

Granite nodded. "It is true for all of the young born from a dragon human mating. No silver, no gold, no black flecks to show that they are Earth dragons. There's just an outline. This is the second time he has breathed fire." He pulled in a deep breath. "Truth be told, I hoped that it wouldn't happen again. Thing is, Declan is perfectly normal. It only seems to be Quake who can do this... breathe fire." The male ran a hand through his hair. "Blaze is not going to like this."

"No shit," Tide said, turning to Meghan. "The only reason the Fire dragons rule all four kingdoms is because they can breathe fire. It gives them the edge over the rest of us. This though..." He shook his head. "This could turn everything on its head. This could start a war."

"Surely not." Meghan's eyes were wide, her skin pale.

"The kingdoms are working together but it's tenuous at best. There is a shared interest—"

"Tide," Granite warned. The male shook his head.

"I wasn't going to say anything more."

"I should hope not," Granite chided.

Tide had said too much... again.

"You said that Water dragons can breathe underwater," Meghan stated, directing the conversation at Granite, taking the heat away from Tide. He was appreciative. "What about Earth dragons? What is your special power?"

"We can blend into our surroundings like a

chameleon."

"And Air dragons?" she asked.

"They have the ability to create lighting from the air. It can be used as a weapon. Not as powerful as fire, but it is a good ability to have."

"Interesting." Meghan looked deep in thought.

Granite unfastened the snaps on Quake's onesie and peeled the material from his chest. The little one kicked his legs and moaned. He knew from experience that babies disliked being undressed.

"Oh my god!" Louise covered her hand with her mouth, her eyes wide.

"That gold wasn't there before." Granite looked shocked as well.

For the most part, there was still an empty outline where the child's mark should have been, only now there were flecks of gold here and there.

Louise unclasped Declan's outfit as well. "See," she said, her voice animated. "This is what it looked like before." There was a dark outline and otherwise, where the silver or gold coloring would have been, was blank.

"You need to inform Blaze," Tide insisted. "This can't be kept quiet."

Granite's mouth became a hard line and his jaw tensed. He finally gave a nod. "Yes, there is no longer any doubt, my son can breathe fire." There was awe in his voice but also a nervous edge. "I will call a meeting of all four kingdoms," Granite added. "Earth, Air and Water will need to stand together. This could be a new anomaly that affects us all."

"I will talk with Torrent. Maybe the three kingdoms should meet first," Tide said

"We don't want to be seen as banding against Blaze. You remember what happened last time." Granite shook his head.

"All too well." Tide grit his teeth as memories accosted him. The conference room becoming engulfed in flames. Everyone present was injured. His own skin had melted. The left side of his face, his chest, his hair had been scorched. The pain was unbearable. It was nothing compared to what Thunder had suffered. The male had almost died. It took him a full week to recover.

"What happened, honey?" Louise asked, looking up at her mate. Little Declan began to fuss.

"The boys are hungry. We will talk later." He smoothed the hair from her brow. His mate nodded.

"Before you go," Meghan pulled another one of the test tube things out of her bag, "I need a sample from you as well, please, Granite. It would be a test sample for an Earth dragon's DNA."

This hadn't been part of the plan. Tide held his breath. How would Granite react to this request? The male seemed to think it over before finally nodding his head. "Fine." He opened his mouth and Meghan took the swab, sealing and labeling the test tube like she had with the twins' samples. "You'll let us know what the findings are?" Quake had also started to fuss.

Meghan nodded. "It will take a week to ten days. I will definitely let you know."

Granite narrowed his eyes as they landed on Tide.

"Have Torrent call me."

"I will," Tide said as the male retreated to the bedroom.

"Fuck," Ice choked out as soon as the door closed.

The human male busied himself packing up.

"No one speaks a word of this. Am I clear?" Tide ordered, looking at each of them in turn.

"I'm not sure what this is all about." Meghan frowned.

"You don't need to know at this time. It's politics. Let's leave it at that." He looked her head-on, waiting for her to argue.

"Okay," she finally said, and he breathed out a sigh of relief.

"Not a word," he addressed Ice. The male nodded. "Blaze especially is not to hear of this. He will be told but it needs to be handled correctly."

"Absolutely," Ice agreed.

"Hey," George held up both hands. "It has nothing to do with me."

"I won't say anything unless directly asked. I'm not comfortable with lying," Meghan said.

"Fair enough." There would be no reason for Tide to start that type of conversation with her at this time. He needed to get back. He needed to talk with Torrent. They would be expected in the dining hall for lunch though. "Let's eat and head out. Thunder is expecting us this afternoon. Not a word to him either."

CHAPTER 12

"Doctor Roberts, how lovely it is to see you again so soon. My brother, Granite, mentioned something about you being here today." It was the shifter she had met yesterday.

"Nice to see you again, Shale." She couldn't help but smile. He was charming.

"We're over there if you need us." George gestured to a table in the corner. Ice was already taking a seat.

"Okay," Meghan said.

Shale hooked his arm with hers. Just like all the other shifters, he was huge. "Come and sit with me."

"Leave the human." Tide had that hard, gruff edge to his voice. "We're not staying long." She wasn't sure whether he directed the last to her or to Shale. It was probably to both of them.

"It's just lunch, Tide." Shale had sandy blond hair and the most incredible golden brown eyes. His lashes were obscenely long.

"Don't you have to be somewhere? Preparing for a certain mission maybe?" Tide asked, looking angry.

"Everything is taken care of." Shale grinned. "Thanks for all the hard work, by the way."

"Yeah, no need to thank me, just stay focused and do a good job. That's all I ask."

"Don't worry about it. I won't fuck it up. I'll—"

"There you are." The same woman from the hall earlier, gripped Tide's arm. "I saved you a seat." She winked at Tide, flicking her long black hair over her shoulder. "Or we could skip lunch and…"

"We need to leave soon," Meghan blurted. *Shit!* She didn't want to come across as jealous. "I can't be late for the next meeting." She locked eyes with Tide as she spoke.

"I need to stay with the human." He kept his eyes on her even though he was addressing the shifter lady.

Meghan bristled. *The human! The human?* Like she was some sort of burden.

"I'll stay with Doctor Roberts," Shale said. She smiled at Shale. At least he was polite.

"Not happening," Tide's voice was still gruff. Then he smiled, looking at the woman at his side. "Why don't you join us?" Without waiting for a response – of course, a guy like Tide would automatically assume her answer would be yes – he turned to them. "This is Topaz. Topaz, this is Doctor Roberts. She's helping us with our silver affliction."

"Oh, that's great." Topaz didn't even look her way. Her focus was solely directed at Tide.

"Let me get that for you." Shale pulled out her chair, gesturing for her to sit.

"Thank you." A total gentleman, unlike other people

she knew.

Topaz plunked herself in Tide's lap. *How inappropriate.* She wrapped her arms around his neck. *Don't look!* It didn't matter anyway. Meghan was so not interested in Tide. Sure, he was attractive but that was where it ended.

Someone gripped her shoulders from behind. "You're welcome to join us," George said.

"I'm fine. We're leaving soon, so eat up." She was amazed at how normal her voice sounded, even though Topaz was kissing Tide's neck. *Kissy, kissy kissy. What the hell?*

"You sure?" George widened his eyes. Her friend knew her well. He knew that this would be rubbing her the wrong way.

"Yes, of course," she lied. All out lied and did it with a straight face. She wasn't sure about anything right now. Only that she hated Tide. Hated. Him. He was clearly a jackass and a slut.

Shale handed her a menu. "I would recommend the steak and salad."

"Hey," Tide gripped Topaz's shoulder and attempted to pry her off of him, "I'm working right now."

Meghan snapped her eyes back to the menu in her hand. "Mmmmmm…" She pretended to study it. "Sounds great." She put it down in front of her, noticing how Topaz was pouting. *Did women really act this way?*

"You'll have to come back real soon for a visit." She touched the tip of his nose and winked again.

"Sure." Tide picked her up and put her down on the chair next to him.

"How about tonight?" Topaz had her back to Meghan, blocking Tide off completely.

"Did you get everything you needed today?" Shale asked her, forcing her attention back to him. "Did you meet my nephews?" he continued. Unfortunately, she missed Tide's answer. *No! It was for the best.* What he did was his own business. She didn't care either way.

"Yes," she blurted when she realized that Shale was waiting for an answer. "I got everything I needed. The twins were adorable. Thank you. So you're going on a mission?"

"Yeah, I'll be gone for a while. I take it there's no one waiting for you at home." She noticed how his nostrils flared.

"No, my work keeps me very busy. I don't have time to date."

"Surely you must make time on occasion, I mean, you and Tide?" He raised his brows.

"That was a mistake. A huge mistake."

Shale chuckled. "I'm glad to hear it. Maybe we could—"

"Let's go and get lunch." Tide stood up. "I'll bring your food, Meghan. You said you wanted the steak."

"It's Doctor Roberts." She looked up at his imposing form.

His jaw clenched. "Doctor."

Shale stood up as well. "I would be happy to get your lunch, Doctor Roberts. May I call you Meghan?"

"Let me do my job," Tide growled at Shale, hands fisting at his side. "You do yours and I'll do mine. *Doctor Roberts* happens to be my responsibility."

"Sure." Shale shrugged. "Knock yourself out."

Topaz stood up, clinging to Tide like her life depended on it. "I'll go with you," she gushed and actually fluttered her eyelashes at him. It was sickening.

Meghan held back a sigh. Although Tide seemed jealous of Shale she knew it wasn't the case. Like he had stated, he was just doing his job. "I can get my own food." She stood up, Shale fell in beside her and they headed for the counter, standing in a line. Why oh why had she thought this would be a good idea? Tide and Topaz were ahead of them. The tall, willowy dragon shifter whispered something in his ear. He said something back and she laughed. Then she nuzzled into his neck. Tide didn't do anything to encourage her, but he also didn't do anything to stop her either.

She shouldn't care either way. It would be best if she tried not to look. "So, you're a prince?" she blurted, glancing at Shale. What a stupid thing to ask. Of course he was, he had a golden chest. Granite was his brother, so it stood to reason. She needed to take her attention off of Tide and Topaz. So what if she and Tide had spent the night together. It was ancient history. Like she said, a mistake. Him groping her yesterday had been to prove a point. Tide clearly wasn't interested in her and even if he was, she didn't want a guy like him anywhere near her anyway.

Shale ran a hand over the marking on his chest, drawing her eye. "Yeah, I'm a prince. Can I come and visit you later? Maybe we can have dinner together?"

Tide turned sharply, forcing Octopus Arms to let go of

him. Topaz gave her a dirty look and folded her arms. Tide narrowed his eyes. "*Doctor Roberts*," he emphasized the words, "has to work late. We're up early. Not that it's any of your business but the human is meeting with Blaze and needs to be fresh and on top of her game so—"

No damned way. He wasn't telling her what she could and couldn't do, was he?

"Actually…"

"Actually nothing. You can't join Doctor Roberts for dinner. Not tonight. Not ever."

Tide had no right. "*Actually*, that sounds great."

Shale grinned broadly. "What time should—"

"Are you hard of hearing?" Tide's eyes were narrowed. His frown was so deep it might end up being permanent. Those muscles on the sides of his neck roped. Come to think of it, his biceps looked huge too. He took a step towards Shale.

Shale clenched his teeth and took a step towards Tide. His soft brown eyes seemed to darken. "I think Doctor Roberts can speak for herself. She may be your responsibility but you're not her keeper."

"No, she can't speak for herself and yes, technically, I *am* her keeper."

No way! "Yes, I can speak for myself and you are most definitely not my keeper." Tide was too much. Making his own arrangements to see Topaz while, at the same time, banning her from seeing Shale. Treating her like a child. *Double standards!*

"Excuse us a moment." Tide gripped her hand firmly in his much larger one.

"I don't need a moment," she spoke under her breath.

"Oh yes, you do." He marched towards the exit, pulling her along with him.

"Why do you insist on trying to rule my life?"

"We'll talk in a moment." He kept on walking, even picked up the pace, which forced her to jog to keep up.

Once they were outside in the hallway, which was also pretty busy with people coming and going, he kept on moving, stopping at every door they encountered. It was only when they reached the fourth door that he paused and sniffed. Then he knocked, cocking his head and narrowing his eyes. He pushed the door open and ushered her inside, closing it behind them. "Shale wants inside your pants. It's as simple as that."

"So much for the preamble. Why don't we just get down to the nitty-gritty?"

"Exactly. We don't have much time here. Shale wants to fuck you and it's not going to happen on my watch. We spoke about this."

"*You* spoke about this. I disagreed. Shale wants to have dinner with me. That's all, just dinner." There was a squeak to her voice. It was of utter disbelief. She couldn't quite believe what she was hearing.

"That's bullshit. Just like cleaning the stain off my shirt was bullshit. Just like those leftovers you promised me were bullshit." He got right up in her face. His eyes looked even brighter. Damn him, even more beautiful.

"No." She shook her head. "He's a nice guy. A sweet guy. Unlike you." She put her hands on her hips. *Take that, asshole!*

Tide laughed. "Unlike me," he muttered. "Yeah, okay, sure. At least I'm honest about what I want and what I don't want. Trust me, Shale does not want to make small talk, he doesn't want dinner and candles and all that other bullshit. He wants inside that tight pussy."

She did that whole choking on her spit thing again. It had never happened to her before meeting Tide. She had a feeling it would happen again several times before her time in the dragon lands was done. "You're a pig and a male slut. You have no leg to stand on, as far as I'm concerned. None whatsoever. Just because you have a dirty mind, doesn't mean that every other man out there does."

"Oh yes, they do. We all do." He shrugged. "I'll admit wholeheartedly, I have a seriously dirty fucking mind." He gave a half-smile, it was feral looking, like he was thinking up a couple of dirty things right now.

Something clenched deep inside her lower belly. Meghan didn't like how his words affected her. "There! Exactly. I told you. You get to go and have as much fun as you want while expecting me to—"

"Oh…" He smiled. No, make that grinned. Tide all out grinned. "So that's what this is all about – you're jealous. I should have known."

What a prick! Her hate went up a couple of notches. If that was even possible. "Jealous! Like hell I'm jealous, you are such an asshole. Did I mention how big your ego is?"

"Several times." He was still grinning. "But this isn't my ego talking. It's a straight fact. You don't like the idea of Topaz and I together, so you're agreeing to meet with

Shale to get back at me or to prove some or other point. Is it an attempt to make me jealous? Because, if it is, you're barking up the wrong tree."

"That's not what it is at all. Not even close. I think it's plain wrong that you get to do whatever it is that you want while expecting me to sit at home alone. It's a double standard and I won't stand for it. For the record, I think *you're* jealous."

Tide chuckled. "No fucking way. It's not a double standard because my life is not on the line here, yours is."

"I don't agree. Shale has been nothing but kind. So what if I was to date him? It would be exclusive, so there would be no fighting amongst the guys." Although Shale was sweet and attractive, she only saw him as a friend. Tide didn't need to know that.

His eyes turned stormy. "You have no idea what you are talking about. Anyway, I thought your focus was on your work?"

"It is, at least during office hours. What I do after that is my business. In fact, do me a favor and go and see whats-her-name tonight. Please. I beg of you. Just don't get in the way of my dinner with Shale. You'll be off duty anyway so—"

"It's not fucking happening," Tide growled.

She swallowed thickly, a little afraid of how his eyes blazed. His muscles were all roped and thick. His chest was practically against hers. The lower part of his chest, at any rate, he was just that tall in comparison to her. He wasn't going to hurt her though. Meghan could be confident of that fact. Especially after how he protected her when he thought Granite was a threat. "Yes, it is happening."

He groaned, the sound laced with frustration. Tide turned and walked to the other side of the room. He squeezed the back of his neck and just stood there, the seconds ticking by.

Meghan wanted to talk. To say something. Anything. But she forced herself to stay silent. The ball was in his court. "Fine," he said when he finally turned. "I'll stay away from all females. No rutting. If that's what it takes, then I'm fine with that." He rolled his eyes. "No double standards."

"You think that's what this is about?"

"You're uppity because I get to do as I please while you need to live by certain rules, despite the fact that I've explained that those rules are for your own good."

"I wouldn't call it uppity, I'd call it justified but yes, it's the reason I was unhappy to sign that non-fraternization policy in the first place. Double standards. I can't stand them."

"What if the same rules were to apply to both of us?" he asked.

"So, *neither* of us gets to have sex?" She raised her brows.

"Exactly. No sex for either of us. If that's what it takes to do my job and keep you safe, then so fucking be it."

"Don't sound so hard done by." It wasn't like she had planned to have sex with anyone anyway. She liked the idea of Tide suffering. She'd get a kick out of it. In fact, she had to work hard to keep from laughing her ass off.

She pursed her lips for a few seconds instead, pretending to think it over.

"Do we have a deal?" Tide folded his arms.

"Yes, fine, we have a deal."

Tide held out his hand. She tried to take it but he gripped her by the wrist and gave her whole arm a big shake. "It's done." He huffed out a breath. "You're a pain in the ass for such a tiny human."

"Oh, and stop referring to me as 'the human.' You..." *Flip*. She felt her cheeks heat. "Should also stop referring to that night."

"What night?" He narrowed his eyes and his lips twitched. The bastard wanted to laugh.

"You know very well which night. Stop referring to it and for the love of god, stop referring to... parts of my anatomy."

"What parts?" He smiled. "Oh, yeah, you mean your pussy."

"Stop it," she whispered.

"I told you, not talking about it won't make it magically unhappen. We fucked, multiple times and you enjoyed the hell out of it. So did I, human, so did I. Very fucking much!" He turned and walked out of the room, holding the door open for her.

Meghan picked her jaw up off of the floor, pulled back her shoulders and walked out. She wasn't sure if she'd just made things better or worse.

CHAPTER 13

"You've got to be kidding me," Torrent growled, throwing another log on the fire before sitting back down.

"Wish I could say that I was, but I'm not. Flames shot from the whelp's mouth. We all saw it. The child was upset after Doctor Roberts touched the silver needle to the inside of his arm. He screamed blue murder and flames shot from his mouth. It lasted a couple of seconds. Thankfully no one was hurt and nothing got scorched. It was a shock, I can tell you that much."

"You said it was the second time this has happened?" Torrent took a sip of his whiskey, swirling the liquid around in his mouth before swallowing.

"Yes, Granite mentioned another time. His mate saw the incident. They were hoping it was a one-time thing. That's why it was never reported. I can't say I blame Granite."

"What the hell does it mean? An Earth dragon capable of producing fire?" Tide could see that his brother was mulling it over. "I can't believe it... and just as the kingdoms are starting to get it together."

He took a sip of his own whiskey. It burned its way down his throat. "I don't know. It has to be the human blood. Or maybe it's the human, Earth dragon combination. Then again, only one of the twins can breathe fire so that can't be it."

"You say everything was fine at Thunder's lair when you visited. There were no problems with his whelp. Everything seemed – for lack of a better word – normal?"

"Yeah, the whelp seemed normal." Tide huffed out a breath. "His baby is only three weeks old, so it might be too early to tell. His chest marking is just an outline. The baby also showed signs of suffering from the silver affliction; so far that has been standard with all of the whelps."

"So, tomorrow you are heading to the Fire lair?" Thunder asked.

"Yes."

"Don't mention the fire incident." Thunder gripped his glass tighter. "I discussed it briefly with Granite. Earth, Air and Water are meeting to discuss what this means. Also, how to break this to Blaze along with the possible implications. We might be reading too much into this whole thing but I'm worried about how Blaze is going to take this."

"I don't think he will take it well." Tide shook his head, watching as the flames licked up as the newly added wood caught alight.

Torrent took another sip. "You said that the non-fire-breathing youngster," he scrunched up his eyes in thought,

"Declan, is the heir to the throne, right?"

"Yup, Declan was born first."

"That is at least one good thing." Torrent nodded. "If this is isolated, and so far everything points to that being the case, then I doubt Blaze will be too concerned. However, if there are more of such cases in the coming years…" He shook his head, looking grave.

"What will Blaze do? Eradicate innocent children?" Tide sighed. "I can't see it happening. The male is hard as nails, but he's not evil. Killing children…" It was too much to contemplate.

"There are many things he could do. I've thought this through." Torrent was frowning. "He might take the infant and raise him as a Fire dragon."

"Let him try. Granite is protective of his young," Tide chuckled. "We're all possessive at the end of the day, will do anything to keep our own safe."

"Exactly. Granite will not allow it." Torrent drank again, finishing the last of the whiskey. He grimaced as the liquid went down his throat. "We're all possessive as hell. This could still spell war. I only pray that Blaze thinks things through. That he treads carefully. Let's hope none of the other children exhibit this trait."

Tide knew that Torrent was thinking of his own unborn son and heir. If the boy somehow had the ability to breathe fire, he would be at risk. Even if Blaze shrugged it off and pretended to be comfortable with this new development, he knew that the male might change his mind at any time in the years to come. Power could do strange things to a male. Terrible things. After all, the Fire king would be just as protective of his own family and future. A sliver of dread appeared in the back of his mind but he pushed it down. It wouldn't help to jump to conclusions or to speculate on outcomes. Not at this stage of the game.

"How is it going with the healer?" Torrent walked over to the wet bar and poured himself another whiskey.

"Fine," he answered simply.

Torrent turned, narrowing his eyes on Tide. "Fine… really? I don't like the sound of that."

"She is a good healer but a handful."

Torrent chuckled. "She's a human female. They're hard to understand. Is she doing her job though?" His whole demeanor changed. "Does she seem capable?"

"She handled herself well with Granite and Thunder. So far, yes, I'm impressed but it's early days yet. I will let you know if things change."

"You do that." Torrent took another sip of his freshly poured drink. "I want no risks with my female or my children. If anything were to happen." He squeezed the glass in his hand so tight that it cracked. He made a growl of frustration and threw the shards of glass in a nearby wastepaper basket. Blood dripped onto the floor and he clenched his fist to staunch the flow.

"Are you okay? Can I get you a towel?" Tide stood up.

Torrent shook his head. "No, I'm fine. The bleeding has already stopped." He sighed. "Am I an idiot to be this concerned?"

"Of course not. You might be a king but you still have feelings. You love your family."

Torrent swallowed thickly. "More than anything."

"Doctor Roberts is good at what she does," Tide assured him.

"It's up to you to make sure that her focus stays on the job at hand."

He took a step towards his brother. "You can rely on me."

Torrent made a snorting noise. "I've heard the males talking. They would like nothing better than to get their hands on that female."

"Let them try." His voice was a deep rasp. "I've explained things carefully to the healer. She understands what would happen if word got out that she was free to rut at will."

"An available human female in our midst. The testosterone levels in this place would go through the roof. It could escalate out of control quickly. They would declare it open season."

"You don't have to explain it to me. I know exactly what would happen. A bun fight of note would ensue." He chuckled. "And she sure has a decent set of buns on her."

Torrent smiled even though he still looked troubled. "That's not funny. You of all people are not supposed to find her attractive. You had her already remember?"

Tide shrugged. "I'm not blind, I didn't lose my sense of smell either." He watched as Torrent's frown deepened. "Relax, she's sexy but I'm not an idiot. I know my duties. I will do everything in my power… whatever it takes to keep her safe and to make sure that her focus stays on her work. I doubt she's a spy or a terrorist, but you never know. I'll keep a close eye on her."

"That's what I'm afraid of." Torrent grinned.

"Not too close, asshole." He rolled his eyes.

Torrent laughed. "If you say so." He turned serious, looking him in the eyes. It was like he was trying to find something.

Tide wasn't sure what it was that his brother was looking for, only that he was barking up the wrong damned tree. "Let me fix you another drink."

Torrent shook his head. "Candy and Rain are waiting for me to get back. I can't be late for dinner."

"Just a quick one." Tide picked up the half-empty bottle of single malt. It wasn't like alcohol really affected them. Aside from warmth in the pit of the stomach and a two-second buzz, it was useless. Dragons liked the taste of it though.

"No can do. Duty calls." By the look in Torrent's eyes, he could see that calling it a duty was not true at all. Going back to his family was the complete opposite. Something he cherished and looked forward to. Tide poured himself another drink. It wasn't like he had anything better to do.

CHAPTER 14

Meghan swabbed Blaze's inner cheek, carefully sealing and labeling the container before packing it away. She zipped the bag closed and gave it a pat. The last of the samples she needed had been obtained. "Thank you for your time," she addressed Blaze, his mate Roxy as well as Coal and his mate Julie. The ladies smiled. There was giggling and the pitter patter of little feet as their two boys toddled after one another.

"I look forward to hearing the results," Blaze said.

"It will take a week to ten days, and then I will need a day or two to put a report together."

Blaze nodded. "I think it would be best to call everyone together, especially if there is something of importance to convey."

Meghan nodded. "No problem. I will certainly let you know if that is the case." She felt her cheeks heat, quickly turning away, returning her focus to her notepad and documentation. She was bound to doctor-patient confidentiality. It was not her place to speak of the events of the previous day. Of what had happened on Earth territory. She sucked in a deep breath.

"So," Coal stepped forward, "all of the children resulting in pairings between humans and dragons have produced offspring with the dreaded silver affliction."

Meghan turned back to face them. "Yes, I'm afraid so. That's why I'm here. I will work tirelessly over the next couple of months. Hopefully one or both of the children born to Sky and Candy will be allergy-free."

"Do you really think it will be possible to develop a vaccine?" Julie asked.

"Yes, I do." Meghan licked her lips. "Although, it might not be possible on the first try."

"Just to be clear," Roxy asked, "one of the children born needs to be allergy-free first."

"Yes." Meghan nodded. "The hope is that they will develop the necessary resistance in the womb. A vaccine will be created from the infant's blood. I won't go into too much detail. It's groundbreaking technology and highly complicated but I truly believe that it's more than possible."

"I hope so. It would be life-changing for us, for our children and our future." Roxy's voice wavered as she spoke. Her eyes began to fill with tears.

Blaze put an arm around her. "Yes, a lifelong dream."

"I will do my very best. Of that, you can be assured. My sister almost died from an allergy similar to yours. I was very close to finding a cure for her illness as well. What I learn here will help me when I return to Dalton Springs. The techniques for curing the illness are similar. Know that I also have a big stake in this. I'm not just doing it for the money. Any money I make from working here will go into continuing my research. So, this has nothing to do with money directly. It's important to me that you know that."

"Thank you for sharing." Roxy reached and gripped her hand.

"Yes, we appreciate it." Sincerity shone in Julie's eyes.

"Thank you, Doctor." Blaze shook her hand. "We look forward to hearing the results. Again," he chuckled, "I'm sorry my son almost burnt you to a crisp." He pulled a face.

"I'm getting used to it."

He frowned. "What do you mean 'getting used to it'?" He was frowning heavily.

Take it easy! Breathe normally! "Oh, George threw a couple of logs onto the fire last night and sparks went flying. I had to duck out of the way."

Blaze smiled. "I must say, you do have great reflexes."

"Thankfully." *Phew!* She'd almost let what had happened yesterday slip. She finished packing the paperwork away and everyone said their goodbyes.

They made their way in silence down the hallways. Tide stepped in next to her. "That was close."

She made a sound of agreement. "I'm sorry, I'm not used to hiding things."

"Thank you for not saying anything."

She nodded. "Sure thing. I don't like it but I do understand."

George and Ice walked up ahead, they were in deep conversation. The two of them had become fast friends.

As per normal, people they passed stopped to stare. Some of the dragon men openly stared at her, looking her up and down. Tide growled if any of them tried to approach. He sounded like a vicious lion or cougar, wild and untamed.

Great! The first woman they passed grabbed hold of Tide. He didn't growl at her. *Oh no!* "Hi honey, long time no see." She fluttered her lashes at him. *Gag!*

"It's good to see you, Scarlet." She leaned in and hugged him. The woman had long red hair and even longer legs. That feeling was back in the pit of her stomach. Meghan had no place being jealous. Especially over a guy like Tide. For a moment, she wanted to pull back her shoulders and keep walking but she didn't, instead, she stood her ground. She had been walking with Tide. They might not be friends but she'd been in the middle of a conversation with him when they'd been interrupted.

Tide put a hand on the redhead's back for a second and then let go. Scarlet held onto him for a few seconds more before finally letting go.

"So how are you?" Scarlet asked. "You're looking really good," she added, giving Tide the once over.

"So are you." Tide smiled.

Meghan had to hold back an eye-roll. *Here we go again.*

Tide glanced her way. His smiled widened. "This is Doctor Roberts."

Scarlet turned to her for a second. "Hi." Clearly not interested in engaging with Meghan, she turned back to Tide. "When are you coming to visit me again?"

Her meaning was clear.

"I'm very busy right now," Tide replied.

"Surely not that busy." She used a sing-song voice.

"I'm afraid I am." He stepped away from her, moving towards Meghan. "We're on a tight schedule, I need to go now. You take care, Scarlet." He winked. *Double gag!*

More of that pouting she'd seen yesterday. Scarlet waved at Tide using only one finger. "You're welcome to come and visit anytime, and I mean *any*time." She made kissy lips, eventually actually blowing Tide a kiss. Really and truly.

Tide smiled. "Take care of yourself." He turned away and began to walk down the hall, pausing so that she could catch up.

Meghan fell in step next to him. They walked in silence for a few minutes. The Fire castle was bigger than the others. More opulent in its design and finishes. It was clear they were the ruling dragons. From their pure unmarred chest markings to the way they carried themselves in general. "You didn't have to blow her off like that," she blurted. "If you want to meet her later you should just do it. Don't let me stop you."

Tide glanced her way. "Of course I had to blow her off. We have a deal. I keep my word."

Why did it bug her so much that he'd only turned Scarlet down because of their deal? What was with her? Why did she care? They'd had a one-night stand. Nothing more. One measly little night. She wasn't in the least bit interested in Tide, yet she still felt disappointed and maybe a bit jealous.

"Still, you should go for it if you really want to. I don't mind either way."

"Well I do mind. We have a deal. No fucking around for either of us. I'm taking it seriously and I expect you to do the same." Why did he look so angry all of a sudden?

"You don't have to get so weird about it."

"Yes I do, because you clearly don't take our agreement seriously. If making it an equal playing field keeps you happy then so be it. I wasn't interested in taking Scarlet up on her offer anyway."

"I take it you've had her already, so she doesn't hold much interest anymore."

"Something like that."

"You really are an asshole," she muttered.

"Most females tend to become clingy if I rut them more than once. They start to think we're in a relationship or something. Humans are the worst at that. If that kind of thinking makes me an asshole, then so be it. I'm very honest about my intentions."

"Fuck and run."

Tide choked out a laugh. "That's pretty rude, doc. I might be rubbing off on you."

"That's Doctor Roberts, not doc, or Meghan, or human." She looked him in the eyes. "It's the truth though. Don't you ever get lonely? Don't you ever want something more?"

He sighed. "I guess I have moments where I feel I could settle down, but unlike every other red-blooded male in the four kingdoms, the thought of the hunt doesn't blow my hair back."

"The hunt? What hunt?" She felt herself frown.

"Oh, you've never heard about the hunt?" He grinned broadly.

"No, never." Her frown deepened.

He chuckled. "Someone should have briefed you better before you decided to take this position. I guess Blaze and Torrent wanted you on board so badly they failed to inform you of a couple of things." Then his smile turned into a frown and he grabbed her by the arm, pulling her o the side. "Please tell me someone told you to take birth control? I remember you saying you weren't on anything the last time we… that night." His voice was deep.

For once he didn't refer to what they did. Tide kept it civilized, he looked anxious, which in turn worried her. "Yes, I was told to go onto something, so I had a copper IUD inserted because…"

He huffed out a heavy breath and grabbed his chest. "Thank fuck. Dragons are very base and instinctual creatures."

"So you keep saying."

"Look, keep taking whatever it is you're on."

"I don't have to take anything. An IUD was inserted into my uterus. A Para Gard can last up to ten years, so I think I'm good."

"I take it, it's effective?" He rubbed his chin, the stubble catching.

"Yes, of course. It's one of the most effective methods of birth control. Look, I'm not sure why we're even having this conversation because I'm not in a relationship and nor do I plan on sleeping with anyone anytime soon. We have an agreement, remember?"

"Just trust me on this one, it's a good thing you're on birth control and it's a good thing you're celibate while on dragon soil. I can sleep easier."

"I plan on doing my job. I think we've talked about this enough over the last few days. I'm pretty sure George and Ice will be wondering where we got to and I need to start working on these samples. Until all of the DNA has been analyzed, I won't know what we're dealing with."

Tide gestured with his hand down the hall. "Let's go then."

"By the way," she continued, "don't get any funny ideas, we're not friends or anything. In fact, I'm going to go back to ignoring you now."

Tide chuckled. "You're still pissed at me because I won't fuck you again."

She tripped on nothing, almost falling on her face. Tide gripped her elbow and pulled her back upright. His chuckle only grew louder, which aggravated her. "That has nothing to do with it. You're very wrong. Totally off track." She wanted to say more but forced herself to shut it.

"Okay, why are you pissed at me then?"

"I'm not pissed at you. I just don't like you – simple!"

He looked at her like she had just lost her mind. "You don't like me? I'm sorry, I find that hard to believe."

"You would," Meghan huffed. They were walking slower and slower, the balcony was just through a double set of doors at the end of the hall up ahead.

"What is that supposed to mean?"

"You're so full of yourself. That's all. The end."

He raked a hand through his hair and stopped walking entirely. "You don't like me because I'm confident and honest?"

It was her turn to laugh. It burst out of her, taking a good few seconds for her to compose herself enough to talk. "I don't like you because you're full of yourself. You call it confidence and I call it arrogance."

"Oh yes, you prefer brains to brawn, right?"

"That's right." She nodded. Tide could go to hell.

"Berries and cream." He grinned and out popped those dimples.

Meghan looked at the double doors just ahead of them. That was the other thing she didn't like about him. He was an asshole and too damned good-looking for his own good. Or was it too good-looking for *her* own good? It didn't matter. Probably a bit of both. "Berries and cream? What does food have to do with anything?"

"That's what you scent of." She snapped her head back in his direction. Tide was right there. Just an inch or two away. "When you're aroused. Berries and cream, doc. Thick, ripe and sweet."

Her heart-rate picked up against her will. She tried to control her breathing because her chest was rising and falling far too quickly. Her reaction would give him the wrong idea. It would give him the impression that he was onto something.

"Don't think I haven't noticed you sneaking little looks at my dick when you don't think I'm watching."

"I have not—" He put a finger over her lips silencing

her.

"Yes, you have. Deny it all you want. Pretend all you want. Your scent changes, *you* may not want me, but your pussy sure as hell does."

Meghan felt her eyes grow huge and she made a squeaking noise. She still couldn't talk with his hand in the way. The bastard was grinning at her. Tide shrugged, his grin disappeared in an instant. He licked his lips, his intense gaze still on her. "In another time, another place, maybe I would've given you another go." He finally removed his hand. "Too bad it's not possible."

"Not if you were the last person on earth," she whispered since a group of people was coming up behind them. Her cheeks felt hot. Her whole body felt hot. She vibrated with anger. *How dare he? How dare he say those things?*

She was appalled to find that she vibrated with something else too. *Need.* It was there, in the pit of her stomach. Unwanted and yet undeniable.

Tide sniffed the air, he raised his brows, his grin widening by the second. "If you say so."

"I do." She stomped off ahead of him, blustering through the doors that led outside. George and Ice were still chatting away. Oblivious to the turmoil around them. George waved when he saw her, then immediately resumed his discussion with Ice. Tide chuckled as he walked past her. His beefy ass on display. Naked. No tan lines in sight. He walked up ahead and then turned, all but thrusting his cock out at her, a smirk on his face.

Her mouth fell open, he was semi-erect. His manhood out on display. Meghan tried to look away. She tried really hard and failed. He gave the tiniest circling thrust of his hips. It had felt so good when he had done that… inside her. He did it again. Did no one else see this? She looked around the large balcony. There was a small group to the side of them, but they continued to go about their business, no one paid any attention to them.

Tide made a big show of sniffing the air. Then he groaned like he liked what he smelled. *Her.* He was smelling her and liking it. *Shit.* Come to think of it his you-know-what was bigger, harder, longer. Tide put a hand over himself and looked at her. Like he blamed her for his erection. There was a hunger in his stare as well. His eyes narrowed, his skin grew taut. She'd seen that look before. When he'd pushed into her. She couldn't take her eyes off of him.

"You ready?" Ice asked, his gaze on Tide.

"Yeah." Tide turned away from them and erupted, he growled loudly as he changed. The sound filled with… pain and definite frustration. It seemed to take longer than normal as well.

Meghan stuffed her hair into her hood and tightened it up. Then she pulled on her gloves, making sure that her backpack straps were firmly on her shoulders.

So, Tide knew that she was still attracted to him despite not liking him one bit. Thing was, Tide was just as attracted to her. Even though he had teased her, he didn't seem to like the idea. Well, it didn't sit right with her either.

What the hell were they going to do about it? Nothing that's what. Absolutely nothing.

CHAPTER 15

"Nothing?" George laughed hard before sipping his hot chocolate. "You still want him but you're not going to act on it?"

"Exactly right. I don't like him."

"Who cares." George put his mug down and turned to face her. "You don't need to like him to have a good time. You haven't said anything about that night but I'm going to assume that if you want a repeat he had to be good."

Meghan pulled a face. "Yes, dammit. He was incredible."

"I knew it!" George shouted.

"Quiet. These guys have excellent hearing." She turned up the volume of the music they were listening to. Some or other pop song about never getting back together, which was rather appropriate. Not that she and Tide had ever been together in the first place. Why was she even thinking about Tide when it came to the stupid love song in the first place?

"Tide's not out there is he?" George asked.

"No," she shook her head, "Bay's on duty, but still, I

don't want this getting back to Tide. He's so big-headed as it is."

"Are you talking about his head or his *head?*" George cackled wickedly.

"You know I didn't mean it like that but he does have a big... head. And I'm not talking about the one on his shoulders."

George lifted his eyes and did this side to side motion with his head while making obscene noises. "His cock is exquisite. Everything about that man is hot."

"Unfortunately, I have to agree with you and just for the record, I *don't* want a repeat."

George looked at her like she'd just grown horns or turned purple or something. "You *so* do."

"It doesn't matter because I'm not allowed to have sex with anyone while here."

"Why not? We didn't end up signing that particular policy."

"Something about all the guys catching wind that I'm available based on my scent and going mad and fighting each other to the death for me."

George stared at her with big eyes for a moment.

"They would be able to smell the sex on me. It would make them crazy or something. They'd lose their minds. Have you ever heard anything so stupid?"

George's mouth hung open. "That sounds amazing, I want in."

Meghan burst out laughing. "You can't be serious."

"Of course I'm serious. I want all of these seriously hot men fighting to have me. It's a pity most of them are straight."

She shook her head. "Most of them, huh?" Meghan took a sip of her own hot chocolate. "What about Ice? You guys seem awfully cozy."

"He's straight as an arrow. Really nice guy though. We get along like a house on fire. Thank god he's straight or I'd be tempted to settle down. He's that gorgeous and that sweet." George sighed.

"So, there's no romance brewing or anything?" She looked at him over her mug.

"Nah! I've seen one or two guys giving me the eye, going to bide my time till I meet one of them. In the meanwhile, there's plenty of eye candy, I'm enjoying chatting with Ice and I have my hand." He held it up, waggling his fingers. "Not a long-term plan but for now," he shrugged, "it'll do the job." He narrowed his eyes on her. "What about you? It sounds like you're headed back to nunhood even though you have to see Mister Sexy-ass every day. You might just self-combust."

"I packed my dildo."

George burst out laughing, even covered his mouth with his hand. "Oh my word, it must be bad. You finally took that thing out of the packaging. Does it even work after all these years?"

She felt her cheeks heat. Meghan had bought the dildo on a whim, years ago. One of their mutual friends had gotten married and there had been a lady selling sex toys and clothing at the Hen Party. Needless to say, it had stayed in it's wrapping all of this time. Well, until now. She looked away, her face on fire.

"Oh my god!" George slapped his thigh. "You've used it. I can't believe it. You actually used that purple monstrosity."

"So what if I have?" She grit her teeth, trying to sit tall. "I'll have you know that it did a fantastic job."

"It's not as good as the real thing." George made a face. "I refuse to believe that."

"It has three settings, the rubber is real feel."

George rolled his eyes. "Real feel my ass." Then he realized what he'd said and covered his mouth while choking out a laugh.

Meghan smiled. "It has a double action stimulator."

"A what?"

"Double action stimulator…" She widened her eyes. "You know, *double action*, and it does the job, so I'm happy."

"Yeah right! A real man would be a ton better." Then he looked at her all weird. "I take that back, a shifter would be so much better."

"Well it's not going to happen, so I'll just be content with my big, purple dildo thank you very much."

"Whatever blows your hair back."

"Exactly. I'm perfectly fine. Definitely not some sex-starved person."

"If you say so." George looked at her like he didn't believe her.

"I'm not!" She said it like she meant it because she did mean it, dammit!

Fucking hell!

Fuck!

Tide bit down on his lower lip so hard he almost broke the damn skin. She was bending over again. For the sixth time that morning. Six times in only three hours. Her ass was per-fucking-fection. Full and round and pear-like and so damned squeezable, bounce-able, bite-able. Not to mention fuckable.

He'd never wanted a female's ass before. He might make an exception for Meghan... Doctor Roberts. Would she make him call her that while he was balls deep inside her? He longed to find out.

Ice chuckled next to him. So softly he barely made a sound. The male gave the air a sniff and glanced down. Tide clasped his hands across the front of him, trying to hide a monster erection.

Tide shrugged. "Human female," he mouthed, knowing that Ice would hear what he had said.

The male nodded once. "Understandable," he mouthed back.

She sat back down at her desk, and put her pen in her mouth, sucking on the tip. Tide swore that he could feel the pull on his tip... all the way to his groin, which pulled tight.

"You have it bad." Ice chuckled again. His shoulders shook but he didn't make a sound.

"I'm horny." Tide shrugged. Was that all it was? Or was it her. *Yeah right... no!* Even if it was her — and it wasn't — it was her body and then only because they had been so compatible. Maybe he should speak with Torrent about getting himself replaced.

Fuck that!

He was the best choice for this assignment. He trusted Bay implicitly. Otherwise, there was no one else. He couldn't risk it. *Wouldn't!* That's why he even checked in on her during Bay's shifts. At odd times, he'd just swing by and make sure everything was kosher and so far it had been.

No, he was here to stay. It was less than three and a half months until his next stag run. He could do this. He could. He had to. Then again, he probably couldn't go on that either. A deal was a deal. *Fuck!* His hand would have to be enough. There was just no other way.

CHAPTER 16

Nine days later . . .

They entered his brother's office.

Torrent smiled. Tide noticed the worry lines on his forehead. His eyes looked bloodshot. "Come in. Welcome."

"Thanks for agreeing to see me," Meghan said.

"Of course. I've been waiting in anticipation for the results of the tests."

"I thought we could go over the findings first before setting up a meeting with all of the royals."

"Yes, I'm glad you did that. You said that your findings were out of the ordinary."

"They were... not what I expected, no." Meghan frowned.

Torrent gestured to a chair. "Take a seat, please." Then he glanced over at him. "Tide, I'd like you to join in on this meeting as well. You can be both my second-in-command as well as Doctor Robert's guard."

Tide nodded. "Sure." He took a seat next to Meghan.

He noticed how she moved over as far as she could to get away from him without making it obvious, of course.

"Can we get you anything to drink?" Torrent looked up at Creek. "My PA can get you anything you want." His brother smiled at Meghan.

Creek stepped forward, a huge smile on his face. Too fucking big, in Tide's opinion. "Juice, water, soda? Maybe a hot beverage?"

"A tea would be great."

"No problem."

Creek was on his way to the door when Tide cleared his throat. "I would love a double espresso with a shot of hazelnut syrup and just a pinch of cinnamon."

Creek's back stiffened. "My apologies, my lord, right away." He quickly scuttled from the room.

"Since when do you take a pinch of cinnamon in your espresso?" Torrent went on before Tide could answer, his brother grinned. "And a shot of hazelnut syrup. Do we even have such a thing?"

Tide shrugged. "It will teach him to forget his place."

Meghan shook her head. "What, are you ten?"

"I'm a prince. A male must know his place, even when there is a pretty human in the room. I'm surprised you didn't give him a kick up the ass for not taking your order."

"He has my order," Torrent said. "Took it before you arrived."

"Insolent, little prick," Tide bristled. "I hope it keeps him busy for the rest of the morning."

Meghan cleared her throat and opened the file on her

lap. "Good thing I didn't really feel like that tea."

"Good thing," Tide said. The meeting would be over by the time Creek found the hazelnut syrup, *if* he ever found it.

"Okay, let's get on with it, I'm keen to hear what you have to say," Torrent urged, leaning forward.

Meghan nodded. "Okay, well, I have to say I was shocked at the findings."

This was interesting, Tide also leaned forward in his chair.

"I'm going to use layman's terms here."

"Please do, spell it out if you have to. All of those medical terms end up getting lost on us," Torrent said.

Tide nodded.

"The reason it's taken so long is because I ran all of the tests twice, just to be sure that I wasn't missing anything or misinterpreting my findings."

"Oh, were they really that different to what you expected?" Torrent asked.

"Completely." She swallowed. "Deoxyribonucleic acid or DNA is a molecule that carries the genetic instructions used in the growth, development, functioning and reproduction of all known living organisms. You find duplicate DNA strands inside the cell nucleus." Meghan must have seen their blank looks because she cleared her throat. "The exact make-up or strand sequencing differs from species to species and is ultimately unique from one to another. We can, of course, break it down even further and say that it's unique from one individual to another, but I didn't need to take sequencing analysis that far…

thankfully." She giggled, sounding nervous. She must have realized that neither he nor Torrent got her joke because she pursed her lips together, smoothing her skirt before continuing.

Meghan turned a couple of pages, finding the one she was looking for. "I used whole genome sequencing to determine the complete DNA sequence of each dragon species. As expected there were minor differences from one dragon species to another."

Torrent nodded.

"Each of you has different unique abilities, so it stands to reason that sequencing is slightly different as well. The results of your offspring, however, were baffling. I'm specifically referring to the children that resulted from a dragon shifter and human pairing."

"Interesting. Go on." Torrent sat back in his chair.

"Well," she puffed out a lungful of air, "it's as if all of the offspring are a species of their own."

"I don't understand." Torrent shook his head, he leaned forward once more, clasping his hands over his thighs.

Tide felt his forehead knit together. Felt his whole body tighten.

"Regardless of the dragon species, all children born of dragon shifter, human pairings have the same DNA sequence."

"English, doctor," Torrent said.

"It's as if they are a species of their own, a new species, similar to their parents and yet not. You have Earth dragons, Air dragons, Fire dragons and Water dragons. Well, now you have a fifth type."

"I don't understand." Torrent had a bewildered look.

"The fifth type have the same DNA. It is ever so slightly different from the other four, yet it has characteristics of each of the four, an amalgamation if you will."

"A fifth type of dragon? What does that mean exactly?" Tide asked, shocked to his core.

"Yes, a fifth type. I'm afraid I'm not sure what it means. It's highly complex and—"

"Will all of these, new species of dragons be able to breathe fire then?" Torrent asked.

"As it stands, there is no way of knowing. It's possible and yet it may not be the case. One would need to dig even deeper. I would need to isolate that specific gene… in order to find out if it was autosomal dominant or recessive. I'd need to ascertain the mitochondrial inheritance pattern and, like I said, it would be complicated," she spoke quickly.

"A new species," Torrent sounded bewildered.

"An amalgamation." Tide looked just as shocked.

"Yes, essentially."

"A new breed of dragons." Torrent stood up; he was smiling. "Finally, equal footing… something that binds us as one. Our children."

Meghan nodded. "Yes."

"Let's not get ahead of ourselves here," Tide cautioned.

"This is cause for celebration. Even Blaze would need to see the merit in a new species. We will finally have something in common." Torrent smiled broadly.

"The general population are not aware that the babies

do not have royal markings. They may still be shunned as royals. This might not be a good thing," Tide said, shaking his head. "Our offspring might be outcasts in the end." He hated being the bearer of bad news but it was true.

"I refuse to believe that," Torrent growled.

"Why haven't the royals presented their heirs? Why does no one know of their chest markings or lack thereof?" Tide asked. "Because you're afraid of the uproar. You're afraid of the fallout."

"This is a new species though, a stronger species." Torrent's fists were clenched.

"I'm sorry, brother, but you might be wrong. They might not be stronger and even if they are, they might be viewed as being weaker. No markings and human blood." Tide shook his head.

"You have some serious work to do, Doctor Roberts." His brother looked Meghan head on. "You need to cure their affliction. Make our young immune to silver. It might be their only salvation."

Looking resolute, Meghan nodded, closing the file on her lap. "I will do my level best. Of that you have my word."

"Good! Let's call a meeting with Blaze and the rest of the kings, otherwise, this needs to stay quiet."

"Agreed," Tide said.

"No problem," Meghan replied.

CHAPTER 17

It was too much. Far too much. Seeing him every day. Being so close to him. Knowing the pleasure he could give her and not being able to do anything about it. Well, there was one thing she could do. Only one.

It was late, she'd eaten supper and watched a mindless program on TV. She'd tried hard not to think of him but had failed. Especially when she'd showered, the droplets running down her skin. The hot burst of water on her nipples. The soft scrape of the towel between her legs when she'd dried herself off.

She looked through her closet and pulled that particular shirt on. *The shirt.* The one she'd worn every night for the last week. She turned up the volume on the stereo so that no one would hear her. Then she went and lay down on her bed, on top of the covers and reached into her drawer, pulling out the purple warrior. Meghan wasn't even sure why she'd brought the thing with her on this trip. It was all Tide's fault. She'd lived quite happily without sex for a whole year. She'd barely even touched herself during that time. Even before that, it wasn't that she didn't like sex, she just didn't particularly need it either. It was like, if she was seeing someone and having sex, then great, and if not, well, that was fine too. Only, since spending the night with him, things had changed. They'd changed for the worse. It was like her libido had been reawakened and with a vengeance. All she could think about was sex lately. Not just that, all she could think about was sex with Tide.

She could still remember the noises he had made. Little grunts and pants. Moans and growls. Just thinking about it was making her feel achy with need. Then she remembered his eyes. How blue they had been, how intense, how focused on her. Of course that led to thoughts of how he had touched her, with his hands, his mouth, his...

She moaned, opening her thighs as wide as they would go. Oh well, a girl had to do what a girl had to do. Feeling this way was perfectly normal. She was a healthy woman, at the peak of her fertility, with hormones running rampant. Sex was completely normal and in times of drought, masturbation was normal too.

She'd start on the first setting. Meghan flicked the switch and her purple warrior began vibrating in her hand. She positioned the device so that the smaller head was directed at her clit.

Double stimulation. Was there any other way? The sex toy slid in easily, she was that wet, that ready. A moan escaped as it breached her... there. The word 'pussy' echoed around her mind. Only, it was Tide saying it in his deep, rough rasp.

She didn't allow the smaller head to touch her clit just

yet, didn't want this over too soon. Even that was different. Before, any form of masturbation would result in racing for release as quickly as possible. Not anymore. Meghan enjoyed drawing out her pleasure, just as Tide had done.

In, out, in, out. *Buzzzzzz*... The vibrations moved through her, making her moan. Slow and easy. She pictured Tide covering her body, his weight pressing against her, his mouth on her neck, sucking, licking and nipping. Kissing her, his beautiful blue eyes open and on her. A hunger reflected in their depths.

Why him?

Why?

It was just sex. Not even real sex. Pretend sex. She could picture whomever she wanted and she wanted to picture him. Only him. She envisioned Tide naked. Broad shoulders, pecs, abs and well-muscled thighs. His cock... yes, his thick, long... She moaned, louder this time. She was working the dildo faster, harder, deeper. The second head bumping her clit every so often.

So good.

She pictured him doing that circling thrust, only, her hands were digging into his meaty ass. His cock was deep inside her, so deep. "Yes," she moaned. "Oh, yes!"

Shit! She needed to slow down. At this rate she was going to come soon. Meghan eased off. In... pause... out... pause... in, easy... Another moan escaped and her hips jerked forward.

"Oh." Her legs shook. Her whole body shook with the need to come. "Oh, oh, oh," she moaned with every penetration. Every slip and slide of the rubber. By now, he'd be holding her down, pinning her with his big body. His thrusts would be relentless. His grunts loud. She'd hear the slap of his body against hers. She so wished it was real. That it was actually happening. His face would be taut with his pending release, his brow creased. Almost like he was angry.

She could hear the greedy slurping noises her body was making, sucking onto the dildo with all its might. There was another bump of the second arm of the dildo against her clit. She moaned louder, his name on the tip of her tongue. It was the one thing she hated in all of this. How she couldn't come without saying it.

Tide.

Tide.

Tide.

Not today. No. She'd hold it in. Another bump and she cried out. "T-T... aaahhh..." *No!*

If this were real, he might stop at this point, flip her over onto all fours. Cage her body with his own. His big cock grinding back into her. Hitting that spot each and every time. "Oh my... oh... oh my good, g... oh..." His breath hot in her ear. His grunts so loud at this point. His touch hard, almost bruising. He'd whisper her name, almost in awe as he strummed her clit. The second part of that vibrator was on her bundle of nerves now. Brushing against it with every hard thrust. The vibrations at her core, flinging her over the edge. "Tide!" She shouted, as her orgasm moved through her. Ripping her from the inside out. She continued to thrust, her whole arm tired from the exertion, she ignored it. Her heels dug into the comforter, her free hand clutched at her cotton-clad breast, squeezing as she came down.

Good.

So good.

Not satisfying unfortunately. She pulled the dildo out, feeling almost as turned on as when she started. "What's wrong with me?" she muttered, still panting hard. "What did that asshole do to me?" She squeezed her thighs shut, trying to ignore the ache. Unfortunately, if she made herself come a second time – something she now knew was more than possible – it would only make it worse. It would make her needier and achier than before. It was moments like this that she went back to hating him, even more than before.

"Good evening." Tide rounded the corner.

Bay jumped. As in, his feet left the ground. He reacted like he had done something wrong. Like Tide had caught him red-handed. Even his eyes were wide. Too wide. Tide could also scent nervousness – it was sour and hit him in the snout as he took a step towards the male. "What's going on?" He felt alarm. Adrenaline raced through him. "Is the female okay?"

"You need to trust me, she's fine. More than fine. But you have to leave." Bay put a hand out towards him and took a few steps in his direction, like he was trying to usher him away. "Go right now," he added, with a growl.

"Why? What's got you rattled?"

A moaning noise punctured through the wall. It was drowned out some by loud music but he knew what he had heard. Tide's head snapped in that direction. "Is Meg... Doctor Roberts, okay? What the fuck is going on?" Then he heard something else. "What's that funny noise?" He walked towards her front door, but Bay stepped in front of him blocking him from going any further.

They stood chest to chest. "Leave. Just go... please." Bay's eyes were narrowed, his jaw tense.

"Don't tell me what to do."

"As Doctor Robert's guard, I will and I must. Go."

"Yes." It was Meghan, her voice clear as a bell despite the music. "Oh, yes!" It was laced with... *Fuck*. It was laced with pleasure. No doubt about it.

"What the fuck!" he snarled.

Bay put a hand to his chest and shoved, hard. Tide was forced to take a step back. "It's not what you think," Bay said, urgency in his voice. "She is alone."

"Alone?" he growled, his hands still fisted, adrenaline still coursed, every muscle was still bunched and ready. "Oh..." He frowned. "Alone. You mean..."

She moaned again, the sound thick, pulled out from somewhere deep in her throat. He'd heard her sound like that before. When he'd fucked her. When he'd been so deep inside her... That buzzing. *Wait a minute. Wait just a goddamn minute.* The heavy moan was followed by a softer. "Oh!" The sound and knowledge of what she was doing tugged on his balls. Every drop of blood in his body went south and all at once.

"Go!" Bay advanced on him. "You can't be here."

"I'm not leaving." What was he saying? He couldn't stay. He definitely couldn't go to her which was what everything in him told him to do.

"Oh, oh, oh…" Followed by another long drawn out moan that had his balls pulling tight. He'd never heard anything more erotic. Anything more beautiful. More… Tide bit down on his lower lip. He needed… wanted…he… Bay slapped him.

His head was whipped to the side, his cheek stung as he staggered back a step or two. "Go! Turn around and walk away."

Tide shook his head. He didn't want to. Wouldn't!

"Yes!" Bay growled under his breath. "You have to. You can't touch her, Tide. Use your brain for a second. I won't let you fuck this up, you will regret it, do you hear me?"

His dick throbbed. *Shit!* Bay was right. Tide turned and ran. He fucking ran as fast as his pathetic legs would carry him. At least one good thing had come of this, he could trust Bay to do the right thing. He needed to stay far away from Meghan after hours. No more visits during the night. What was this fixation he had with her? It was getting in the way of things. He had almost fucked up and badly.

A realization hit – he needed to excuse himself from this detail completely. He would do so first thing in the morning.

"I don't understand." Torrent stood up, staying behind his desk. "Why? What happened to make you change your mind? You wanted this detail. You insisted that Shale take the mining assignment."

Tide was also still standing. He'd burst into his brother's office and had announced his decision to be taken off the detail. "Nothing changed. I just... I think it would be best if someone else took over. That's all. It would be my recommendation that Bay take head guard position."

"Shale is already—"

"Not Shale! Anyone but fucking Shale."

Torrent frowned. "What has gotten into you, Tide?"

"I was wrong when I said I'd had her and that I was over her," he blurted. "The female winds me up in knots."

"Are you saying you have feelings for her?" Torrent growled, pushing his chair back so quickly it fell backwards, clanging as it landed. Torrent ignored the ruckus, he kept his eyes on Tide.

"No! Fuck no!" he sighed. "I'm in serious lust with her. We were highly compatible. I guess I can't stop thinking about fucking her again."

"You're going to walk away from this assignment because you can't control your urges? You're a grown male, for fuck sakes. You're a prince."

"Exactly, that's why I'm here. If I stay on that detail, I'm going to fuck up. Look, I feel like a failure standing here admitting weakness but it's that or sticking my hand in the cookie jar."

Torrent choked out a laugh. "It's not your hand we're worried about though, is it? Why not go on the stag run this weekend? Get it out of your system."

Tide shook his head. "It's not my turn."

"You're the prince, I think you're permitted an extra stag run once in a while. No one will—"

"Nope, I don't think it would help. I want her... Meghan... Doctor Roberts."

"Shit!" His brother frowned. "Are you sure you don't have feelings for her?"

"Yes, very sure."

"Okay."

"Okay what?"

"Doctor Roberts is working on the final," he made a face, "DNA sequencing report for the meeting with the royals next Wednesday."

"And?" Tide had no idea where his brother was going with this.

"Fuck her. I'll give you this one pass. Get it out of your system but no one is to know. Not a single soul. Maybe Bay and Ice and that would be it. For the next few days, she will need to be kept from the public eye..."

Tide felt his jaw drop. "What are you saying? Have you lost your mind?" He failed to keep the growl from his voice.

"No! You need to get her out of your system. You're fixated on this female and I don't like it. Doctor Roberts is important to our people. She's important to my family."

"Exactly, that's why I'm staying far away from her." Tide chuckled. "No wonder you nearly lost Candy early on in your relationship. How does your mind work? The last thing I want is to use Meghan or to hurt her. Not that I want any kind of a relationship with her either. We're not even friends, but I guess I respect her as a person. I will end up hurting her if I sleep with her again. I don't want her developing feelings for me. Right now, she hates me and I want to keep it that way." She did hate him, but she definitely wanted him at the same time. It was a recipe for disaster. He was staying far away from Doctor Roberts.

"Oh my god!" Torrent scrubbed a hand over his face. "You *do* have feelings for her."

"What are you talking about? I just told you it's strictly sexual."

"You don't want to hurt her."

"What's wrong with that? Meghan is a good person. She's sweet and…"

Torrent was pacing. "Oh my fuck, you care!"

"I care about our people. I care about our future heirs. We can't have our geneticist heartbroken because I fucked her and ran." He used her words, which made him smile.

"Okay," Torrent sighed. "I guess that makes sense. Fine. I'll make Bay head guard. You might need to hang tight the next few days while we find your replacement. Also, Shale's doing a decent job at the mine. I doubt Blaze will want to pull him for no reason. Are you sure you want this?"

"Yes," he answered without hesitation. "I don't think I have much choice."

"Okay then, I'll get the ball rolling."

Tide nodded, already regretting turning down a night with Meghan. It was for the best. The thought of hurting her – even potentially hurting her – didn't sit right with him at all.

CHAPTER 18

M eghan filed away the last few pieces of documentation. Her desk was still a mess but it couldn't be helped.

"Are you just about ready?" George asked, already halfway to the door.

Her stomach gave a growl before she could answer and they both laughed. "I'd say that's a yes," she said.

"I'd say it's…"

"Actually, I need to have a word," Tide spoke from his place on the far side of the room. He was looking at her. When she didn't reply, he turned to George. "You guys go ahead. We'll meet you in the dining hall in a couple of minutes."

"Okay, sure." George looked hesitant but agreed. "We'll see you in a few?" He raised his brows, looking at her. It was sweet of him to double-check with her before leaving.

Meghan sighed softly and nodded. What crazy, idiot request did he have for her now?

Ice fell in behind George, they closed the door behind

them as they left. "Do I need to sit down?" she asked, turning to face Tide.

"No, it's nothing like that." He smiled. "I just wanted to let you know that I've been reassigned."

It took her a few seconds for his words to sink in. "Reassigned?" As in, leaving? No longer her guard? What?

Tide nodded. "Yeah, reassigned. Bay will take over from me, we still need to finalize my replacement and then I'm out of here... out of your hair."

"Oh, I see." She widened her eyes. It was weird, she'd grown used to his company. A couple of weeks ago she would've been thrilled to see the back of him. Now, she wasn't so sure.

"I thought you'd jump up and down once you found out." He was frowning.

"So did I," she said, simply.

"So," he folded his arms and gave her a cocky half-smile, "you're sad to see me go, aren't you?"

She choked out a laugh. "I wouldn't go that far. I guess I'm used to having you here, it's going to be weird not having you around."

"You'll miss me, won't you? Might as well admit it."

She laughed again, this time rolling her eyes. "No... forget that. You have the biggest head."

"Yeah, I do." He gripped his... his cock.

Her mouth went dry and dropped open. The air in her lungs rushed out.

Tide let go of his cock, the outline of which had become easy to see through the thin cotton of his pants. Especially since he was semi-erect. As hard as she tried, she couldn't make herself look away. She really should look elsewhere on account of her making a fool out of herself.

Tide sniffed the air. "Berries and cream. You really shouldn't look at me like that. You won't like where it would lead."

"Maybe I would." It slipped out and she instantly regretted it. She didn't try to take it back, how could she when she meant it?

Tide clenched his jaw, his eyes darkened. "You'll have to trust me then, doc, because you wouldn't. I know you wouldn't, so don't tempt me."

"Like I could tempt you. You already had me remember?" She smiled, trying to make light of it.

"You'd be wrong on that note, very wrong." His pale blue gaze was intense. His whole stance was tense. He pushed a breath out through his nose. His words were unexpected. The shock must've registered on her face because he quickly added. "Maybe we should talk about something else. Something less dangerous."

"What's your new assignment?"

"That's strictly need to know and you don't need to know."

"Fair enough." It was a reminder. They were nothing to one another.

"We'd better get to lunch."

"Yes, let's do that." The atmosphere had turned from heated to awkward. "Good luck! I know you didn't really want this assignment, babysitting me. I hope whatever you do next is more exciting."

"I hope so too, not that I minded this assignment." He said it like he had no idea where he was going next, which was nuts. What was all of that 'need to know' nonsense?

"You said you'll leave as soon as a replacement is found?" she asked as they walked to the exit.

"Yes."

"So, tomorrow then? I'm sure there are a ton of guys who are more than capable."

"No, there aren't." His voice held a gravelly edge. "I don't trust most of them... make that all of them. You are important to my people. Not just the Water dragons, all of us."

"Hey..." She touched the side of his arm and he sprang away like he'd been burned by her touch. "Sorry."

"No, I'm sorry." He shook his head. "What is it you wanted to say?"

"Our deal will still stand... after you're reassigned. I'm not going to jump into bed with anyone, so you can put anyone onto this detail. You just have to trust me, that's all."

Tide nodded. "That's good to know. I do, I just wish I trusted myself."

"What? Why?" What did he mean by that? She'd pretty much offered him sex just a few minutes ago and he'd turned her down flat. He could trust himself. Maybe he wasn't talking about trusting himself around her. Maybe he was talking about trusting himself with other women. What then?

"It's not important." Tide pushed out a heavy breath. "Let's get to lunch. They'll start to wonder where we are soon." He walked ahead, stopping and waiting for her to catch up. Then he fell in behind her. Resuming his position as her guard and putting an end to their conversation.

CHAPTER 19

"This is a fetal heart-rate monitor. It's perfectly safe to use as it works with sonar and not radiation," Meghan explained as she stuck the Velcro in place. "These discs," she pointed at the two situated on either side of Candy's tummy – there was barely a bump there – you wouldn't say she was even pregnant if you didn't know, "will pick up on the baby's heart-rate. They're attached to this machine and…" Meghan turned the dial, instantly, the sound of a galloping heart could be heard.

Candy grinned. "That's him. That's our son?"

Torrent clutched his mate's hand tighter, his eyes were wide and shone with excitement. "My boy." He smiled broadly.

"Yes, and as you can hear, he sounds perfectly healthy." She pointed to the monitor. "A normal fetal heart-rate is between 120 and 160 beats per minute. Your son is right within that range at around 145 beats per minute. We will keep the heart-rate monitor on throughout immunotherapy. If at any time his heart-rate goes up, particularly above the range I just mentioned, we would need to assume that he is in fetal stress and we would discontinue therapy immediately."

"But we're going to take things really slowly to ensure that it doesn't get to that, right?" There was a deep growl in Torrent's voice and he was frowning heavily. Even his eyes were narrowed.

He looked angry and pretty darned scary. Meghan knew there was nothing to be afraid of. He was just highly protective of Candy and his unborn child. It was really sweet actually. She only hoped that someone cared for her as deeply one day.

Meghan smiled at Torrent. "Yes, that's right. I've upped the schedule from the recommended two sessions a week to three, however."

Torrent growled so loudly that she flinched. His lip curled back and his eyes were narrowed on her. Even his teeth seemed longer than normal.

Tide stepped forward. "You need to calm down." It was weird to see him step out of position. Although he was always there and she was continually aware of him, he never actually said or did anything.

Torrent's eyes flashed to Tide. "We are talking about my mate and our unborn child." He sighed, looking back at Meghan. "You must please forgive my reactions. I am... nervous."

"Of course, it is completely understandable."

Torrent pulled in a deep breath. "Let's try that again. Why are you increasing the recommended sessions, is that not dangerous?"

"As previously mentioned," she needed to tread

carefully, "it is not completely without risk and it would be wrong of me to advise you otherwise, but I will do everything to minimize the risk as much as possible. One of the reasons we have stepped up the sessions to three is so that I can lower the contact with silver significantly. We'll meet more often and take a safer route rather than upping the contact time or dose. I hope that makes sense."

Candy nodded. "Yes, it does. We would like nothing more than for our son not to have to suffer from this potentially life-threatening allergy and to see a cure come about for the rest of the dragon shifters. At the same time, the lower the risk, the better."

"It's a balancing act. I will monitor you and the baby every step of the way. With you, it's more important because you don't suffer from the allergy, but chances are almost a hundred percent certain that your baby does. Sky just left about half an hour ago. It is helpful that she can tell me if she's not feeling well. We can look for symptoms of discomfort and illness because if she's feeling it, then the baby certainly is as well. With you, that's not the case, so we'll need to take it much slower, just to be sure." She paused. "On the other hand, you are not as far along, so we have a little more time."

Candy nodded. Torrent clutched his mate's hand, holding on for dear life. His focus was on her belly.

"Shall we begin?" Meghan asked.

"Yes, I'm ready." Candy smiled, but she could see that the other woman was tense.

Meghan glanced at Torrent but he still wasn't looking up. She could see deep frown lines on his forehead.

"It's okay, honey." Candy squeezed his hand and Torrent grunted once, not sounding convinced.

Meghan opened the pack of needles, removing one. "This contains the lowest dose of silver. It didn't seem to have any effect on the babies, even the newborn. For this first session, I will touch the silver needle to your skin. I don't expect it to have any effect, but it is a good place to start."

"So the needle won't actually penetrate my skin?" Candy asked.

"No. We'll keep it at five minutes of contact time only. We can progress to…"

"But you said that the babies had no reaction whatsoever?" Candy frowned. "Surely just touching me with that needle won't help anything?"

"We said we'd rather keep the risk to a minimum."

"But within reason right?" Candy asked. "I know I said I wanted to keep the risk down, but at the same time I'm hoping for results."

"Listen to the doctor, my love. She knows what she is doing."

"It just seems silly. I remember you saying that the more sessions we can fit in the more chance of him not having the allergy." Candy cleared her throat. "I don't want to take unnecessary risks but I also don't want to waste any time. We have a real chance of this working."

"It is possible but I don't want you to get your hopes up either." Meghan shook her head. "Maybe if we used you as a test subject, Torrent." She had heard of this working in the past when parents were nervous about procedures, or when children were worried. Let the parent experience it first.

"What would it entail?" Torrent asked.

"A few minutes of contact time with the needle to begin with," she said.

"Hun, please hold that needle," Candy spoke to Torrent. It was quite comical because he did exactly what she asked without question, picking it up.

Torrent did frown however. "You really should listen to the doctor…"

"And?" Candy raised her brows, looking pointedly at the needle.

"And nothing – but I'm a grown male in my prime. I'm the king. You can't compare me to an unborn whelp."

"Even though you sometimes act like a big baby," Tide said and from right next to her. "Did I give you a fright, doc… Doctor Roberts?"

Her heart raced. She swallowed hard. "Yes, I didn't hear you move."

"I'm really light on my feet for a big SOB."

She turned her head and there he was, grinning down at her. So close she could smell him. *You're working, Meghan. Stop your shit!*

"Go back to being a guard. You're not invited to this therapy session," Torrent said, between clenched teeth.

"You're being prickly and downright aggressive." It wasn't lost on her how Tide put himself between her and Torrent.

"I'm not going to hurt the female," Torrent snarled.

Candy gasped. "Stop it you two, please." She tried to sit up.

"No, stay where you are," Meghan said. "Stay calm. The baby's heart-rate has gone up a little."

"What?" Torrent snarled.

"Calm the fuck down," Tide cautioned, voice low.

Torrent bashed chests with Tide. "I *am* calm!" he roared.

"Like hell you are," Tide's voice was even. "Get yourself under control or get out."

"I'm not leaving Candy or the baby." He sounded less aggressive.

"Then calm down."

"I told you, I won't hurt her."

"Not on purpose but…" Tide sighed. "I wouldn't let you hurt the doctor. You would have to go through me. Do you hear?"

"No-one's hurting anyone." Meghan stepped forward. "How is your hand feeling?"

Torrent looked down, she could see that he had completely forgotten that he was even still holding the needle. "I'm fine." He frowned, looking shocked. "It feels absolutely fine."

"Let me take a look." She took the needle from him and sure enough, his skin was unblemished.

"That's a good thing, right?" Torrent asked.

Meghan nodded. "Yeah, it would be great if we could prick you with the needle. Then we'll wait a minute or two to test for a reaction. If that's clear, we can insert the needle and leave it in for a little bit longer. Then maybe, if you're both okay with it, we can try the same with you, Candy?"

Candy nodded.

"Okay. Let's test it on me first. I like that idea." Torrent held out his arm and she pricked the soft tissue of his inner arm, removing the needle immediately.

"How was that?" Candy asked.

Torrent shrugged. "I didn't feel anything. It feels fine. It was not bad." He breathed out in one big exhale, looking relaxed for the first time since coming.

"I think I'll leave you to it." Tide had this little half-smile. When she looked his way, he winked. "I think you have things under control, doc."

"Thank you," she mouthed to him. Even though Tide had been doing his job – it hadn't been anything more than that – she was still grateful he had stepped in. It wasn't always easy to stand up against your superior, even if the person was family. The shifters seemed to take hierarchy even more seriously, so it would have been difficult for him.

Tide winked at her a second time. This time there was a definite flirtatious edge to it. It made her feel... something. She wasn't sure exactly what. More lust. Must be. He looked so damned sexy when he winked. It was a good thing he wouldn't be around for much longer. Better that way.

CHAPTER 20

The group of males sat in stunned silence for a few moments. Or maybe they were waiting to see if Meghan was going to say anything more. When she didn't, the whole room erupted and everyone spoke at once. The only males not shouting some or other question at Meghan was him, Torrent and Blaze. Everyone else was yelling, growling, or shouting.

Coal was on his feet. "Silence. Silence!" he commanded, his voice drowned out by the madness. Okay, so Coal was yelling, but not questions like the others.

Blaze slapped his hand on the table. Every glass vibrated. One of them even fell over, smashing and spilling its contents. "Quiet!" He looked around the table. Everyone calmed. Those standing sat back down. The feeling of stress still reverberated around the room.

"I realize that this is a lot to take in. An amalgamation of the four species?" Blaze shook his head, he looked at Meghan.

"Yes." She nodded. "In essence, the human-dragon

shifter offspring are a completely new species," she went on.

"What?" Thunder barked, jumping to his feet. "I'm not sure I understand what it is you are saying."

"Sit down," Blaze said, still completely calm. He paused until Thunder obeyed. The male still scowled heavily. "You heard the healer. She explained things very clearly. Young born of a human-dragon mating all have the same DNA. They are, in essence, the same. It does not matter if the father is Earth, Water, Air or even Fire."

"That can't be." Thunder was frowning darkly.

Granite looked deep in thought. "Interesting." He rubbed his chin. "What are the implications? I mean," he paused, "will they all be the same in their abilities?" Tide knew precisely why Granite had asked the question. He wanted to know more about his own son's ability to breathe fire. Tide wondered if the male would come clean. Torrent had urged him to do so.

"I don't know. Not at this stage," Meghan answered.

"Would you be able to research and find out?" Blaze asked.

"I'm not sure. It could take months. I'd need to ascertain the mitochondrial inheritance pattern. Find that specific DNA sequence. In short, I'd have to dig much deeper. These things start to get very involved when we have to isolate specific… it's complicated."

"Is it possible though?" Blaze asked.

"Yes, but my main reason for being here is to find a cure for your silver allergy. I'm here to develop a vaccination. That would need to be my key focus." Tide loved how she stood her ground, even against a male like Blaze. The Fire king was powerful and dominant. Even a human would pick up on that and yet she didn't flinch under his gaze.

"There is something I need to… mention," Granite said.

Here we go. Tide exchanged a look with Torrent, who sucked in a deep breath. Meghan sat at the head of the table. There were four males between himself and the healer. He didn't like it. Hadn't liked it when he'd been instructed to sit there earlier. Truth be told, he hadn't expected the Earth king to come clean.

"Something happened," Granite went on, "something that I need to disclose."

Blaze shook his head. "This is not the forum—"

"Actually," Granite swallowed thickly, "it is. My son, my second born, Quake… it happened the other day. He was upset, crying and it just… happened." He paused. They had agreed that Granite was not going to mention anyone else having been witness to the event.

"What happened? Why is it pertinent?"

Granite huffed out a breath. "It's very pertinent. Our children are a new species. They are unique. It stands to reason that we do not know what to expect. It was a shock when flames shot from his mouth."

Thunder shot to his feet. "You must have been mistaken!" he yelled.

Blaze frowned deeply. He shook his head. "That cannot be," he said, almost to himself.

"I know what I saw. My mate saw it too. There can be

no mistake, Quake can breathe fire. He has done it again since."

Tide's gaze shot to Torrent who shrugged. His brother hadn't known about the new development.

"His chest has flecks of gold within the mark," Granite continued. "At first it was just an outline and then there were golden flecks. They appeared after he breathed fire for the second time."

"What of Declan?" Blaze asked. "Has he too breathed fire?"

"No, his markings are still just an outline and there has been nothing out of the ordinary."

Blaze was taking this well. He looked calm and together. "Have you seen anything out of the ordinary, Thunder?"

"No." The male shook his head. "Nothing! My son's markings are but an outline."

"What of your son, Blaze?" Torrent asked. "Any sign of anything untoward?"

Tide held his breath.

"No!" Blaze raged, his fists clenched. *Oh shit! Here we go.* "And before you ask, Coal's son has not exhibited any strange abilities either." He looked like he wanted to say something and then thought the better of it. "I think that this needs to be explored, Doctor Roberts." He turned to her, eyes blazing. "Shall we bring a second geneticist on board or will you be able to tackle both projects?"

"I will do my best, but I need to warn you all that it could take time."

Blaze nodded. "You will let us know if you need more

staff?"

"Yes, certainly. I understand the reluctance to employ more outsiders. I will do my best with the time I have."

Tide breathed out, feeling some of the tension drain. Again he marveled at how well Meghan had handled herself.

The Fire king looked calm again. "I appreciate that," Blaze said. "In the meanwhile I need you all to report any incidences. Do so immediately." He looked from one male to the next. "One more thing. There was a child born to one of my warriors. The boy is a result of a human-dragon pairing."

"What?" Torrent asked, eyes narrowed. "Why were we not told of this?"

"The child has the same marking as the royal young – there is no silver to speak of. He should probably be tested—"

"We should have been told!" Thunder roared, slamming his fist onto the table, which made a cracking noise. "It was my understanding that there were only royal children born of human matings. What is this?" he added with a snarl.

Tide looked at Meghan who had sunk back in her chair. He wanted to jump to his feet, to go into protection mode and shield her with his body, but he was afraid that one move could provoke violence. The peppery scent of anger was strong around the room. It was that and adrenaline with a good dose of testosterone. A potentially disastrous concoction.

"I chose not to disclose—"

"That wasn't your decision to make!" Thunder shouted, his focus on Blaze.

"I am the fucking leader, I—"

"I am also a king. Yes, we follow you and yes, you ultimately rule but there needs to be honesty and respect or it won't work. Not telling us—"

"Was a decision I made and one I stand by," Blaze's voice was raised. "It was not pertinent at the time." His neck muscles roped.

"Not fucking pertinent? Fuck!" Thunder roared, smashing the table a second time. The crack evident at this point. One more blow and the entire thing would break up into pieces. As it stood, every glass was smashed, the various contents spilled over the gleaming wood, dripping on the floor below.

"Do not forget that the human female is still in attendance." Tide held up a hand. "Please, can everyone calm down?" This was getting more and more out of hand by the second. Tide rose to his feet. He gestured for Meghan to do the same. Her eyes were wide, her face pale. She might not have his senses but she could feel the brewing violence. She nodded once, doing as he said and doing it slowly and carefully.

Thunder narrowed his eyes. "This new breed of lessers and royals are indistinguishable. That's what you're saying, right?"

"All except for Granite's second-born." Blaze was frowning deeply, his eyes bright. Too fucking bright for his liking. Tide carefully made his way to Meghan, putting an arm around the female. He eased her behind him, stepping away from the table and towards the door.

"Does that mean that Granite's second-born will rule all of the kingdoms then? Since fire breathers are the ones in control." *Thunder hadn't just said that.* "Because it seems to me that whoever can breathe fire wins." The male wasn't thinking before opening his trap.

"It means..." Blaze said, his voice too deep, his muscles flexed. *This was bad.* "You need to shut the fuck up. The healer will do her job. We will soon know exactly where we stand. All of us. We'll soon have a greater understanding of the situation and will be in a better position to make decisions." Although Blaze's voice had returned to calm, a tendril of smoke wafted from his right nostril.

"You mean *you* will?" Thunder muttered.

"Hold your tongue." Blaze pointed at Thunder. "Or you will lose it!"

"I won't keep quiet!" the normally easygoing Thunder roared. "You mean *you* will know where *you* stand. The rest of us—"

"I already know where I stand." Blaze vibrated with anger. His eyes glowing, his teeth sharp.

Thunder smiled. There was no humor there. "Your son on the other hand..."

Tide turned and covered the human with his body, pulling her to him and enclosing his arms around her.

Hot.
White hot.

She screamed, squeezing her eyes shut and burying her face in Tide's chest. He roared, his whole body seemed to turn to stone. More roars and screams came from behind them. She smelled burning. Smoke filled the room, filling her lungs. Tide was moving though, dragging her. No, carrying her. Still shielding her body with his. The door was slamming shut and he was picking her up, carrying her. Running now. His face a mask of determination. His forehead dripped with sweat.

"Tide, we're okay now. You can stop." She coughed, her lungs still affected by the smoke she'd inhaled.

He shook his head, running faster. They burst through the double doors and out into the sunshine.

"Stand," he growled, setting her on her feet and stepping away. He shrieked as he changed. It was a terrible sound. Like he was in pain. But he looked fine.

Before she could think about it, he was scooping her up and flying for home. Going so fast that she felt nauseated. Her hair whipped about her face, stinging her. She moaned.

Her fur coat was still in the conference hall, as was her bag and the rest of her things. Then again. They were probably burned. There had been so much smoke. So much chaos. She'd never seen that kind of anger before. Blaze's eyes were terrifying. There had been scales showing on one of his arms and across that side of his chest. The other king, Thunder, had been just as angry. Blaze had blown fire. She hadn't seen it happen but she knew that it had. Thunder must be gravely injured along with the others. She took stock of herself. Nothing hurt.

She hadn't so much as broken a nail. Tide had kept her safe.

Meghan shivered, her teeth clattered together. Her eyes tightly shut against the wind. Tide made another shrieking noise. It didn't sound right. She cracked an eyelid. Was that the lair up ahead?

Then he was dropping. Meghan screamed. They fell a few feet before Tide's great wings flapped again. Harder and yet they weren't gaining much ground. They were slowing. He roared, his grip on her slipping. Meghan grasped his claws tighter. "Take us down!" she shouted, not sure if he heard her. "Are you hurt?" she screamed, feeling like an idiot for asking. Of course he must be.

They inched towards the lair. The few hundred feet felt like thousands. He nearly dropped her a couple more times. By the time they made it to one of the balconies – it wasn't the usual one, this one was much smaller, but closer and not as high up as the main balcony – by the time they made it there, her arms were shaking from holding on. Tide dropped her from about eight or ten feet. She landed hard, falling onto her knees and scraping them. Tide crashed on the ground beside her, he rolled once, smashing into the glass, which cracked. Thankfully it didn't actually break but a zig-zag pattern formed along the middle.

"Tide!" Bruised and scraped up, Meghan jumped to her feet and ran over to the giant beast. The dragon that was Tide was breathing heavily, his eyes closed.

"Oh my god." She covered her mouth. His back was a raw open wound of singed scales and flesh. His wings were perfect, as was the front side of him. "What should I do?" She needed to get help. She needed to get him to an emergency room or clinic. She needed medical supplies.

He opened his eyes. Pale blue and slitted, blinking a few times. He breathed in deeply and then exhaled. Breathed in again, seeming to hold it in his lungs and gave a shake of his massive head. Then he changed, folding in on himself. It was slow and cumbersome. The seconds ticked by, Tide stayed in mid-shift. He groaned, shifting some more. His jaw was too long, he still had a partial tail and scales. His hands were still curled into claws. Only they were smaller. With a loud shriek that hurt her ears, he shifted completely, lying in a heap on the stone floor.

His chest rose and fell quickly. His breathing came in loud pants. Sweat covered his body in a sheen. She knew he needed a few moments to recover. The shift had been hard on him. He lay on his side, so she moved around him to get a better look at his back.

Meghan swallowed thickly. His hair at the back was singed. His upper back, a black charred mess. "Oh no," she whispered, her heart racing. She felt her eyes prick with tears but sucked them back. She couldn't fall apart. She needed to stay strong for Tide.

"Is it that bad?" His voice sounded surprisingly normal.

"Um…" She cleared her throat. "You have first degree burns covering two-thirds of your back." She couldn't lie to him.

"I'm a dragon." His voice was a deep rasp. "Help me up."

"You shouldn't move. Let me fetch help." She blinked

again.

"No need."

"Don't be stubborn. You've sustained major injuries and need—"

"What I need are a few hours to heal and maybe a glass of water."

"Water?" She burst out laughing. It sounded a tad hysterical. "Look, I had to study to be a physician before I majored in genetics. I did my residency at our local hospital and I've—"

"I'm a shifter, doc. I have advanced healing capabilities. You can keep your degree. I don't need it." Tide turned onto his stomach in a surprisingly graceful move. He sucked in a deep breath and then pushed himself up. It took effort, his muscles strained. Tide grit his teeth, his face a mask of pain.

"Wait." She gripped his upper arms. Tide held onto her, he looked out of it. "Let me call someone."

"No," he groaned. "Need to keep you safe," he muttered.

"I'm fine. It's *you* I'm worried about."

He grunted as he got to his knees.

"Hold on," she instructed. "Let me stand and I'll help you up." She got to her feet and took hold of his biceps, which were almost too big to grasp with her hands. Stubborn, stubborn shifter. He needed his head examined, followed by his back.

"I just need a little leverage." He grunted again, louder this time, lifting one leg to stand on his foot. He gripped her hips and pulled. So did she.

Meghan nearly fell over but somehow they managed to get him on his feet. Tide swayed, his eyelids at half-mast. She grabbed him by the hips. Tide held her shoulders and swayed again, almost pulling them over. He was breathing heavily again. "Damn, Blaze," he muttered.

"Yeah, I can't believe he did that."

Tide chuckled. "Emotions." He shook his head, looking a little drunk.

"Let's get you inside."

They slowly shuffle-walked until they made it to the door. Tide leaned against the glass that made up the wall, while she opened the door. They shuffled inside and Meghan shut the door with her foot. Then they continued over to the large bed situated in the middle of the room. It was unmade. There were signs that the apartment was occupied. A towel thrown over a chair and a pair of cotton pants on the floor in the bathroom, which was open.

"It's mine," he said, almost too softly for her to understand.

"Sorry?" she looked at him.

It took a second or two for his eyes to focus on her. "My chamber." It took a lot of effort to say the words.

"Oh… oh, I see." She nodded. "Let's get you to bed."

Tide chuckled, his laugh turned into a fit of coughing. He leaned into her, burying his face in her shoulder, swaying a little.

"Are you okay?"

He nodded. "Just wish I was stronger, since you're taking me to bed that is." He chuckled again. Flip, he was acting like he was completely out of it. Definitely not thinking straight.

Tide fell onto the bed as they reached it. All sprawled out, his body on the mattress and his legs hanging off of it. He spent a long minute catching his breath before pulling himself up so that his head was on a pillow.

His back looked really bad. "I need to find you help. Medication—"

"No," he growled the word. "Water… thirsty."

"I'm not arguing with you," she spoke over her shoulder as she walked to the kitchenette. "I'll bring you a water." She rummaged in his fridge, snagging a bottle of water and made her way back. "Once you've had a drink, I'm finding you painkillers and—"

"I don't need it." He lifted himself onto his elbows.

Meghan uncapped the water and held the bottle to his mouth. Tide drank deeply, his throat working with each swallow. Broken, burnt and weak, he still somehow managed to make the act of taking a simple drink look sexy. How was that possible? She felt bad for even noticing.

Careful not to touch his injured back, she put the bottle down where he could reach it, leaving the cap off. Against the stark white of the sheets, his flesh looked worse. Raw, charred. Just horrible. She tried not to react, not wanting to scare him. "I'll be back within the next ten minutes. I'll get help and a first aid kit. I saw one in—" She screamed when he grabbed her wrist and yanked her not only onto the bed, but right next to him.

Then he gripped her hip and flipped her around. He was still so strong despite his injuries. "No." A whisper.

"Stay here." He wrapped his arm around her and pulled her against him. Right up close. Her back flush against his front. His very naked front. "Few hours." His words were slurred. "Safe." Then his breathing deepened, telling her that he was falling asleep. She expected his hold on her to ease as he sank deeper and deeper, but that didn't happen.

Great, he was gravely injured and wouldn't let her leave to get help. Tide was not human, so she couldn't think in human terms. He was going to heal up. *Hopefully!* A couple of hours though? That seemed just a little too optimistic.

What if his wounds became infected? With first degree burns like that, he might even go into shock. Her heart began to race but she forced herself to breathe slower. To calm down. She needed to find help, one of those dragon healers. What if he slowly became worse instead of better?

Damn. The stubborn idiot needed help. She tried to pry his arm off her but he was holding on too darned tight. Meghan attempted to slip out from his hold but he held her even tighter, muttering in his sleep. Then he hooked a thigh around her legs, completely trapping her.

Shit.

He was heavy. She was stuck. Unable to move a muscle. Okay, she could wiggle her toes but that was pretty much it. At least he was warm. Very warm. *Too warm?* Her heart raced again. What if he was running a fever?

Calm down! Stop it! There was nothing she could do. Not a thing. He had said he needed time and that he was going to be fine. She only prayed he was right.

CHAPTER 21

Tide woke up with a start. One second he had been deep in sleep and the next he was wide awake. The room was dimly lit, the sun setting. *Where? What? Fuck!* Why was he in his chamber? His mind was fuzzy.

He sniffed and closed his hands around… her… Meghan. She was in his bed, flush against him. His cock hard and straining against her ass. In one hand was her hip. Fucking lush, and in the other was on one of her breasts. Doubly lush. He squeezed, feeling her nipple harden against his palm. He growled softly as his nostrils filled with her scent. Why was she here again? Surely to rut? Yes, to rut. He rubbed his shaft against her ass. Why was she wearing so much?

Then it came back to him. What had happened. The flames. The burns. He'd nearly fucking dropped her. Did drop her? *Yes!* He could recall how she had fallen onto the balcony, crying out as she landed.

With a hard growl, he turned her around. Her eyes were both wide and hazy with sleep. "What?" she muttered.

"Are you okay?" he asked, cupping her chin. There was

a smear of blood on her blouse. "You hurt?" He yanked the fabric aside. Her stomach looked fine, unmarred by scratches or bruises. "Did I hurt you?" He felt along her arms, her hips.

"Hey," she said. Her tone soft and soothing. "I'm fine. You don't need to do that… I'm alright," she added as he checked her legs.

Tide growled. "Your knees. They're scraped and bruised. Fuck!"

"Hey… Tide… I'm fine. Listen, it's nothing. What about *you*? How are *you*?" She pushed against him, trying to make him lie back down. "You're going to hurt yourself." Her voice was thick with… worry? *No, surely not!*

Tide looked up at her. Her eyes were filled with tears. "Did I hurt you? I didn't mean to. Please don't cry." He cupped her cheeks.

"I'm not hurt," she said more forcefully, trying to break out of his grasp. "I need to check your back. Let me look." Another tear streaked down her cheek.

He couldn't help but grin. "Oh, doc. Are you worried? About me?"

"Don't you dare smile like that." She used a harsh tone. "Don't tease me either. This is very serious, Tide." Another tear fell. "You are seriously injured. You need medical attention." Then she frowned. "You *do* seem a bit better… thank god. Still, you're not out of the woods yet." She spoke quickly, looking worried. "I can't believe I fell asleep," she muttered to herself, clearly angry she had done so.

"You're right, I do need attention." He couldn't help

himself. She was walking right into this.

"Yes, you need medical attention."

Using the pad of his thumb, he wiped away the tear. "I do need attention, doc, but not of the medical kind." He leaned in and brushed his lips against hers.

She squirmed and then she sucked in a shuddery breath, and then she kissed him back. He dug his fingers into her soft hair. Slanted his lips more firmly against hers and... She pulled away. "I can't... we can't... you're hurt. Stop this, you're not thinking straight."

Tide let her go and moved onto his belly. It wasn't easy. Not with a throbbing erection in the way. "I assure you, I'm feeling fine and that my mind has not been affected."

Meghan sucked in a deep, shuddery breath. "Oh my word. I can't believe it. It's gone." She ran her hand over his skin.

He bit back a groan because the area was still very sensitive.

"It's a little pink, but—" She yelped as he turned her onto her back and slid on top of her.

Meghan clasped his shoulders in her little hands. He wasn't sure whether she was pushing him away or pulling him towards her, maybe a little of both. "What are you doing?" Her eyes were wide, her legs open, knees bent, skirt crumpled up around her hips. His dick fit perfectly between the juncture of her thighs. Her panties, the only barrier between them.

"You were worried about me." He kissed her softly, pulling back immediately.

"I would have been worried if it was anyone." Her heart

was racing, her chest rising and falling in quick succession.

He chuckled. "Bullshit! Just admit it. You were worried because you care about me."

She swallowed thickly, the column of her neck worked. "No, I…" Then she sighed. "Fine. I care. I was very worried."

"Good," he growled. "Because I care too. A whole damn lot. I almost lost you." His chest tightened. "You could have been hurt."

"I wasn't," she whispered.

"Thank fuck," he growled, slipping his hand between them and ripping the cotton that covered her sex.

Meghan groaned, she reached up and kissed him. He lifted her thighs and pushed into her wet heat. Tide broke the kiss, keeping his forehead to hers as he pushed all the way home, all the while, biting back a snarl. "You feel fucking amazing."

"So do you." She was already panting heavily.

"I've wanted you for the longest time," he murmured, eyes on hers.

"Same here," she struggled to get the words out.

Tide pulled back, ripping her blouse open and shredding her bra. Then he began to move, watching as her eyes first widened and then rolled back. Her head fell back as well and she groaned so deeply, it had his sacs pulling up, his skin tightening. He was already so damned close.

He leaned down and suckled on her nipple, taking the turgid flesh between his teeth before suckling some more. She cried out, gripping his hair and arching her back, almost making him come then and there. All the while, he kept thrusting into her hard, and yet slow. So deep. She took him, all of him. All. Of. Him. Into her tight confines. He was grunting hard with each rough thrust. Lost in her, like an animal. Even his scales rubbed him raw beneath his skin. He looked down, between them, to where they were joined. To where his cock pummeled into her welcoming flesh. Then her arms were tightening around him. Her breath came in sharp pants. She cried out as her pussy spasmed around him. Meghan called his name with a strangled wail and he was done for.

Tide first groaned and then roared as his sacs emptied inside her. He jerked hard, picking up the pace as his back bowed. His gums ached. His teeth sharpened. The need to bite hit him and it hit him hard. Made him come harder. His mouth was right by her neck. Right there. One turn and she would be his. Tide bit the pillow instead, hearing it rip and he continued to slam into her. *Must not hurt! Must not damage!* He eased his hold, eased his thrusts. Let go of the pillow, which was in tatters.

She was breathing hard. Holding onto him tightly.

"Are you okay?" He looked down at her, still inside her.

He tried to pull away but she held onto him, giving him a lazy smile. "Yes, I'm fine."

"You sure?"

She nodded. "Yes, but what did that pillow ever do to you?" Meghan was panting heavily, her eyes hazy, her lids droopy. She smiled, even that was drunk looking. *Good!* He had sated his female. *His.* What the fuck?

"Oh, um, yeah, I told you we can be base and intense

and pretty savage. You saw that today."

He eased out of her, still hard. Still wanting more. "I'll be back." Tide went to the bathroom. He quickly cleaned up, taking a towel back with him. He handed it to Meghan and climbed back into bed, on his side next to her. She had removed what was left of her shredded clothing. That had been hardcore. He had never wanted a female more. There were pieces of shredded clothing and feathers from the pillow everywhere.

"Thank you." She blushed, taking the towel and using it to wipe between her thighs and legs. Tide would have liked to have been the one to have done it but he somehow knew that she would prefer to do such a thing herself.

"You said you're on birth control?" He had to bring it up. "I'm sorry, I didn't check that you were okay with rutting without a condom. I guess," he rubbed the back of his neck, "I wasn't really thinking clearly. You can't get anything from me and…" he paused. Fuck, he sounded like a complete pussy but Meghan needed to hear it, so he would say it. "I haven't had sex with anyone else in some time. The last time was with you."

"Oh." She frowned, looking shocked. Then she smiled looking… happy, relieved maybe. "That's good to know… that you're clean, that is, and yes, I'm on birth control."

"Good. You smell really good." He reached out and touched the side of her arm. "I'm pretty sure it's just because of what happened with Blaze."

"How is it that nearly burning to death makes me smell better? And, what does smelling better have to do with birth control?"

"I told you dragons are emotional. I freaked out because you could have been injured."

"And that changes the way I smell?" She smiled, looking up in contemplation.

"Yes. I've wanted back inside you almost from the day you arrived on dragon soil. You almost got hurt, first in the fire and then because of me."

"No…" She narrowed her eyes and shook her head. "You protected me."

"I nearly dropped you. Your knees, the blood… I freaked out a little. It made me want you even more. I needed to touch you and hold you and—"

"I'm fine." She reached out and grabbed his hand. "I didn't realize that *you* cared so much." She tried to sound flippant and failed.

"Well, I guess I do. I didn't realize it either. I thought my feelings were strictly sexual."

She turned onto her stomach looking away so he couldn't read what she was feeling. He couldn't help but look at the line of her back and her lush ass.

She cleared her throat, making him realize that she had turned back and caught him staring. "Sorry, you have one hell of an ass."

She laughed. "That's what George says, he says I'm all tits and ass and that—"

He didn't hear the rest of what she was saying. "Who is George to you?" he all but snarled.

Meghan's eyes widened and her mouth fell open for a few seconds. "Excuse me. What the hell was that?"

He was losing it! It couldn't be helped. "I don't know." What the fuck was happening to him? Tide got up off the bed and walked to the other side of the room. Then he walked back. "I'm jealous. I'm seriously fucking jealous." He could hardly believe it himself.

"What?" She frowned, her eyes hazy. Meghan sat up, using her hands to cup her breasts. "You can't be jealous. What happened to not liking me? We're not even friends."

Tide got back onto the bed. Her pupils dilated, her breathing picked up a notch or two.

"That's the thing, I *am* jealous. Just tell me who he is to you. You aren't fucking him... were you fucking him before?"

"Oh my god! You can't be serious."

"I am serious. Deadly serious. You're right, we're not friends. I don't want to be friends with you Meghan, I want more, I want it all."

"All?" She sounded panicked. "You don't know what you're saying. We don't even know one another. It's been a couple of weeks, we've had sex twice. Wanting it all at this stage of the game is impossible."

He cupped her jaw. "I'm a dragon."

"Why do you keep saying that?" She seemed angry.

"Because you don't seem to realize what it means." He let go of her.

"I've seen you shift. I know what it means, dammit." There was a growl to her voice.

"No, you don't. I can't believe this is happening but it is." He brushed a kiss to her lips.

"What's happening?" she said, against his mouth.

"This. Admit that you want me. That you think of me touching you, fucking you? You want me now, don't you?"

Berries and cream. Fuck but she was delectable. "Yes, but that has nothing to do with us being together."

"It does. I swear we're compatible and it's more than just sex."

"You can't say that. We don't know each other well enough yet."

"Oh, but I can and I am." He lifted her onto his lap. "Straddle me."

"Why?" she asked but still did as he said.

"I want you again. I also want you to admit that there is something between us. More than just sex."

She looked him in the eyes for what felt like a long time. Then her gaze softened. "Yes," she finally huffed. "I'll admit it. There's more there."

"Good," he growled. "I'm having you again."

"I would like that." She wrapped her arms around his neck. "By the way, he's my colleague and my best friend."

"Who is… you mean George?"

"Yes." She moaned when he circled her clit with the tip of his finger. He loved that she was still wet. Loved how tight and swollen her little nub was. Ready for him.

What the hell were they doing?
What was he saying?

Did he want a relationship with her? It felt like he had gone from being in lust with her to… something more…

and all because of what had happened earlier. Was that even possible?

Tide was a dragon shifter. That made him more intense and oh so good with his hands. She moaned and squeezed her eyes shut as his thumb slipped over her clit, moving ever so slowly. Too darned slowly for her liking.

"He's gay by the way." She was panting but didn't care.

"Are you still talking about George?"

"Yes," she whispered.

"Well stop. I'm going to fuck you now and I don't want you even thinking of another male. Do you hear me?"

"You're still jealous." Her words were strained but it couldn't be helped. *Oh, that finger.*

Tide palmed his cock with one hand and lifted her onto it with the other. His face became strained as his tip breached her. Meghan swallowed hard, loving how he felt inside of her. A little afraid of just how good – and she wasn't just talking about their physical connection. Meghan eased herself onto him, inching down and lifting up and inching down some more. Slowly, slowly. They both groaned as she hit his hilt. So full. So stretched. It stung a little but it was a good kind of pain.

He gripped her ass. One cheek in each palm. His jaw tight. His eyes bright. His skin taut.

She could only imagine how she must look. Hair wild. Eyes wide. Panting heavily even though neither of them was moving... yet.

Tide licked his lips and then leaned in and kissed her. Slowly and softly. He did that circling thing with his hips and his cock hit places inside her that had her crying out.

He swallowed up the noises, his thumb back against her clit – rub, rubbing. Barely touching her. He circled those hips and then gave a little nudge, circled and nudged.

Wow!

Oh wow!

She was breathing through her nose, the sound obscenely loud. "More," she moaned, planting her feet on the bed and gripping his shoulders.

Tide pulled back, he sent a feral half-smile her way. It just about had her coming there and then. "No problem, Doctor Roberts."

He gripped her hips and lifted her just a smidgen, essentially carrying her weight. It was so hot. "Hold on," he growled.

Good lord almighty up above. Tide growled, gritting his teeth as his hips surged upwards. His abs crunched with each thrust. Tide was ripped. So darned gorgeous. He lowered her a little as he thrust, and lifted as he relaxed. His biceps bulged with each lift. She might just come from looking at him in action. His lids were half shut. His jaw tight. Those little grunt noises he was making were ultra sexy as well.

Her own mouth hung open in a gape. She made the most obscene noises with each thrust. She was about to come. Meghan grabbed her boobs to try to stop them from bouncing so hard. Might give herself a black eye and at just the wrong moment.

"So fucking tight," Tide snarled, sounding more like an animal than a human. She loved it.

His name hovered on her lips as her muscles began to

tighten. His name was right there as heat pooled in her belly. As her skin seemed to shrink.

"Oh, oh…."

"So goddamn beautiful," another hard rasp.

That did it. The way he looked at her. The way his hands tightened on her hips. The way his thrusts turned desperate. The way his mouth pulled into a grimace because he was holding off.

She grabbed his arms as she went off like a rocket on concentrated jet fuel. Meghan yelled his name. As if that wasn't good enough, she moaned it as well.

Tide roared as he jerked into her. She could feel him come inside her in hot bursts. He grit his teeth, which looked sharper. His eyes glowed. Tide slowed his movements. His gaze firmly on her neck. "Shit!" He was still grunting with every circular thrust. Slow and easy. Still good. She was startled to find that she was shaking a little. Meghan collapsed onto his chest, she sounded like she'd just run a marathon. Tide wrapped his arms around her. "I almost bit you."

She smiled against him. "Like a kinky nibble or a…"

She felt Tide shake his head. "Like, I almost sank my teeth into you." She pulled away. His gaze had moved back to her neck, that look of hunger was back as well.

"Why would you do that?"

"Don't be alarmed. Biting is mating behavior." He paused. "This is serious."

"That's crazy talk." She tried to get off of him on account that he was still inside her. Still hard. This was not a conversation to have… like this.

"I know and if it helps any, I'm feeling just as freaked out about this."

"We're not even supposed to be having sex, are we? Unless I missed something." She frowned.

"No, we're not." He looked like he wanted to say something and thought the better of it. "I'll talk to Torrent. I don't think it will be a problem." He pushed some hair behind her ear. "I want to spend more time with you. I want more sex. More of everything to do with you. What do you think? Is that something you would want as well?" He looked at her with such focus. There was a vulnerability in his stare. It was endearing considering he was usually so alpha.

"You're actually asking me? I can't believe it." She pretended to be shocked.

He flipped her onto her back. "No, Doctor Roberts," Tide grinned, there were dimples everywhere, "I'm telling you. There was no question mark at the end of those sentences. At the same time, I'm trying to be nice by pretending to ask you."

"Oh, really?" she chuckled.

"Yes." He kissed the tip of her nose and then brushed a kiss on her lips. "So, what do you say?" That vulnerable, nervous look was back.

Her heart did a little flip in her chest. *No!* It was far too early for that. She was just being a girl. A 'I've slept with him, so I have to add emotion' girl. "I thought you had been reassigned and that we weren't going to see each other anymore?"

"That was bullshit. I asked to be reassigned because I

wasn't going to be able to keep my hands off of you any longer. I knew that I was desperately in lust, what I didn't know at the time, what I was trying hard to deny was that there was more there."

Her heart did that little flip thing again. Harder and faster this time. She couldn't deny it or make an excuse for it. She was falling for him. "Yes, I'd like to see where this goes."

"Good." He pulled out and thrust back into her, biting his bottom lip. Two more thrusts and she was already moaning. What was wrong with her? She couldn't seem to get enough of him.

His face went from pinched with lust and hunger to serious. He stopped moving. "I'm not sure my brother will agree."

She frowned. "To us dating? Why not? It wasn't like we planned for this to happen."

"I know but," he pushed out a breath, "this is not how we do things."

"It's normal for men and women to meet, date and… well… to go through the normal steps."

"Not for dragon shifters." Tide shook his head. "We'll talk about it after I make you come." He nuzzled her neck, circling his hips.

"Okay…" she moaned. "Oh, and, Tide?"

"Yeah?" He groaned as he thrust back into her, pausing while waiting for her to continue.

"If we're going to be dating, you should probably call me Meghan."

He pretended to think it over. "Meghan? Nah, I think

Doctor Roberts has a ring to it, especially while I'm fucking you."

She choked out a laugh. "You're kidding me."

"I don't kid around when it comes to sex. Fucking is serious business."

"Oh!" she yelled as his finger found her clit. It was firm and unrelenting. Her eyes widened.

"We're not going to date, by the way. Don't call it that."

"I thought you said...?" She panted, trying to get her brain to work. "No dating." She moaned. "What are we going to do then?"

"Practice." He pushed into her and then pulled out. That finger kept strumming.

She licked her lips, her hips rocking. "What are we practicing?"

Tide thrust back in, causing her to moan. "We're practicing at being mated."

She wanted to answer. Wanted to say something but he was pushing her legs over his shoulders. His thrusts insistent. That finger never letting up on her clit. She screamed his name as he pushed her over the edge. It had taken less than a minute. Less than a freaking minute. Tide didn't let up. Didn't slow.

"Again," he growled.

No! Surely not. "Can't," her voice was strained.

"Oh yes, you *know* you can, Doctor!" His voice was strained as well. Tide thrust harder, the finger on her clit eased up a whole lot, but at the same time, it didn't stop its slip and slide. Her clit felt like it was throbbing. "Doctor..." *Thrust, grunt.* "Roberts..." *Thrust, grunt.*

She moaned, strangely turned on by his silly chant.

Tide picked up the pace, fucking her deep and quick. One thrust per syllable. "Doc... tor... Rob...erts... Doc...tor... fuck... fuck... Doc... shit... Doc...tor... Rob..." Meghan threw her head back, gritting her teeth as she came again... hard. Stars exploded behind her eyelids. She felt this orgasm move through her entire body.

CHAPTER 22

"What the fuck!" someone snarled.

Tide leapt from the bed, adrenaline pumping. *Had to be an intruder.* Who dared enter his chamber? He gripped the male by the throat, closing off his air and almost crushing his windpipe. Once the threat was immobilized, he glanced back over his shoulder. Meghan gasped. Although she was mostly covered by the sheet, her legs and part of her ass were exposed. Her eyes wide, she clutched the sheet to her chest, thrashing about as she pulled the sheet completely over herself.

Better, but not great. Bay might not have a working cock but he was still a male, for fuck sakes. He still had eyes. "How dare you," he snapped. "This is my chamber. I should kill you." Even as he said it, he wanted to do it. His hand even tightened just a smidgen. There was a nagging voice in his head that stopped him.

Bay made a choking noise, his face was turning red.

Tide set his jaw, working hard to get himself back under control. *Maim. Kill. Defend what is mine. Mine.*

He sucked in a deep breath and then pushed it out

before sucking in another one. Bay was his friend. His friend. He still couldn't release the male.

"Tide!" Meghan sounded afraid. "Tide, let him go."

She touched the side of his arm and a growl was torn from him. Her touch calmed him enough to allow him to open his hand. Bay crunched over his middle and coughed. He choked and spluttered, his hand clutching at his neck.

Tide wanted to turn back to his female, so that he could reassure her. Her heart was racing and he could scent fear. He couldn't take his eyes off of Bay long enough to do so. Protect and defend. *Mine.*

"This is a fuck up," Bay finally managed to choke out, his words a rough, grating rasp.

"Leave now," Tide managed to grit out between clenched teeth.

Bay shook his head. "Before you kill me," he said, his voice still gravelly, "the female is in heat."

"What?" His brain was fuzzy. *Heat?* Tide sniffed. Smelled good. "Leave!" The word left his chest in a deep rumble.

"I can't do that. You need to stop before you get her with child."

"That's impossible," Meghan said. "I had an IUD fitted… Oh shit." His female paused as her eyes moved up in thought. "It's the copper kind, no hormones." She was mumbling to herself. "Oh… I understand now. Shit!"

"I'm fine. I'll speak with Torrent. You can leave now."

"I'm not going anywhere." Bay folded his arms.

He was going to break those fucking arms. Meghan

moved in front of him, standing between him and Bay. The sheet was wrapped around her but her shoulders were bare. He looked over her at Bay who wasn't looking at his female. Lucky for him. "Go!" he roared.

Bay shook his head. "Look at you. Dammit!" he yelled and then began to choke, cough and splutter all over again. "You might hurt her," he finally rasped, his eyes watering from the effort it took to speak.

"I wouldn't ever hurt—"

"She's in heat."

His mind cleared some. "No, you're wrong." He turned to look at Meghan. He frowned. "You said you were on birth control." He sniffed. "But... Fuck, you're in heat... or will be soon. Within the next couple of hours."

"I *am* on birth control. It was never specified I needed to specifically be on a hormonal method." She widened her eyes. "You can tell all of that by my smell?"

"Yes, I can." He understood the question, but the rest of it may as well have been in another language. If she was on birth control, she wouldn't scent this way. Thing was, Meghan wasn't the type to lie. "English, doc."

"I still ovulate... go in heat." She sounded flustered. "But, I can't get pregnant. No one ever said anything about preventing ovulation."

"I guess we assumed wrongly that if you were on birth control, you wouldn't go into heat."

"At least you've calmed down," Bay said. For a second there he had almost forgotten that the male was in the room. He turned back with a snarl.

Bay put up his hands. "I'm not going to touch your

female."

"Leave."

"No! I don't trust this birth control where a female can still go into heat. I don't trust you with her either."

"I trust Meghan. If she says it works, then it must work."

"Okay, fine. The other problem is that you are not thinking rationally."

"I'm fine." Even as he said it, he knew it wasn't true. His mind was hazy, his body tense. Adrenaline still pumped through his veins and for no reason. A female in heat would do crazy things to a male, especially since he had feelings for Meghan. *Fuck!* He still couldn't believe it. *When the hell had that happened?*

"It would be better if you left. I will take care of this."

"Fuck that!" he snarled. A rational side of him knew that he wasn't being illogical. It knew that Bay wanted to genuinely help, but instincts could be a bitch. "You want her all to yourself." He clenched his teeth and worked hard at getting himself back under control. It wasn't working.

"Look at yourself. Try to think clearly here." The male looked at his… at his… dick. "I know you like me, but… that's just ridiculous." Bay pointed at his cock.

Tide glanced down. *Fuck!* His dick was jutting from his body. Hard, thick and proud. This while another male stood just a few feet in front of him. "What the…?" Tide covered his cock with one hand. He left the other one free just in case Bay tried something.

"Look," Bay put up both hands, "you can be thankful it's me here right now and not one of the other males. It would be open season otherwise."

Just thinking about others brought on a fresh surge of adrenaline. *Fight. Protect. Mine.* Tide growled low, his whole chest rumbled. His eyes narrowed in on his target.

"Easy." Bay kept both his hands up where he could see them. They were open, palms forward and his shoulders were hunched. His gaze was on the floor. Everything spoke of submission. It eased something in him, just a smidgen. "I don't feel a thing. I don't get sexual urges anymore. Not at all, remember?"

"You are still a male."

"Hardly." Bay frowned as he looked up. There was a whole mountain of sadness reflected in his eyes.

Tide pushed out a breath. His instinct was still to fight, to protect but he was able to override it now… mostly.

"The female needs to be taken somewhere safe," Bay said.

"Yes." *Why hadn't he thought of that?* "I will take her," he quickly added.

"Um…" Meghan said. "What do you mean I need to go somewhere safe? I *am* safe, aren't I?" She moved in next to him, showing him that she did feel safe despite his behavior. *Calm the fuck down!*

His little internal dialogue with himself didn't work at all. The instinct to protect her rode him hard. Tide put his arm around her, pulling her back behind him.

"Hey, I can't have a conversation if—"

"Stay," he ordered.

"Listen to Tide, doctor." Bay kept his eyes on the ground and his posture submissive.

She sighed. "This is crazy…"

"Tide is being ruled by his hormones at the moment. His instincts are telling him to take you, to mate you and to breed you."

"Breed me?" Her voice was breathless. Not fearful and angry like he had expected.

"We can't have this conversation right now. Speak to my brother. Tell him that I took his advice." He clenched his teeth. "Fill him in on the birth control problem." He began to walk towards the door. He put Meghan in front of him. "We need to go and hole up."

"Wait… stop!" Meghan tried to turn, but he held onto her, ushering her towards the balcony. He had to get to his cave. It was isolated and ready. "I can't go dressed like this."

"I'll wait in the hall," Bay continued, his jaw tight, his eyes blazing. "Hurry up, if anyone catches her scent—"

"Dress." Tide picked Meghan up and ran to the closet. "There isn't much choice," he growled. "Here," he handed her a pair of his sweats, "you'll have to fold the top over at the elastic until it fits." He handed her a shirt. "Put this on."

"Wait, we can't just leave."

"Trust me! We have to. It won't be long before they scent you."

"Who?" Her eyes were wide.

"The other males. All two hundred-odd unmated males in the Water dragon territory. You are unclaimed, in heat and scent of sex. Get dressed. I will be challenged soon."

"Why would someone challenge you?" She sounded

panicked. *Good!*

"For a chance to rut you." He sniffed… it made him feel light-headed. It made his dick twitch and his balls pull tight. "Hurry up or I will need to rut you here and now despite the threat."

"What's wrong with you? What the hell, Tide! I understand that my ovulation is affecting—"

"Hormones, instinct, need. I'm not human. You need to try to remember that. Hurry up!" he urged, staring at her breasts. Her sheet had fallen. Just off of the one shoulder. It was lush and full… so fucking full. Her nipple tight and dark like a cherry. So ripe. He began to salivate, his teeth sharpened. He wanted a taste, a nip. "Fuck!" he growled turning away, gripping his hard cock. His balls were in his throat. He could scent her pussy. Wet, hot…

"You're breathing funny." He could hear the rustle of clothing. She was getting dressed. *Thank fuck!*

"I'm desperate to fuck you." Might as well be honest.

"Oh…" she sounded shocked.

"It's how every male within sniffing distance will feel."

"Oh!" Extra shocked. "I'm dressed," she announced.

He turned, Meghan was folding the top of the sweat pants. His shirt was huge on her but it would have to do. It was at least half an hour to his cave, she would freeze dressed like that. He had another look in his closet and found a long leather jacket in the back. That would work fine. "Here." He grabbed it and handed it to her. "I might need to fight."

"Oh my god! This is really happening. I thought you were exaggerating." She put on the coat, still buttoning as they began to walk towards the balcony.

Tide shook his head. "I wasn't. I wish to god that I was, but I wasn't. I might need to fight and you need to trust me and do as I say."

CHAPTER 23

Bay roared out in the hallway.

"We're out of time," Tide growled. His eyes were a bright, glowing blue.

There was an answering snarl. Definitely not Bay and whoever it was sounded pissed. Then came the sound of bashing and thuds that were clearly flesh against flesh. There was a full on fight going on out there. Another loud bang and a picture fell off the wall, landing with a crash. Tide was pulling her outside.

"Bay. What about Bay? He's going to—"

"Bay can take care of himself," Tide replied as they made it outside, then he was changing. He howled, the sound so agonized it had goosebumps rising on her arms. It took a long time for him to turn. Half a minute. His dragon form finally took shape and stayed.

Tide, the dragon, shook his great head, like he was trying to regain his senses. His giant body shook. And then he reared up, his tail thrashing, and took to the sky, his great wings displacing the air so that her hair whipped about her face. He reached down with his taloned claws and picked her up.

Her stomach gave a lurch as he ascended, rising at an alarming rate. Then they were off, moving so quickly. The air rushed past her face. Her hair stung her cheeks and tears formed in her eyes, which she could not open. The wind was too strong.

Tide roared and slowed. Her stomach gave another lurch. Meghan moaned, she opened one eye and then the other. *Oh no!* Another dragon advanced, chest a bright silver. Tide roared again, louder this time, the sound-induced fear even though it wasn't directed at her.

The other dragon also roared. It kept coming at them, both claws facing forwards, aimed at Tide. They looked sharp and lethal. Its big slitted eyes seemed to focus on her.

Flip! There was no way Tide could fight this dragon — even though it looked to be smaller than he was. He had to keep holding her, which meant that she was a handicap to him. He was essentially fighting with half his weapons in use. What if he crushed her while fighting the other dragon?

No, she couldn't think like that. She needed to keep quiet so that he could concentrate and stay still and out of his way. She also needed to trust that he could save her and look after himself in the process.

Tide roared again as they crashed together. Meghan's body jerked in his hold as Tide's body suddenly came to a halt, mid-flight. She heard jaws gnashing. One of the dragons screeched. The other dragon clawed Tide, it's enormous claws slashing into his chest. Tide bit into its shoulder. Then they ripped apart, the other dragon falling. Tide flapped his wings and they began to fly away. Not even ten seconds later, Tide whipped around. The other dragon was coming for them. What scared her the most was the sight of five more dragons taking flight from the main balcony. It looked like they were headed their way. She was shocked to find how far away they were. Tide had made good time in those first few minutes after leaving the lair.

Tide screeched so loud it hurt her ears, he swung around cutting off her view of the lair with his body. The other dragon was on them again. This time Tide let go of her. He let go. His big claws opened. She tried to hold on but his body jolted as the other dragon collided with him and she was ripped away, her fingers clutching air as she began to fall.

Free-falling. *Down. Down. Down.* Blood rushed in her ears. Meghan screamed, looking up, reaching up. The dragons fought and she fell. Did Tide even know that he had let her go? She looked down, and already the ground rushed up to meet her.

When she looked back up, Tide seemed to be in a free-fall as well. So was the other dragon, one of its wings ripped clean off. Blood, there was so much blood. She looked back down, realizing that he wasn't going to make it to her in time. Her heart raced. Her lungs hurt. It was hard to breathe. His talons closed around her middle but they continued to fall, although slower and slower. Then they lurched up, just as they were about to hit the treetops. The force of the jolt brought her heart into her throat. It had her lungs expelling every molecule of oxygen and her blood rushing to her head. Everything went black.

She could feel her eyelids flutter as she tried to wake up. Meghan felt warm and safe and… She opened her eyes with a start, sucking in a breath.

"It's okay." Tide leaned over her, smoothing the hair from her face. "No-one will find us here."

"There were a whole lot of dragons after us. I counted five just before I passed out—"

"I'm sorry about that, it was the G-forces. I had to react or you would've hit the tops of those trees. And yes, we were just in time." He continued to touch her hair. "Too close for comfort and there were fourteen after us by the time you passed out."

She gasped. "I can't believe we managed… *you* managed to get away from them."

Tide frowned. "Have a little faith in me, Doc. I'm strong and fast. I'm gold." He touched a hand to his chest. "A royal… much stronger than all. Okay, all but one."

"One?"

"My brother, the king. He is the only male in the Water kingdom who is stronger than I am." He said it in such a matter of fact way. For once, there was no arrogance or over-confidence, just pure fact.

"Okay. Well, I'm glad. That other dragon, the one you hurt." She pulled herself more into a sitting position. "Is he going to be okay or…?"

"You shouldn't care, he was after you. Might have hurt

you. Not willingly of course."

"Exactly. I do care. He fell from a serious height and lost a great deal of blood." She shook her head. Healing from burn wounds like Tide had was one thing. Falling from that height and surviving was another thing altogether.

"River will be fine. He'll hurt for a day or two, but he'll be just fine. Even his wing will grow back."

"Oh, good." She scanned their surroundings. "A cave." Her voice was filled with shock. It was exactly as one would expect a cave to be. A narrow entrance comparative to the main body. The light that spilled in was weak. High ceiling covered in stalactites – or was it stalagmites? She could never remember which was which.

There were numerous candles lit around the room and a fire in the hearth. It looked like the fire had been burning for some time, judging from the burned out logs and ash. It was topped with fresh logs and was blazing. There was only one item of furniture, the bed they were on. "How long have we been here?"

"We arrived about an hour ago. The sun is setting, it'll be dark soon. I decided to let you sleep. How are you feeling?"

Meghan stretched out. "A little stiff and a bit sore…"

"Where are you sore?" He frowned, running his hands down her arms like he had earlier.

She felt her cheeks heat. "I'm fine. It's not what you think."

His frown only deepened. "Did I hurt you when I caught you as you fell, or was it…" He put his hand on her side, pushing lightly.

"It hurts a bit down there, from earlier." Her cheeks were on fire.

"Where there?" He continued to stroke her body, checking for injury.

"Between my legs," she ground out. "I guess I'm not used to so much sex."

"Oh." His eyes darkened up and his frown stayed exactly where it was. His nostrils flared.

"Are you okay?"

He nodded. "Your scent is growing stronger. I might need to leave or…" He stood up, taking a few strides away from her. She got an eyeful as he got off the bed. *Flip!* His man part stood to attention. Thick and long. She wasn't sure it was possible but it looked bigger than it had earlier. His sacs were pulled tight on his body. Like he was about to come.

"Is it that bad?" She unbuttoned the leather jacket she was drowning in and took it off, placing it on the bed next to her.

He turned, swallowing hard. His Adam's apple bobbed. Tide nodded, his face taut. "You have no idea what your scent is doing to me."

"I think I can tell." She made a point of looking at his cock.

"Don't look at me like that," his voice was deep, "I'm barely in control." His neck muscles roped.

"Come here." She patted the bed next to her.

"You just told me that you're sore. We can't…"

It warmed her that he thought of her right now, even

though he seemed to be suffering. "I can't... but you on the other hand." She gave the bed another pat, ending on a rub.

"Really?" His eyes brightened. "You would take me into your mouth?"

"Yes, I would." She licked her lips and bobbed her eyebrows.

Tide smiled. It was a smile filled with tension. He walked back to her and put a knee on the bed. The firelight flickered on his skin, against his tattoo. He was the most beautiful man she had ever laid eyes on. "Do you want me to stand or to lie down?"

Meghan scooted to the end of the bed, she opened her legs and curled a finger, telling him to come to her.

He did as she asked. "You sure you're..." Tide hissed when she gripped his cock in her hand. *God, but he was big.*

"I'm very sure." She leaned, having to reach up. Meghan sucked on his tip.

Tide groaned.

Meghan swirled her tongue around his rim and took him back into her mouth. Tide threaded his fingers through her hair and groaned again, deeper this time. "So good!"

She looked up while she sucked on him. His head had fallen back and his eyes were closed. His lashes fanned his cheeks. They were long. Too long for a man, and yet he was the epitome of masculinity.

Meghan closed her hand around his sacs and Tide jerked his hips forward, easing his hold on her head. She wrapped her other hand around the base of his cock, fisting him while she sucked and licked.

Tide swore. "I love the hell out of your mouth… oh fuck… your tongue." His hips were making tiny thrusts into her mouth. "I'm not going to last, doc."

She alternated between sucking and licking for a while, trying to draw out his pleasure. Then she took him as deep as she could while rubbing on his sacs.

"I can't wait to fuck you again," he growled. "Love your mouth," he added, gripping the back of her head in his big hand. He was still doing those thrusting movements. "Fucking love—" Then he was grunting hard with every swirl of her tongue.

He let her head go. "I'm going to come," he groaned. "You might… want… to… to stop." She could hear that he was trying to hold on. His hands curled into fists at his sides.

She made a noise of disagreement. By now she was turned on despite being a bit tender.

"Oh, Doc… Doctor… Doctor Rob… Roberts… fuck!" His thrusts became a little more pronounced. Nothing she couldn't handle. Then he grit his teeth and groaned as the first spurt hit her tongue. His come was warm, she swallowed it down. His hips jerked but she could tell he was trying to take it easy. Working hard on staying in control. His jaw was clenched, his eyes squeezed shut. His groan, a deep rumble. His chin dropped to his chest and he thread his fingers through her hair again. So soft and gentle. Meghan eased her hand off of his balls, she still sucked him but kept it soft and easy until finally stopping altogether.

Tide's chest expanded as he took in a deep breath. He pushed it out through his nose, his lids cracking open. Then he grinned. "Wow! That was amazing." He sat down next to her. "Thank you." He leaned in and kissed her softly on the lips.

"I can't help but notice that you're still," she pointed at his erection, "hard."

His grin widened. "I will be continually hard until your heat goes away."

"So that's twelve to forty-eight hours if memory serves."

Tide shook his head. "We'll soon find out."

She huffed out a breath. "Wow, that's a long time to be like that." She widened her eyes.

"Yeah, it is. Try to ignore it."

"Hard to ignore." She laughed.

"You make yourself comfortable, I will go and hunt us some dinner."

"Hunt?" Her heart beat a little faster. "As in kill?"

"Yes, that's how things are done in the wilderness."

"Okay, that makes sense. Do you want me to help you?"

Tide's lips twitched. She could see that he was trying to hold back a smile. "I know you're a competent human. That you're highly intelligent, but I can handle bringing home dinner myself."

"Fair enough." She watched as he began to walk towards the cave entrance. "Do me a favor will you?"

Tide turned back, a sexy half-smile toyed with the corners of his mouth. "Name it."

"Be careful." Tide walked back to her, leaned down and kissed her, again. "Also, before you go, there wouldn't happen to be a hot tub in here?"

His eyes glinted with mischief. "There's a pool in the back of the cave, but I don't want you washing."

"Why not? We had hot, sweaty sex all afternoon. I really need to clean up."

"No washing." There was a growl in voice. "My scent is on you. It needs to stay that way. If you bathe, I will need to put my scent back on you, back *inside* you." He said the last with an even louder growl that was so primal it took her breath away. His eyes brightened up. His brow was heavily lined with a frown.

Her tummy did a flip-flop and her clit gave a zing. Despite being sore, she still wanted him. Tide sniffed and squeezed his eyes shut. "I'd better go." She watched as he walked to the entrance. He turned as he reached the opening, giving her a grin. "Shifting with a hard-on is a bitch. Thank you for easing me. It won't be quite as bad as before."

Before she could say anything, he jumped. He was already changing as he fell out of sight.

Meghan didn't know what to make of this whole thing. Dragons were definitely very different to humans. To think all of those guys had been after them. More than a dozen of them. They had fought so aggressively, blood was spilled and all because she was about to ovulate. Tide was so different towards her. He wanted to date or practice at being mated, as he put it. She couldn't help but wonder if her hormones weren't muddling his brain.

Thing was, she was enjoying the attention. Enjoying the way he looked at her. The things he was saying. Would it last? Would he still feel the same once she finished ovulating and he could think more rationally? Meghan needed to guard herself a little over the next day or two, while they were stuck in the cave. She didn't want to start buying into all of this. Although Tide was the complete opposite of the guys she usually dated, he was someone she could fall for. Yes, she was hugely attracted to him, but there was more there. Tide could hurt her.

CHAPTER 24

Her hands were flat against the bark. The tree trunk thick and sturdy. Her hair so wet it clung to her head. Moisture dripped down her back, down her thighs. He was just as soaked, could feel droplets of water running down his own body. His hands were on her hips, his fingers denting her flesh. *Fucking heaven.*

"Can't get enough," he moaned.

"Me neither," Meghan managed to choke out. She arched her back and cried out. Her ass lifted a little higher, his cock slid in a little further. Tide grunted as he felt himself bottom out inside of her.

Desperate.

It was the only way to describe his current state of mind. Mindless desperation. It had become worse and worse as the scent of her heat had intensified. He'd lain awake the entire night, his cock throbbing. His sacs heavy. Easing himself had helped, but only so much. They'd had breakfast and headed to the stream to wash. The fresh, cold, mountain water was so much better than the pool in the cave. A male could only take so much, and his control had ended once they finished washing. Thankfully she was ready to take him back inside her body. There had been no more patience left in him. No preamble. No time to even get dry or back to the cave. The only thing that mattered was coming inside her – multiple times if possible – and bringing her pleasure in the process.

Her ass shook each time he thrust into her. Her pussy made those sucking, wet noises that drove him insane. He needed to take it easy. Needed to be careful. His balls were already in his throat. His grunts filled the clearing. That and the sound of him slapping against her. "Never felt this good," he moaned.

Meghan was crying out with every hard thrust. Her shouts becoming higher and higher pitched. A sure sign of her pending orgasm. Thank fuck, because he wasn't going to last. Not now. Not with the sweet scent of her heat in his nostrils. He reached around her and furiously strummed her clit. Thankfully, Tide felt her pussy flutter around him.

Her shouts became hoarse as she came apart. Tide yelled her name as he followed close behind. He grit his teeth to keep himself from marking her. It was becoming more and more difficult to keep from doing so.

Torrent was going to be pissed enough when he found out about this. He'd be in unending shit if he marked her as well. Thing was, he didn't think she was ready yet for such a big step anyways. "I'm sorry," he muttered, still moving, still loving the feel of her. "I was supposed to be gentle. Instead I took you like an animal."

She looked back over her shoulder at him, her lids

hooded, her eyes hazy. "You have nothing to be sorry about. You won't hear a word of complaint from me. Are you feeling a bit better now?" She was breathing hard.

"Yeah, much." By her scent, she was ovulating right now, so things would hopefully start to calm down soon. He hoped so. "Although I'm not sure how long it will last." His dick was still firmly inside her. "Also, I would prefer to stay right where I am for the foreseeable future."

"It's going to be difficult to shift while still inside me." She smiled.

"Are you still worried about someone seeing us?"

She nodded. "Yes, is that so weird?"

"We're in the middle of nowhere. That cave up there is mine. No-one will come all the way out here."

"Why do you have a sex cave in the middle of nowhere?"

"I had hoped to have a mate of my own one day." He chuckled.

She turned back towards him, "So you've never been with someone during their heat before? Is that the first time that you've used the cave?" Then she blushed like maybe she shouldn't have asked him that. "You don't have to answer all of my questions. I'm being nosey."

Tide shook his head. "I've never used the cave. We tend to stay far away from females in their heat during the stag run in case we accidentally make them pregnant."

"I guess I should feel special then." She smiled, her cheeks still red.

"You *are* special. I wouldn't rut you right now unless I was okay with you becoming with child." It was all true.

He didn't know when she had started getting under his skin, only that it had happened. Tide forced himself to pull out of her and did so with a hard grunt. He pulled her against him, so that her back was to his front, and kissed her neck. Her breathing immediately became elevated. Despite the trying circumstances, he was enjoying being out here with her. There was a part of him that didn't want to go back to the real world.

It was as if she could read his mind because she tensed. "What will Torrent say about this… about us?"

"I'll handle my brother. Don't worry about that right now."

"Okay." She shivered in his arms.

"Are you cold?"

"You're doing a good job of keeping me warm." He could hear that she was smiling.

Tide pulled away and she turned. He had to bite back a groan. This female was beyond beautiful. Her cheeks were flushed. Her hair still soaking wet. Her lush body. Her scent. Her. He wanted her again. Instead, Tide turned away. "Let's get you back to the cave before you catch a cold." He handed her one of the towels they had brought along with them. He watched her dry off and get dressed. It eased something in him now that his scent was back on her. He was beginning to realize that he wouldn't be able to completely relax until his teeth were in her flesh, until she was truly his. Tide knew that there were still a few hurdles ahead of them. He would gladly face them all.

The next morning…

Meghan stretched, a soft groan escaped. Everything hurt. Every muscle in every part of her. There was a deep ache between her legs that spoke of hours of sex. While it had mostly been frantic, it had also meant something to her. Had often felt like lovemaking rather than fucking. At least, to her it had.

Tide had been tireless and infinitely careful with her. Then again, there were a couple of bruises on her hips and more on her thighs. She had stubble burn on her neck and breasts and down there… between her legs, she was sure. Meghan smiled, biting down on her lip.

Tide was still sleeping. His chest rising and falling in a deep rhythm. His erection was finally gone, she suspected that she was no longer ovulating. Thankfully. There was a part of her that was sad they would be going back, but it was time to face life. The real world.

Thing was, she needed to get back to work. She'd already missed her next immunotherapy sessions with Sky and Candy. It couldn't be delayed.

It was also time to face their true feelings. What was going to happen with Tide now that her heat was over? Was he still going to feel something for her or had this all been about lust? What was Torrent going to say? Her stomach was in knots.

Tide stirred. A few minutes elapsed and his eyes opened. "Morning." His voice was croaky.

"Morning. Did you sleep well?"

"Like the dead." He yawned, holding his hand in front

of his mouth. "I didn't sleep the first night we were here." He rubbed his face. "Right." He sat up and stretched. His back was broad and muscled. "We'd better get going. We need to get back ASAP." Her sentiments exactly. "Can you be ready in the next half hour? We'll eat breakfast back at the lair."

"I take it that I'm back to normal."

"Yeah. How are you feeling?" He looked almost sheepish. Like he felt bad about something.

"I'm fine."

"Good." There was no kissing. No hugging. No lingering looks when she sat up and the sheet pooled fell to her hips. "Do you want to bathe first or should I?" Tide was all business. In fact, he seemed a bit uneasy. There was worry in in his eyes. A tension in his stance.

"Go right ahead." It almost felt like they were strangers again. She forced a smile.

"Perfect. I won't be long." Tide headed to the hearth where he spent a couple of minutes getting a fire going. Then he disappeared to the back of the cave. She heard a splash as he washed. Disappointment welled up in her. She needed to have a talk with him about where they stood with one another. It would be better to know now, before things progressed any further. Before she really began to have serious feelings for him. They hadn't just had sex over the last two days, they'd talked a lot as well. She really felt like there was something there. They both had responsibilities to get back to, so the immediate need was to return.

She couldn't help but feel that things had changed now

that her heat was over. It was almost like he'd had his fill of her. Sex was one thing. A relationship was another. He'd never made her any promises. Meghan was a strong, independent woman. She didn't need a man to complete her. The sooner she knew his feelings the better.

CHAPTER 25

Tide gently descended to the balcony and carefully released Meghan. He moved to the far side and shifted back into his human form. He had to speak with Torrent. He felt stressed and anxious. There would be no relaxing until he'd had it out with the male.

"Are you okay?" Meghan touched the side of his arm. "You've hardly spoken since we woke up."

"It's just that—"

"There you are." Bay walked out onto the balcony. "I'm glad to see that the both of you are okay." The male sighed.

"I'm glad you're here. Stay with Doctor Roberts. I need to go and see Torrent."

Bay shook his head. "With all due respect, my lord. Your brother has requested that I notify him immediately upon your return."

"I'll notify him myself," Tide said.

"I need to do it or I'll be disobeying a direct order." Bay widened his eyes. "The king is in a bad mood."

"I'm sure he is, but…" *Fuck!* Bay turned away from the

balcony and headed into Meghan's chamber. All Tide could do was follow, and by the time he made it into the room, Bay was already gone. He ran a hand through his hair and sighed. Tide couldn't leave Meghan. He had to keep her protected. Although the peak of her heat was over, she still smelled of sex. There would still be those who would try their luck, which was unacceptable. His muscles bunched and he clenched his teeth.

"I take it that your brother is angry."

"Understatement of the century." He turned to her. Meghan pushed out a breath.

Tide didn't want Meghan to witness his brother's anger. Torrent was generally pretty easygoing and they had a good relationship, but the male had a serious temper on him. It might get violent. "Stay out of the way of Torrent when he gets here."

"You really think he'll be that upset? Surely he'll understand. You did what you had to do. No one explained things to me. It's…"

The front door crashed open. "Glad you could join us." Torrent sniffed the air. He raised his brows. "I hope you enjoyed yourself over the last few days?" His brother folded his arms, clearly waiting for an answer.

"Yes we did," Tide told the male what he needed to hear.

Torrent nodded his head. "Bay explained things. I'm not thrilled, but I understand why it was necessary for things to unfold as they did. Taking the female to your cave was the best solution. You pretty much killed two birds with one stone. Right?"

Tide hated how his brother spoke of Meghan like she wasn't in the room. For the umpteenth time, he found himself sympathizing with Torrent's mate. No wonder Candy had left him. No wonder it had taken Torrent crawling on his knees for months to win her back. He didn't always think before speaking. He knew that Torrent didn't mean it the way it sounded. Torrent could be an oaf.

"Yeah, pretty much. Where is Bay?" He didn't want to antagonize Torrent.

"He's outside." Torrent was far more relaxed than he expected him to be. "There's one thing I want to mention while the two of you are here. It's why I asked Bay to call me the moment you returned. I was at your apartment, just in case you went there."

Tide folded his arms.

"I'm glad you took my advice," Torrent said.

"About that—"

"No. You get to listen right now." And there it was, a growl to his voice and a narrowing of his eyes. There was anger there, he was just doing an excellent job of holding it in check. "I said you should get your attraction to Doctor Roberts under control by sleeping with her again and I hope that the two of you have done that. I don't want a repeat of this. Doctor, you need to go on a birth control that prevents heat."

Meghan had a faraway look. She didn't talk for a moment or two. "You told Bay to tell Torrent that you took his advice." She narrowed her eyes for a moment and they flared with sadness.

"Yes, I said it, but just to appease my brother. I knew

he was less likely to get too upset if he thought this was purely sexual."

"It was. You went into heat," Torrent pointed at Meghan, "and you, as her guard, needed to keep her safe. And get this whole thing out of your system."

Meghan looked distraught. He could scent her pain. She quickly schooled her emotions.

"It wasn't like that," Tide insisted. "I meant everything I said to you." He implored Meghan with his eyes but it didn't seem to help.

"What are you saying?" Torrent growled. He knew his brother was going to explode when he told him he had feelings for Meghan. He couldn't do it with her in the room. Needed to protect her. He would explain it all later.

"I need to speak with you alone," he told Torrent. "I need you to trust me." He turned back to Meghan.

She shook her head, her eyes welling with tears. Then she blinked a couple of times.

Torrent called for Bay to come into the chamber.

"Stay with the female," Tide directed Bay once he was inside. "Do not leave her side. I'll be back." Once again, he tried to convey his feelings for her with his eyes but she turned away, seeming to fold into herself.

Fuck!

He forced himself to put one foot in front of the other. The sooner he dealt with Torrent, the sooner he could come back to her and explain.

Meghan wasn't sure what to believe. What to feel or

think. It would be better to try to put it out of her mind. It was her heat. Nothing more.

No!

That couldn't be. It had to be though. She needed to try to clear her mind or to do something to stay busy. She quickly changed and headed for her laboratory. Bay fell in behind her like a silent shadow. She needed to get back to work instead of obsessing over Tide. It seemed like all she did lately was think about him. Ever since she came here. It felt like most of her thoughts outside of work revolved around him.

"How have things been here at the lair?" she tried to make small talk.

Bay smiled. "Interesting."

"Why, what happened?"

"You will find out soon enough," was his cryptic reply.

"You're not going to give me a hint?"

Bay shook his head.

"Come on, just a little clue."

"Okay," he sighed, looking wistful. "It has to do with love."

"Argh!" She pulled a face.

He chuckled. "Not one of your favorite subjects right now?"

She shook her head. "No."

"It's so damned complicated, isn't it?" he said. "I was in love once. She was a beautiful Fire dragon. I was young and stupid." His features tightened. His already dark eyes darkened up a whole lot more.

"Oh, what happened?"

"In hindsight, I probably wasn't as head over heels in love with her as I imagined I was. I decided to go on a stag run. I'd never been before and didn't know what the bid deal was. I was curious and stupid. Did I mention stupid?"

"What?" She cocked her head. "As in, you went into town with the sole purpose of having sex with a human woman? That was stupid."

He made a face. "Yeah it was. I was young. I found pleasure between a female's thighs for the first time and thought I was in love. If it was true, my friends would not have been able to convince me to go on the stag run. You see," he paused, "I had not yet made any promises to Ember. I convinced myself it was fine. I would go on the stag run and then settle down with her, only…" He paused again, staring off at the wall for a long while. They had stopped walking.

"I take it she found out and that she was mad?"

"Fire-breathing mad and unfortunately she got her hands on a silver blade. Not that she knew it was silver. She grabbed the knife, burned me to a crisp and then stabbed me four times. I almost died. There were days when I wished I had."

Meghan gasped. She covered her mouth with her hand. "I don't care how much she loved you, she was raving mad. What happened to her?"

"Females are in such short supply, especially the fertile ones. Ember was given a slap on the wrist. She has since mated a Fire dragon. I am told they are very happy together."

"And you?"

"Let's just say that I am not the male I once was and leave it at that."

What did that mean? Oh… oh…

He smiled. "You don't have to look at me like that. I am at peace."

"The silver knife. She…" Meghan made a slashing motion with her wrist.

Bay nodded. "Yep. That's exactly what happened. She blasted me with her flames, rendering me helpless and…" He made the same sweeping motion with his own hand.

Meghan made a squeaking noise. "That's terrible. You have no…" She couldn't say it. Couldn't even think it.

"Oh, it grew back."

"Oh thank god. You must have been in agony."

"It grew back, but it doesn't work." He made a pained groaning noise. "I don't know why I'm even telling you all this. I guess, I just wanted you to know that even though you're feeling down, things could be worse." Bay began walking towards the lab, which was just up the hall.

"I'm so sorry!" Meghan said as she caught up with him.

"I'm not looking for sympathy." He looked at her pointedly. "You can trust Tide. He is a good male. I shouldn't talk out of turn, but I think he has feelings for you. I've seen the way he looks at you."

She rolled her eyes. "With lust, yes."

"No. Although yes, he does give you those kinds of looks too, but there is more there. I have never seen him look at a female like he looks at you. I know he has always wanted a mate and children but he has never been eager to join in on the hunt."

"I've heard mention of this hunt," she said, as they reached the laboratory door. "What is it?"

"We are here." Bay looked at the sizable beveled door before them.

It was clear, by his body language, that he was done with the conversation but went on anyway. "It is an ancient dragon tradition. One Tide can explain to you if it comes to that."

"The hunt." Whatever it was, it didn't sound like anything she wanted to be a part of.

Bay held the door open and she walked in. George dropped the notepad he was holding. "O.M.G! You're back," he shouted and ran over to her, throwing his arms around her.

Meghan laughed. "It's only been two days."

"I was worried." George put his hands on his hips. "Apparently you were in heat and had to be whisked away for your own safety." He rolled his eyes. "These dragons are so dramatic."

Meghan laughed. "Talk about the pot calling the kettle black."

"Who me?" he said with extra gusto as he cocked his head comically.

She chuckled. "Yes, you. I assure you that nothing about what happened was overdramatized."

George turned serious in an instant. "How so? Spill."

Meghan went on to tell George all about what had happened at the meeting with Blaze. How Tide had been injured and what had happened after that. She didn't go into detail though.

"You slept with him?" he whispered under his breath, his eyes glinted with excitement. "I was wondering when the two of you would get it on again."

"Yes, I did and really? You were wondering?"

"You two eye each like nobody's business."

Meghan ignored the comment and went on to tell him about how the other dragons had come after them. She also mentioned the fight and then the cave.

"So, did the two of you end up having a fun-filled two days then?" He bobbed his eyebrows.

Meghan felt her cheeks turn decidedly heated. "Yes, we did." She forced herself to smile. She didn't feel like talking about Tide right now, because she didn't know how things stood between them. She didn't know whether to be angry with him. One thing was for sure, Tide had some explaining to do. "Enough about me, what's been going on with you? How are things here?"

"Lots of things have been going on," George gushed. He grabbed hold of her hands, his face animated. "I'm in love."

Her mouth fell open in an all-out gape. It took her a few long seconds to close it. "What? How did that happen? Who's the lucky guy? I'm sure I can guess." There were several more questions floating around in her head but she stopped herself from bombarding him.

"It's Ice. It's been happening for a while. It became official the day you left. We had the hottest sex of my whole entire life."

"I didn't know Ice was gay."

"You know me, honey." George laughed. "I can turn

straight guys like that." He snapped his fingers. "Only kidding. Ice is bi."

"I see."

"We get along so well. We talked about everything under the sun. I so enjoyed his company as a friend. That was until," George smiled, "until I caught him checking me out. Then all bets were off."

"And? Are you dating?"

George shook his head. "No dating. Dragons don't date. They tend to fall in love fast and hard when they meet the right person. I never thought love like this was possible." He clutched his chest.

"That is so amazing," she gushed. "You're so lucky."

"Yes and no." George frowned. "Torrent was mad. Unbelievably mad! He was pissed at Ice. He ordered that he be strung up in a cage."

"Oh no." Meghan clapped a hand over her mouth. "Please tell me you're joking."

"I wish. It's a big bird type cage that hangs out over the valley. The cage is silver-infused. It makes the occupant feel ill. It didn't matter how much I begged and pleaded," he pursed his lips together, "he just wouldn't listen."

"Silver would do that since dragon shifters are allergic. I'm sorry this all happened and that Torrent wouldn't listen. How long does he need to stay in there for?" Meghan went on before he could answer. "I can't believe he would do that."

"Dragons are so barbaric. I guess it's just as much a pro as what it is a con. Ice was only in the cage for a couple of hours." George licked his lips. "Torrent called us both in for a meeting since then, and he's given us permission to be together."

Meghan felt everything in her relax. "That's such good news."

"He hasn't made it that easy."

"How so?" She wasn't sure she wanted to hear this.

"I have to take part in the hunt in ten days' time."

"Again with the hunt. What the hell is a hunt? I'm going to assume you're not all getting dressed up in camouflage gear and going to hunt deer or something?"

"The hunt is where a group of people, normally women, are dropped off in the middle of nowhere. They are given a couple of hours' head-start. Most of the single guys in the four dragon kingdoms then hunt them. They have to stay in human form the whole time. They generally tear each other limb from limb to win a woman. If a dragon shifter catches you, he gets to keep you for a couple of weeks to try to convince you to mate with him."

"That's crazy, George. You can't tell me that you're going to actually do it."

"Of course I am." He swallowed thickly and blinked hard a couple of times. "I love Ice and he loves me. We have to at least try. I'm lucky in that most dragon shifters are straight so, we're in with a fighting chance. Anyway, I have a plan."

"I'm not sure I want to hear it, but what's your plan?"

"I'll kick anyone else who tries his luck in the balls."

Meghan choked out a laugh, even though her stomach was wound in knots.

CHAPTER 26

Torrent opened the door to his office and gestured for Tide to go in ahead of him. His brother closed the door behind them. "What did you need to talk to me about in private? I'm hoping it's not what I think it is."

It was best just to get it out in the open. "I'm in love with Doctor Roberts… Meghan. It wasn't something I expected to have happen, it just did."

"Firstly, what happened to not rutting the same human female twice? Don't answer." He held up his hand. "We've already discussed this. It was something I could still cope with." Torrent went on. "But this…" He shook his head. "Love! I thought you said you took my advice. This was not what I advised you to do. I told you to get her out of your system."

"Meghan could have been hurt or killed when Blaze lost it. I could've lost her. It made me realize that it's more than just lust. It's more than just wanting to rut her, although I want to do that too… all the time. Even now that she's over her heat. I couldn't stand being near her this morning and not…" He ran a hand over his face when he realized how horrified his brother looked. "Too much information." Tide chuckled despite feeling nervous, maybe because of it.

"Far too much. You're lucky." He was amazed at how relaxed Torrent looked. How accepting he was. This was not how he expected things to go down.

"Lucky? How so?" It also worried him a little.

Torrent sighed. He actually looked upset. No, that wasn't it. The male looked apprehensive. Torrent looked at the far side of the room before locking eyes with him. "Ice came to see me too."

"What does this have to do with Meghan and me? We want to take our time to get to know each other."

"That's not how dragons do things."

It felt strange, surreal even, having his own words thrown at him. "I know how things are done, but it's not necessary in my case. I know who I want and I'm certain Meghan wants me back. Given time we can—"

"Forget it. That's not how things work." A little more forceful this time. "Bringing up Ice is related because he came to see me the day you left." He squeezed the bridge of his nose. "We should have had both of them sign that damned non-fraternization policy."

"Both of them…?" Tide frowned. He wasn't sure where Torrent was going with this.

"Yes! Both of them. Meghan and her assistant, George. None of this would have happened."

"Now you don't believe that, do you? That a piece of paper would have kept Meghan and me apart? Would a piece of paper have kept you from falling in love with

Candy?"

"Don't bring up my mate," Torrent snarled, his muscles tightening and his eyes darkening. "You don't get to speak of her or my children. You have put the entire therapy program in jeopardy. The reason I chose you for this assignment was that I thought I could trust you with what was most precious to me... my family."

Fuck! "I'm sorry. I know you trusted me and that I betrayed that trust but this doesn't have to end badly. I want Meghan as my mate. That means that she'll become family and stay here indefinitely. She'll be here for Candy, for the pregnancy and to help with the immunization. All of it."

"You have this all planned out, don't you?"

"Yes, it'll work out. We just need some time. Meghan— "

"No! Stop!" Torrent's voice boomed. "Hear me out. Ice came to see me because he and George are in love. He wants to take George as a mate."

"Oh." Tide smiled. "I didn't see that coming. Good for them."

"I was furious," Torrent went on. His jaw was tight. "I put Ice in the cage for a time while I figured it all out."

"The cage? Was that really necessary?"

"Yes, damn you," Torrent growled. "There is a doctor stationed on Earth territory. Blaze is interviewing four final candidates for the Fire and Air kingdoms. All four candidates are female and even if they weren't..." He huffed out a breath. "Look at what happened with George and Ice. Point being, these humans are vulnerable. We have rules in place for a reason. Look at what happened with Doctor Roberts and all because you couldn't keep your hands off of her."

"It was also partly due to her heat. You should have informed her of what kind of birth control she needed to take and why it was important," Tide said. He immediately felt guilty for the outburst. He was ultimately the one who had put Meghan at risk. His need for Meghan had had very little to do with her heat and everything to do with being desperately in love with her. He was trying to shift some of the blame. "I'm sorry, you're right, it was my fault. I just... I guess I couldn't help myself. My emotions were all over the place, I... I'm making excuses." He made himself shut the fuck up.

"I will take some of the responsibility. Blaze accepts his shortcoming as well. We plan to speak with the vampires. They have had far more dealings with humans. They have strict systems, security measures and rules in place. We are going to request assistance from Zane and Brant to assure we can step up measures here as well. Dragon shifters cannot go around doing as they please. Hundreds of unmated males to one or two human females, it's a recipe for disaster. You talk of how your female was almost injured when Blaze lost his shit, well, what of when you rutted her? You put her in a far more precarious situation. What the hell were *you* thinking?"

"I guess I wasn't." Tide scrubbed a hand over his face. "It just happened."

"Just happened. Males can handle the scent of a female's heat. It is not pleasant or easy but it is manageable. But when you have an unmated human female in heat and add to it the scent of sex, well it's like putting a flame to gasoline. *You* did that."

"I know I did, but I took care of it. I took care of my female."

"You got lucky. You can thank your lucky stars Bay was there to assist you. I don't think you would have made it otherwise. It took the male a whole day to recover. Were you aware of that?"

Tide shook his head. "He never mentioned it. I owe the male my gratitude and a word of thanks."

"You might even owe him your life. Where is the brother I know? You've always been so rational. What happened to you?"

"You're right. I've fucked up big time." He was the biggest asshole who lived. Meghan was right, he was self-centered and arrogant. This was all his doing. "How do I make it right? How do I fix this? I love her, Torrent."

"I understand. I do. Love will make us do crazy things but apologizing isn't going to make things better."

"What do you want me to do? Name it? How do I fix this?

"You hunt."

"What?" Tide didn't think he'd heard Torrent correctly.

"When Ice was out in that cage, I consulted with Blaze about what to do about the situation. We decided to look to the Lores on how to solve the dilemma. I don't want to stand in the way of love, but at the same time, I can't condone these types of actions. I can't and neither can Blaze. There is a hunt at the end of next week. Ice must hunt this male, George. He must win him if he is to mate him."

Fuck! Tide didn't like where this was going. "Ice should stand a good chance of winning George."

"Yes, he does. The same cannot be said for you however."

"What? You can't expect—" Tide bit his tongue. Literally bit into it until he tasted the coppery tang of his own blood. He had been selfish and arrogant. *No more!*

"The Lores are clear. You will need to hunt Doctor Roberts and you will need to win her if you wish to keep her."

Blast and damn! How could he put her through this? How could he convince her to do this in the first place? Did he even want to? "Are there any alternatives?"

"Yes. Doctor Roberts returns home. She ends her time with us."

"That's not right! We hired her. I fucked up! She's done nothing wrong, she—"

"We will pay her out on the remainder of her contract."

"What about her research? What about—"

"We would replace her... eventually."

"That would mean..." Tide couldn't say it.

"Yes, it would mean putting a halt to the whole project."

"I'm sorry!" He'd fucked up so badly.

"You need to hunt and win her to fix this."

"I understand that but I need all the facts. What would happen if someone else was to win her?"

"The regular rules would apply. She would need to stay

with that male for a minimum period of two weeks, after which she would be permitted to return home. If she chooses the hunt and chooses to return home, she forfeits being paid out for her contract."

"That's not fair," Tide snarled.

"Life isn't fair. Make sure that you win her."

Tide nodded. "I will put this to her. It will be Meghan's choice. I am a royal, second to the throne. I will win my female at all costs. I will make this right." He locked eyes with Torrent as he said the last. "I know I can do it."

There was a look of regret in Torrent's stare. "There is one more thing."

More?

No!

The look of regret clouded Torrent's eyes. *Oh fuck!* This wasn't good. "As in accordance with our ancient Lores, and because you are a royal and because you fucked up, I'm sorry brother…" Torrent pursed his lips and gave a shake of the head.

"What? Just tell me."

"You must hunt and win your female but you must do so after being hobbled."

"Hobbled?" Dread filled him and he looked at the ground, his mind running a mile a minute. The feeling of dread worsened, not because of the pain and suffering he would endure but because it made his task infinitely more difficult.

"I'm sorry. You should have had more willpower. You should have followed our Lores in the first place. I wish I could change things."

Tide nodded, he grit his teeth as he looked Torrent in the eye. "Meghan must not know of this."

Torrent frowned. "You have to tell her. She needs to have all the facts before deciding what she would like to do. You said so yourself. You stand very little chance of succeeding, Tide."

"I will do what it takes. I *will* succeed."

"You will be hobbled. Do you know what that means?"

"Yes, I know exactly what that means. You cannot tell her." There was a desperate edge to his voice that could not be helped. "She must not know of this because she will never agree otherwise."

"I don't blame her." Torrent shrugged, his whole demeanor was nonchalant. "If she chooses the hunt and you fail, which, let's face it, you probably will, there won't be any payday for her."

Torrent's attitude infuriated Tide. Then again, his brother didn't know Meghan. Not like he did. "That's not it." Despite the anger and sheer desperation, he felt, Tide practically whispered the words. "Meghan is a good female. A kind female. Do you know why she needs the money?"

It took a few moments for his brother to finally shake his head. "No."

"It's to fund her research. She's trying to create a vaccination for a human affliction called asthma."

"Yes, I remember now. She will make millions if she develops a cure."

"No." Tide shook his head. "She plans on giving the cure away. She's doing it to help sufferers. Her sister and nephew are such sufferers. It's something that's close to her heart."

"You will take this away from her if you go ahead. You need to be honest with her or you need to let her go. You cannot win her."

"That's where you are wrong. Hobbling is designed to make it difficult for a male to win a female. Difficult, but not impossible."

"Don't do this." Torrent swallowed thickly.

"I ask you this… would you do it for Candy?"

"In a fucking heartbeat, but—"

"You have your answer." Tide strode from the room. He needed to speak with his female.

"Tide!" his brother shouted, stopping him in his tracks. He didn't turn. "No rutting between now and then or you forfeit your place in the hunt."

"Understood." He barreled his way through the door and kept on going.

CHAPTER 27

"That's your well thought out plan?" She laughed some more. "You'll kick them in the balls?"

"You have no idea how painful it is," George said. "It doesn't matter that these shifters are huge. Way stronger. Far more aggressive. None of that matters. They fall just as hard and as fast if their family jewels are broken. No!" He looked her in the eyes. "I will use my knees, my feet. Do whatever I need to do to ensure that Ice gets to me first."

"I've never seen you like this. Whatever happened to being footloose and fancy-free?"

"I met the right guy." George fake-swooned. He even clutched his chest and everything. "I'm so in love. So far gone, you have no idea."

Meghan didn't answer. Instead, she chewed on her bottom lip.

"What about you, what's going on with Tide? Do you have feelings for him now that the two of you have spent some time together – and by time, I mean had sex, lots of sex?"

Meghan fiddled with a button on her blouse. She didn't want to answer. "That's not something I want to talk about right now."

"Come on. You can tell me. Talking will make you feel better. Look, I know you're not the type to fool around. I also know you're not the type to fall in love easily. In fact, I don't think you've ever really ever been in love. Until now that is."

"You think I'm in love?"

"Yeah, I do."

"I don't know, I'm too afraid to let myself fall. Not for a guy like Tide. I'm afraid of being hurt."

George nodded. "I can understand that, because—"

There was a knock at the door and Tide stuck his head around the jamb. "Can I borrow you for a few minutes?" He had a pleading look in his eyes.

"Sure." They did need to talk and it wasn't like she was getting much work done obsessing about him and trying to analyze what it all meant. She needed to ask him straight out.

"Hi, George," Tide said.

George waved. "Hi, Tide. We were just talking about you."

"Oh yes? All good I hope?" He smiled and out popped his dimples. She loved those damned dimples.

"Definitely," George chuckled.

"I believe you and Ice are an item?"

George grinned so broadly it lit up his entire face. "Yes, but it's not official yet."

"Don't worry, I'm sure he'll win you. He's a strong male."

George nodded, looking quite sedate for once. "I'm sure he will. And yes, he's very strong, it's one of the many things I love about him."

Meghan walked over to Tide and they left together. They walked in silence. "Where are we going?" They were heading in the opposite direction to their apartments.

"Here we are." Tide opened a door and waited for her to enter. "It's my office."

It was large and very similar to Torrent's. There was a sitting area on one side and a desk on the other. The only thing it was missing was the big conference table. Instead, it had a small round table that could seat six people.

"Let's go through here." He gestured to the sitting area.

"You're being so formal. Should I be worried?" Meghan folded her arms. She could feel herself frown.

"So, you're not in love with me?" He sighed, and ran a hand through his hair which was a little overgrown and a lot mussed. His jaw was covered in stubble. In short, he was sexy as anything. She had a feeling he'd look good covered in mud, wearing a sack.

Then his question registered and her eyes widened. "In l-love… um…"

He half-smiled, rubbed a hand over his jaw, stubble catching. "I overheard the last part of your conversation with George. I'm sorry, it wasn't on purpose."

"Well then you heard the part about me being afraid too."

"Yes, I did and you have nothing to be afraid about." He closed the distance between them and took her hands in his.

"You were acting so weird this morning. I didn't know what to make of it and I guess I was too afraid to ask."

"You have nothing to be afraid of because I am completely, totally and utterly in love with you, Meghan. I couldn't be more in love if I tried."

"Oh." She struggled to breathe. Her heart pounded inside her chest. "I believed you may have felt that way because of my ovulation cycle. I wasn't sure if you would still feel the same way once I—"

"You were wrong." He cupped her cheek.

"Good, I'm glad. You hardly looked at me this morning." Why was she harping on about that? Maybe because her nerves were getting the better of her and in a big way. "I mean, it wasn't the same between us. It suddenly felt so stilted and formal."

Tide let go of her cheek. His eyes clouded. "I needed to speak with Torrent. I was focused. You said that you were afraid, well, so was I. I still am." He let go of her and scrubbed a hand over his face.

He looked completely out of sorts. "It didn't go well, did it?" There was a timid edge to her voice.

His eyes lifted to meet hers. "We have this age-old tradition. It's called the hunt." He huffed out a breath just as Meghan gasped. His eyes narrowed. "You know of it?"

"Yes, I do. George explained hunt basics to me. He told me all about it because Ice is going to be expected to hunt him next week." She narrowed her eyes. "Are you telling me that...?" She let the sentence die as his eyes clouded.

Tide nodded. "I have to hunt you. I have to win you before I can keep you."

Meghan nodded. "What happens if you don't win me? What happens if—"

"I will."

"How can you say that? There are hundreds of unmated guys in the dragon lands. Hundreds, Tide." Her voice was shrill. "This can't be happening."

"Hey." He put an arm around her and pulled her close. "We've spoken about this. You need to have faith. Most of those males are silver. I am gold. I will win you. I *will*." It sounded like he was trying to convince himself. Tide let her go and made a groaning noise. "You don't have to do it. I would understand if you didn't. It would fucking kill me if you didn't, but the thing is…" His gaze drifted to the other side of the room before coming back to her. "If you decide to join the hunt, and I don't win you, you will need to spend time with whomever…"

Anger coursed through her. "How many times do I need to tell you that I'm not interested in some other guy. I wouldn't—"

"I know that. You would still need to spend the allotted two weeks with him before you could return home."

"Home?" She frowned. "I wouldn't want to go home."

"That's the thing. It doesn't matter. You would have to go home. You would be forced to. If it happens that way, you would forfeit being paid out the rest of your contract. If you join the hunt, it would be a choice."

Meghan nodded. "What if I chose not to take part at all?" She was almost too afraid to hear his answer.

Tide took a few moments before speaking. "You will be sent home. You will be paid out in full and will be able to pursue your dream of finding a cure for asthma."

"What would happen between now and the hunt? Do I get to continue my work? I have immunotherapy sessions scheduled. I can't just be replaced."

"Yes, it would be business as usual." He paused, pulling in a breath. "Blaze and Torrent have already begun working on a replacement for you."

"It would be too late for Candy and Sky, for their babies."

"There will be more children born. It would put a hold on things but…"

She felt her lip quiver. The question that had been at the forefront of her mind was on her tongue. "If I end up getting sent home, what would happen to us?" Meghan bit down on her lip and blinked a couple of times, holding back her well of emotions.

"There would be no us. The only way for that to happen would be if you were to risk everything."

"That's outrageous. Why can't we just be together? Take time to explore…"

Tide shook his head. "It's not the dragon way. The hunt is not until the end of next week." He took her hands. "You have time to think it over. Know that I would understand if you couldn't do it."

"I think that it's probably a good idea for me to… to think about it. I need to be really sure." Her mind raced at a mile a minute.

Tide's whole stance softened and he squeezed her hands. "It's a major decision. I completely understand that you can't just—"

"Yes!" She said the word so out of the blue and with such conviction that she gave herself a fright.

"You don't look like you're sure." He cocked his head, really looking at her. "Are you shouting yes for an entirely different reason, or are you saying yes because you want to take a chance on us?"

Meghan shook her head. "Who am I kidding? There's nothing to think about. I want to stay. I want to be with you. I've fallen in love with you too and I would never—"

Tide crushed her to his chest and kissed her. It was a kiss that was filled with so much promise of tomorrow. A kiss that could move mountains. It was a kiss that told her he planned on racing. Not just that, that he planned on winning. She prayed he could pull it off. Thing was, she didn't care one bit about the money. If it came to it, she would make a plan. She would continue her asthma research one way or the other but losing Tide... The thought of that had her heart landing in her throat. Had her eyes filling with tears. Meghan quickly blinked them away. If she was honest with herself, she'd been in love with him for a while now. It had been hard to admit because she was afraid. It just seemed so cruel that they might still be kept apart, despite their feelings for one another.

"It's going to be okay." He must have seen all of her emotions written on her face because he cupped her cheek, his voice deep.

"I know it is." She forced herself to smile. "I have faith in you. In us."

Something flared in his eyes. Panic, fear... maybe? And then it was gone.

CHAPTER 28

The day of the hunt...

Tide had never been more fearful in his entire life. He was sick with worry. His stomach pulled tight and sweat beaded on his brow. He looked over the vast acres of land that lay before him and his gut churned with it. It had nothing to do with fear for himself but fear for her. His Meghan.

Thousands and thousands of miles of wilderness. Thousands of miles of streams, gullies, mountains and fields. Of forests and rivers. There were dangers out there. Wild animals. Meghan could fall and hurt herself. She could drown. He couldn't think like that though. He needed to stay focused and positive. Tide was going to hunt his female and make her his and he'd do it quickly.

"Hello, hello." Shale walked over to him. "It's a great view isn't it?"

"Amazing," he mumbled, not feeling much like talking, especially to a male like Shale. He certainly didn't give two shits about the view. All he saw was the danger. That and distance. With every minute that passed, Meghan was further and further away from him.

"So, you love her that much?" There was a smirk on his face. "I don't think that I would be willing to do it."

Tide didn't say anything. Shale wouldn't understand.

"Then again, she is something alright. Not just beautiful, but—"

Tide gripped the male by the throat. Shale made choking noises.

"Leave him." Torrent seized Tide by the arm when he didn't do as his brother said. Tide released the male, who grinned at him even though he was gasping for air and his face was red.

"Stay away from her," Tide warned. "That goes for all of you. I'll kill anyone who lays so much as a finger on her."

"Maiming only, no killing," Torrent recited the rules to him.

Fuck that. He was going to win his female and if by some small fucked up chance he didn't manage it, he would kill whoever dared touch her. Within minutes, the males went back to talking amongst themselves in groups and he was able to unclench his fists.

Torrent turned to him. "Are you sure you want to do this?"

"Yes." Softly spoken.

"Be rational. You—"

"I'm sure." A growl this time.

A bell sounded. It was five minutes till the start of the hunt. His heart just about beat its way out of his chest.

Torrent frowned. "I don't know about this. It's foolish.

It's…"

"Do it. Time is running out."

Torrent clenched his jaw, he turned and nodded to someone. Tide followed his gaze to Blaze. The male was holding the contraption. It looked like a trap. That's because it ultimately was a trap. A deadly looking thing. It was round and comprised of sharp stainless steel teeth that reminded him of the jaws of a shark. It was, in itself, a vicious contraption, capable of stopping a male in his tracks. What made it worse, was that it was attached to a ball and chain. Dragging that hunk of iron was going to be fun.

The trap was double spring-loaded. It took both Torrent and Blaze to pry the contraption open. Torrent slowly lifted his head, his gaze locked with Tide's. The time to dig deep had come. There was a part of him that was happy it was almost over. The waiting had been tough. Lying to his female had been tougher still. There wasn't much time. Soon the second bell would ring, signaling the start of the hunt.

He quickly made his way to the two males. Tide ripped his pants leg clean off and stepped into the trap. It was different from a conventional trap in that it didn't have a trigger mechanism. No need since this was a choice. The two males lifted the device until the teeth were about mid-thigh, as was customary. His brother looked up at him, a grave expression on his face.

Tide gave a nod. He clenched his teeth, his nails biting into his palms.

"On three," Blaze instructed. The male counted up.

One.

Two.

White hot pain. His stomach rolled, causing him to gag. Tide felt his blood running down his leg. Hot and coppery. It spattered on the ground beneath his feet. It took him a few seconds to realize that his eyes were closed. Tide forced them open. Torrent gripped his arm on the one side and Blaze on the other. "You okay?" Torrent asked.

"Never fucking better," he growled, having to force the words through a haze of pain.

"Good luck," Blaze said.

"Thank you."

"No, I mean it. I said the same thing to Ice. We had no choice."

"I understand." His voice was thick with pain. His leg throbbed in time with his heart. Each beat like flames shooting through him.

Torrent bent down and picked up the iron ball. "I suggest you carry it for as long as you can. Give your leg a chance to heal some. No one can help you with your burden. You need to do this all on your own."

"I know." The bleeding had slowed some, but the pain was just as white hot. Sweat dripped off of him. The idea of moving was hideous. Tide pictured Meghan. Her beautiful green eyes, her smile, her laugh, fuck, even her frown. He loved everything about her. The way she sucked on her plump lower lip when she was in thought. The smattering of freckles across her nose. Her scent. Her.

The bell rang, pulling him out of his reverie. Torrent handed him the iron ball. It was heavier than it looked.

"It's filled with silver," Torrent explained. "It won't affect you, other than weighing you down."

That explained it. Tide took his first step. He staggered. It was worse than he had imagined. Torn muscle and sinew protested. He growled deeply, watching as the others began to run. All out fucking run.

"Better get going." It was Shale. The male still had that smirk on his face.

Tide took a step. *Fuck!* Then another.

Shale was barely moving, staying just ahead of him. "Too slow. At this rate, I'm going to end up with the prize. I know which female I'm hunting today."

"Fuck you," Tide growled through clenched teeth. He picked up the pace, not feeling the pain as much. Not caring that his blood began to flow again as the teeth bit into his flesh.

"Two weeks is a long time. Pretty sure I can make that sweet, little doctor forget you ever existed."

He knew that the male was goading him into a reaction. That the bastard was taking perverse satisfaction from his pain and suffering, but he couldn't help reacting anyway. "I'm going to fucking kill you," he snarled.

"You have to catch me first." Shale winked at him and picked up the pace, widening the distance between them.

He wanted to snarl at the male. Scream at him. He wanted to kill the fucker for even thinking of his sweet female. Tide roared as he picked up the pace. A slow jog was all he could muster. It frustrated him to see the others leaving him behind. He only prayed that his leg healed enough for him to pick up the pace and soon.

"My feet hurt." Meghan sat down on a boulder. She took off her sneaker and massaged her foot.

"You need to get up and get going." George looked concerned. He put his hands on his hips. "Now missy. Hustle." He tried to sound light-hearted. Like he was making a joke, but she could see that something was bothering him. He had been acting weird all day. She assumed, like her, that he was worried about how things would turn out.

"Tide is the strongest of all the dragons. I only planned on taking a five-minute break. We've been at it for hours." Exercise was not one of her strong suits. She had two left feet and no muscles to speak of. It was a good thing that Tide liked his women soft because that's what she was, soft. "Shoot," she muttered as she removed her sock. "I have a blister. No wonder my foot hurts so darned much."

"Put on the sock and shoe and let's get going." George walked up ahead a few steps and turned back to her. "Let's go." She'd never seen him like this. Thing was, George also wasn't much of an exercise fanatic, even though he had been acting like one since they set out. "Tide specifically told you to get as far away as possible. You need to buy him time to get to you before the others."

Meghan put her sock and shoe back on. "What's going on?" she asked as she tied her laces. "You're acting weird. We're both really worried here, George, but at the same time, we need to have a little faith in our men. You didn't see how Tide fought off that dragon that was after us.

How he still managed to outrun the group of shifters who were right on our tail. He is strong and fast and we love each other. He will make it to me first. I have no doubts about that. You're starting to make me nervous." She began to walk. They were headed through a forest. It wasn't too dense beneath the tall trees. She suspected it was because the canopy was so thick. It blocked out much of the sun, making it difficult for the plants to grow. There was plenty of moss and ivy.

George stopped dead, Meghan almost walked into him. "I have to tell you." He covered his face with his hands and made a pained noise. "I promised Ice I wouldn't but I can't keep quiet any longer." He turned around and she noticed how pale he looked. "You need to know."

"What the hell is going on? I'm not just nervous anymore, I'm scared." She noticed that her hands were shaking and folded her arms. "What aren't you allowed to tell me?"

"Tide didn't want you to know. He was afraid you wouldn't go through with this if you did."

Her heart beat faster. Her stomach clenched tight. "Tell me." It came out as a whisper. Dread filled her. It made her feel icy cold. Made goosebumps rise on her arms.

"Tide was hobbled at the start of the hunt."

"Hobbled?" she shouted the word because it didn't sound good. "What the hell is that? What did they do to him?" Her voice was shrill.

"Something about ancient traditions and Lores. I don't know exactly. Ice has never seen it before. They hobble him. Do something to him designed to slow him down.

It's bad, Meghan. Really bad."

"Why would they do something like that?" She felt something on her face and realized that she was crying.

"Something about him being royal and leading by example. He should have had more willpower where you were concerned. He displayed weakness and must therefore show immense courage if he is to save you."

"What the fuck is wrong with these people?" she sobbed, wiping a hand across her face, trying to staunch the flow of tears. "Why would they do such a thing? It would have to be bad to slow him down. Really bad." She remembered how he had made it back to the lair with his back burned.

"That's why we need to hurry. You need to give Tide time to get to you. That's why he told you to get as far away as possible. Ice told me that whatever they did to him will slowly heal given time. He will get stronger and faster and hopefully makeup time."

"He should have told me."

"You wouldn't be here if he did."

"No." She shook her head. "I would never have expected this of him. Hobbled." It sounded terrible.

"He loves you. He'll do anything for you. It was his choice. You said you were willing to give up everything, to risk it all."

"Of course." Tears still ran down her cheeks. "I love the big, lying asshole. I wouldn't have wanted him to suffer though." A terrible thought occurred to her. "What if it's for nothing? What if no matter how hard he tries, he—"

"Hush!" George widened his eyes. "Don't you dare say it."

"I need to go. I need to run."

"Like I was saying, let's hustle."

"Not you, George. Your and Ice's strategy was the opposite to mine and Tide's. You shouldn't get too far. You might end up with a real prince instead of your prince." Tide had explained that royals had more stamina. They could outlast the general population. Ice was not a royal. If George got too far, he risked losing him.

"I can't leave you. You need me." His eyes welled with tears.

"I'll be fine." She wiped away her own tears. Crying was not going to help her. "Thank you for telling me. I appreciate it."

"I'm glad I did. You needed to know. Don't be too hard on Tide. He's carried this since you guys got back. He's going through hell to get to you before the others. He did it because he knows how sweet, kind and genuinely good you are. You would never have let him suffer."

Another tear slipped down her cheek and she wiped it away. "I need to go. I'll see you back at the castle."

"Yes, you will. I might need a day or two though."

"Oh, are you guys going on a honeymoon?"

"No," George winked at her. "To recover. I think you will too."

"I hope so, George." She turned to run.

"Oh, and Meghan…"

She looked back over her shoulder, brows raised.

"I'll try to hold them back. If any of those shifters head

this way, and they're not Tide, I'll kick them in the balls for you." A look of determination took up residence on his face.

Despite the sheer terror that coursed through her, she burst out laughing. "Just don't hurt yourself in the process." Meghan didn't wait for a reply. She picked up a fast jog. Moving as fast as she could through the undergrowth. On and on and on until finally, the forest began to thin out, making it easier for her. It took about a half hour and the trees gave way to a grassy hill, which eventually led to more forest.

It was slow going up the hill. Her muscles burned from the exertion. Sweat dripped off of her and her bangs stuck to her forehead. Breathing was the hardest part of all. She couldn't seem to catch her breath and her throat felt raw. *Water.* She'd take a one-minute break and ease her throat with something to drink.

She unfastened the water bottle on her hip and took a deep drink. Not too much though. That was when she heard it. Dull methodical thuds. With a gasp, she turned. *Oh no! Oh god!* It wasn't Tide. This person had dark hair. She dropped the bottle, the water sloshing out. Meghan turned and ran. Her muscles were screaming in protest. A couple of minutes later, she was on the plateau. She glanced back as she reached the descent. The sound of footfalls was much louder.

Shale.

It was Shale. His eyes were set, a look of determination on his face. Although he seemed to be limping ever so slightly, he was gaining on her big time. She sobbed as she turned back to face the pathway ahead of her. Thankfully the decline wasn't steep or she might end up falling. Any faster and she would risk a stumble.

The thuds grew louder and louder, until they were right behind her. He grabbed her hips and hauled her off the ground. Meghan yelled in both anger and frustration. "Don't!" she shouted as he turned her around. "Get away from me!" *Shit!* She was crying again. Struggling to form words because she was breathing so darned hard.

Shale was covered in sweat and grime. There was a streak of dried blood on his cheek. "You did well, female." She was happy to see that he was also out of breath. He smiled at her. "Not well enough, I'm afraid."

Meghan gripped her side, which was cramping. She pushed past the pain and fatigue and squared her shoulders. "Don't do this. I love Tide. There is no one else for me."

"We don't have any time." Just as he said it, she heard a whole bunch of footfalls coming from above them, followed by a shout as the first of the shifters caught sight of them. "My apologies." Shale pulled her against him and closed his mouth over hers.

Meghan's eyes widened and she clamped her mouth shut. She kicked and railed against him, but it was no use. He held on tight. It was like hitting against a brick wall. A scream built up inside her. *This couldn't be happening. It couldn't!*

CHAPTER 29

"Hurry!" George screamed as Tide jogged up to the couple. Ice had his arm around the male. "They've gone that way." George pointed in the direction the scent trail led. Ice didn't say anything, he just gave a nod of acknowledgment.

He slowed just a smidgen. "Thank you."

George looked like he wanted to say something else but he didn't wait. Tide couldn't. He picked up the pace once more. By now his body had mostly healed around the steel teeth. It remained uncomfortable. He went from carrying the iron ball until his arms shook from fatigue, to dragging it. The ball would hook onto undergrowth and bounce over rocks, pulling on his flesh, reopening the wound some. He felt weak. Not just from pushing so damned hard but he suspected that blood loss played a role as well. Right now he carried the thing even though his arms shook.

What kept him pushing was that he could scent that fucker along with several other males. They weren't all that far ahead of him. Shale's scent was weakest. The asshole was in the lead. He grit his teeth and forced his body to move quicker.

It wasn't long before the forest gave way to open ground. He dropped the ball, growling as the teeth pulled in his flesh. His thigh burned and fresh blood trickled where his wounds reopened. The scent of his female grew stronger and he noticed a discarded water bottle on the ground. Tide picked it up, sniffing it. Her scent was strong. It renewed his vigor. Dropping the bottle, he forced himself to put one foot in front of the other. To keep going. Higher and higher, he climbed. The gradient wasn't steep but he could still feel the burn.

What the fuck!? Tide stumbled when he saw them. It was a group of seven males, they headed towards him.

Towards him?

No!

They were going the wrong way. *Fuck!* His blood ran cold. His scales rubbed. Smoke wafted from his nostrils. Everything in him tightened as adrenaline pumped.

"I'm sorry, Tide," one of the males announced as he drew nearer. "You are too late. Your female has already been won."

"No," he roared. "I will fight."

The male who had spoken shrugged, looking down at his messed up leg. "Suit yourself. Good luck, I hope you win her back."

Tide could see that the male thought that Tide was crazy. That he didn't have a hope in hell.

"Why are you rooting for him?" another male spoke. "Not ten minutes ago you were pursuing the female. You wanted her for yourself."

The male pulled a face. "Nah." Then he grinned. "Okay, fine. You're right, I would've liked—"

Tide punched the male in the face. He heard the satisfying crunch of bone. The asshole gasped, managing to stay on his feet despite the impact. His eyes were wide, his hands closed around the injury. Blood flowed unchecked. The others shifted from one foot to the other. "Anyone else want to tell me how they were hoping to win my female? Mine!" He snarled the last, unable to control the emotions that surged through him.

They all looked at the ground. Most of them shook their heads as well for good measure. Tide didn't have time for this shit. He took off at a run. It wasn't too late. He would fight despite his fatigue and waning strength. He would win. Fuck that, he was going to kill Shale. The decision had been made. He didn't care about the consequences.

The fucker was dead.

Dead and fucking buried.

The incline was a killer, only because of the weight of the ball. It pulled on his thigh. Blood ran down his leg but he ignored it. Renewed energy coursed through him as he spotted his female at the top of the hill. Shale stood behind her. Lucky for him, he wasn't touching her. Maybe Tide would let him live. Maybe.

Shale said something to Meghan and she turned towards him, her eyes lighting up. She tried to run to him but Shale grabbed her around the waist and shoved her behind him. *Fuck him!* Tide snarled and tripled his efforts. He hoped that the male would underestimate him. He hoped to use surprise as an advantage. Shale had folded his arms. It was clear he was expecting a conversation and not the fight that was coming.

Good!

Meghan stepped out from behind Shale, her eyes widening as they landed on his wound. She sobbed something that sounded like 'oh no,' but he couldn't be sure. The injury looked as bad as what it felt. Maybe worse. A mangled mess of flesh and metal. Not to mention the blood. So much blood. She covered her mouth and sobbed into her hands, squeezing her eyes shut.

Shale just stood there, arms folded. "It's about time. You don't have to," his eyes widened and he inhaled sharply, reacting too slowly, "wait—" Tide's fist connected with the side of his jaw. There was a cracking sound and Shale groaned as he went flying to the left. Just as planned. He had to keep Meghan safe. His female screamed. It sounded like she was shouting for him to stop but that couldn't be right.

He was on Shale in seconds. The male held up his hands. "No, stop!" Tide kicked him in the ribs. There was a loud thud. Not quite hard enough. He really was tired and weak. Tide tried again. There was a sickening crack and Shale screamed. Sweet music to his ears. Tide staggered though, only just managing to keep his footing. Unfortunately, he was running low on reserves. He could feel his leg bleeding again. With it, he could feel the last of his energy spattering on the ground.

He wrapped his hand around the chain and pulled the silver-centered iron ball to himself. Even that was hard work. Shale gave his head a quick shake. Trying to shake it off. He could see that the male was preparing to get back onto his feet. Once that happened, it would be over for him. It was now or never if he wanted to win this thing. If he wanted to win his female. He gave an almighty tug, rolling the ball where it landed at his feet. Then he bent over, breathing deeply through his nose. He picked it up. So fucking heavy. His muscles shook with the effort. Tide was going to brain the fucker. No-one touched his female and lived. No-one!

"No, Tide. Stop!"

He lifted the iron ball above his head.

Shale rolled onto his back, his eyes widening as he saw the iron ball in Tide's hands. "No—"

"No!" Someone jumped on his back, making him drop the ball. It landed with a dull thud next to Shale, who staggered to his feet. His face was pale. His cheek was puffy and his lip was split. Tide clenched his fists, preparing to fight on.

"Tide, he's helping us. Tide!" It was Meghan. Her voice was right in his ear. She was on his back. "Don't hurt him."

"The female is yours," Shale assured him.

"Damn straight," Tide growled. "Damn fucking straight she is." He leaned down, helping her off of his back. Tide pulled her into his arms, keeping his eyes on Shale.

"I'm trying to help you," Shale said.

Help him? Like fuck! "What, by going after Meghan, by—"

"No, I never went after her with the intention of taking her for myself. I did it to help you."

"Why would you do that?" Tide narrowed his eyes. He didn't trust the male, could scent him on his female. It irritated him. Rubbed him raw.

"You love each other. I could see it back then already, at the Earth lair. There was something between the two of you."

"So you asked Meghan out on a date?" Tide raised his brows, pulling his female closer.

"I'm a shit stirrer. What can I say?" Shale chuckled, then winced, putting a hand to his chest. "It was fun watching your reaction." He shrugged one shoulder, wincing again. "You broke a rib."

"Just like you enjoyed fucking with me at the start of the race?" Tide snarled. "I wish I had broken all of your ribs."

Shale frowned. "That was to get you going. I wanted to anger you so that you would forget about your leg."

"Are you okay?" Meghan said with a sob. *Shit!* He realized that she was crying. Tears streamed down her cheeks. "You should have told me about this." He could see that she was examining his leg. She touched his upper thigh with the tip of a finger. "You're going to need surgery."

"Surgery," Shale snickered. "Humans are the best. He does not need surgery. He'll be just fine."

Meghan's eyes were wide. "But—"

"He's right." Tide thread his fingers through her hair. "I'll be just fine."

"Maybe we should get the ball off of the chain. Funny that," Shale laughed, "you win your female and doing so, we get to take the ball off the chain. Get it!"

Tide shook his head. "Why don't you want me to kill him again?"

"Because he kept those other guys away by pretending to have won me," Meghan said. "They thankfully didn't put up a fight."

"I was almost too late," Shale said, his gaze on Meghan. "Your friend slowed me down. He can seriously kick." He cupped his balls.

Meghan laughed. "Seriously? George kicked you in the nuts?"

"That's funny to you?" Shale looked horrified.

"George was just trying to protect me. He didn't mean it."

"Sure as hell felt like he meant it." Shale continued to cup his balls.

Tide breathed out through his nose. "I guess I owe you an apology."

"Nah." Shale waved a hand. "I had my own ulterior motives. Meghan is a good doctor, it would have been a shame to lose her. Also, you arrived expecting the worst. I couldn't tell you my plan because you wouldn't have pushed hard enough. I needed you to use every ounce of strength you had and you did. Thing is," Shale shook his head in disbelief, "I don't think you needed me. You would've coped just fine on your own."

"I'd do anything for my female."

"I love you." Meghan caressed his cheek.

He leaned in and pressed a kiss to her lips. Then quickly turned back to Shale. "You dare kiss my female again and I'll—"

"It's not like I had a choice."

"He didn't do it because he wanted to." Meghan tugged on his arm. "He had to do it."

"Yeah right," Tide snorted. "I assure you he wanted to." He kissed her again. "Who wouldn't want to kiss you?" he said, as he broke the kiss.

"This is my cue to leave," Shale said. "I'll help you remove the iron ball."

When Tide looked up, the male was picking up a rock. Tide went down onto his haunches. He put the chain over a flat rock. Shale hit the chain a couple of times. The links eventually gave out.

"There," Shale said.

"Thank you," Tide said as he stood up. "I appreciate it."

"No problem. Who knows, maybe one day you can return the favor."

Tide nodded.

Meghan stepped towards Shale. "Thank you."

"Good luck to you both," Shale said. "Don't try to take that off until you get back to the lair." He pointed at the contraption embedded in his thigh.

"I won't." Tide shook his head. "My thigh has partially healed around the teeth."

"Exactly. You're going to have to rip it out. You'll be incapacitated for a day or two."

Meghan's heart-rate picked up, as did her breathing.

She was worried about him. Tide squeezed her hand. "I'll be okay. I've got you to look after me." He winked at her, trying to look relaxed and light-hearted. It was going to hurt more coming off than what it had going on, but it would be worth it.

They said their goodbyes and Shale shifted. He hadn't won a female, so no need to get back to the lair in his human form. They watched as he lifted into the air and flew away.

Meghan sagged against him. "I'm so glad it all worked out. I can't believe you did this. You should have told me."

"You would never have agreed."

She shook her head. "You're right." Her eyes welled with tears. "Look at your leg."

"I don't have to." He smiled down at her. "I'm looking at you. You are everything to me and I meant what I said, I'll do anything for you. To keep you at my side, to keep you happy and healthy."

"I know." A tear slid down her cheek.

"No need to cry. Everything is fine now."

"I'm crying because I'm happy."

He wiped away the tear. "You seem to have this backwards."

"I have to be honest with you," she chewed on her lush lower lip, her teeth denting the flesh, "I was worried that things between us were moving too quickly." She blinked her beautiful blue eyes a few times.

"I know. We can take it slow. Torrent will try to push for us—"

"No," she shook her head, "that's the thing. When

Shale grabbed me and I thought he had won me…" She swallowed thickly.

Tide couldn't help himself, he growled. It was a low, deep rumble that vibrated right through him. "I'm sorry. I can't help being possessive of you."

Meghan smiled. She reached up on her tip-toes and cupped his cheeks in her tiny hands. "That's what I'm trying to say… when I thought I'd lost you. That I'd have to go back to Walton Springs, that was when I realized how ready I am to take the next step. I don't want to wait. I know what I want and that's you."

Tide grinned. Something eased in him hearing her say it. He knew that there had been a hesitancy there. He couldn't blame Meghan. Humans were different to dragons. Love though, love was universal. It superseded race, color, sex, even species in their case. "I love you so much."

"Love you too," she said. He captured her lips, put his arms around her and pulled her close. Tide couldn't wait for the rest of their lives. He planned on savoring each and every moment.

CHAPTER 30

"We are right on time." Tide looked at the clock on the wall.

"You are half a minute late." Torrent frowned. "Are the two of you taking this seriously?" he directed his question at Meghan, sniffing the air as he asked it. She knew he could tell that they had just had sex. Sometimes she hated their enhanced senses. This was one of those times.

Meghan nodded. "Of course we are."

"We were on our lunch break. We're not late," Tide spoke with a growl. "And you know how seriously Doctor Roberts takes her job, so you can cut it right out."

Despite where she was. Despite just having had sex with Tide, her girl parts reacted when he said her full name like that. He always insisted on calling her by her full name during sex. It had become a thing since they mated almost six months ago. *Six months!* Time flew when you were having fun.

"Leave them, love. They are newly mated," Candy said. "Remember how we used to be?"

Torrent smiled. "Yes, yes." He rolled his eyes. "I only hope you both start trying for a baby soon. You've been mated for a while now. Come to think of it," he looked at Candy, "they aren't *that* newly mated anymore."

"We will start trying for a baby when we are good and ready," Tide said.

"As second-in-command, you need heirs. It is—"

"I know!" Tide snapped. "*We* know." He put his arm around her. "We'll get to it in our own time." He kissed the top of her head.

Megan felt bad. She knew that Tide was more than ready, but she wasn't so sure just yet. They needed to get to the bottom of what was going on with the children who had resulted from dragon-human pairings. More had come to light in the last few months and she was close to having conclusive scientific evidence to back up her findings. Also, she needed to – hopefully – start working on that vaccine. "Shall we get started?" she asked, trying to get the conversation back to the job at hand.

Candy and Torrent looked her way. Candy nodded. "Yes, of course." Torrent inclined his head.

The door to the lab flew open and a very flustered looking George rushed in. "I'm so sorry I'm late." He grabbed his white coat and tugged it on. "I had an extremely important errand I needed to—"

Meghan raised her brows and looked at George in such a way that had him stopping in his tracks. "Dang our improved senses." He huffed out a breath. "I get bust every darned time." He turned his attention to Torrent and Candy. "Hello everyone. My sincerest apologies." He nodded his head at Tide.

"We'll have a word after this meeting," Meghan said, trying to sound stern. She did it more for Torrent's benefit. She was sure he would expect for there to be some sort of recourse.

"Don't be too hard on him," Torrent piped up. "He is newly mated."

Meghan's mouth fell open for a moment. "Not *that* newly mated." She laughed but quickly turned serious. "Shall we continue?"

Torrent's grin disappeared in an instant. He nodded once.

"Okay, so, as you both know, Sky and Lake's baby still has the silver allergy. However, the effects are much less severe because of the immunotherapy during the pregnancy. I had truly hoped to eradicate the allergy altogether." She paused, holding in a breath before slowly letting it out. "I'm afraid, that because of this, I am expecting similar results with little Fjord here." She glanced at the baby in Candy's arms.

Torrent nodded. "We'll go through the same procedure as before?"

"Yes." Meghan nodded. "I'll touch a needle to his arm for a few seconds and then we'll give it a minute before going on to the next one. Each needle will contain a higher percentage of silver than the last."

Torrent didn't look thrilled. Thankfully he'd seen the whole process with Lake and Sky's baby, Flood, so he knew what to expect and was able to be more understanding as a result.

Meghan picked up the first needle. "If he starts to fuss, you can go ahead and feed him."

Candy nodded. "Thank you. It is almost his feeding time, so I might have to."

Meghan touched the first needle to his arm and as expected, there was no reaction. She pushed the stopwatch, checking Fjord's heart-rate while they waited the allotted time. She kept going, taking a higher percentage needle and noting her findings. Sure to check his heart-rate regularly.

Meghan picked up the next needle. "This one is forty percent silver," she clarified.

"You're sure it's safe?" Torrent growled, his eyes narrowed, his whole stance became tense.

"Calm down," Tide said from somewhere next to her. Right next to her.

She gave a little start and clutched her chest with her free hand.

"I'm sorry. Did I scare you, doc?"

"You know you did." She glanced his way. Just as she suspected, he was smiling at her, his dimples out in full force. His beautiful blue eyes were bright with mischief.

"You get back to your place at the wall." Torrent pointed at Tide. "My female is feeding our son."

Meghan looked over at the tiny baby. He was already four weeks old, and yet he was smaller than a newborn human baby would be at this age. She shrieked when Tide cupped her breasts through her white lab coat. He was still behind her. "I have my own mate," he growled. "I do not need to look at yours. My mate has amazing breasts. The best breasts I have ever—"

"Tide," she tried to keep her voice calm, "I'm working. This is inappropriate." Even as she said it, a warmth settled in her chest. *His mate.* She still had to pinch herself sometimes.

"What's inappropriate is him," Tide let her go and pointed at Torrent, "insinuating that I'm looking at Candy's breasts. Why would I do that when I have you?" Something in his gaze softened and she melted. Full on melted, even though he was being inappropriate.

"You two stop it." Candy laughed. "I swear you're like little boys sometimes."

"Take that back," Torrent grumbled, pretending to be upset. Meghan noticed that his mouth twitched with the need to smile. "I am a male in my prime."

"Yes you are, my love."

Torrent leaned in and kissed Candy. It was a quick brush of the lips and then he was turning back to her, a worried look on his face. "I'm not sure I want to do this."

"You don't want to know if our son is immune?" Candy asked.

"What if the whole therapy thing didn't work?" Torrent was looking back at Candy. "I'm worried."

Meghan realized that he was worried about the outcome rather than the actual procedure. "We don't have to do this today. The meeting between the four kingdoms is not taking place for another two weeks. We can postpone. A couple of days won't matter either way."

"Postponing won't help anything. Let's do this." Candy's gaze was locked with Torrent's.

The Water king took his time mulling it over. A whole range of emotions crossed his face. Starting with nervousness and ending with uncertainty. "You do realize that the outcome is even more important now than before?"

"I understand your apprehension, Torrent," Tide said.

"How could you? You don't have a son."

"I'm an uncle. I have a mate. I have some understanding." Meghan could see that Tide was working at keeping his voice calm.

"What if...?" Torrent's eyes were tormented.

"No what ifs, love," Candy said. "Not until we know for sure."

"Any more news on...?" Torrent turned his gaze to her.

Meghan shook her head. "I have a good idea about what is going on with the new species of dragon children, but my findings are not conclusive yet."

"A hint then?" Torrent pressed.

Meghan squeezed Tide's arm. She could feel him becoming agitated. "What if my theories are wrong? What if my assumptions are completely off the mark?" She shook her head. "I need a week – ten days tops – by then, the last of the test results will be in and I'll have conclusive evidence. I do expect the evidence to be firmly in line with the things that have happened."

"What does that mean?" Torrent widened his eyes. "You're speaking in riddles."

"I would rather not say anything more for now," she replied.

Torrent sighed. "I guess we'll have to wait."

"May I continue?" Meghan held up the needle in her hand.

Torrent's frown deepened. It took a few seconds for his features to soften... marginally at least. "Yes, doctor, you may proceed."

CHAPTER 31

Two weeks later . . .

"W elcome back to the Fire lair, Doctor Roberts," Blaze said, opening the file in front of him. "I hope you have some good news for us."

"I do." His mate nodded once. "At least, I believe the news to be good, although it's not exactly what we were hoping for."

Blaze sighed. "Oh boy, is that your way of preparing us for the worst?"

"Not at all." She turned the pages in the file on the table in front of her until she reached the one she was looking for. "First, some feedback on the new dragon species."

"Yes, our children." Blaze smiled and sat back, relaxing in his chair.

"The final results of the DNA testing I conducted came in last week. They are in line with what we are seeing in the children. I will state each case. Firstly, little Quake of the Earth kingdom. Capable of breathing fire. His marking showed flecks of gold. The little one has since also developed the ability to produce lightning…" She paused, expecting a reaction. There was none.

Meghan cleared her throat. "Blue flecks also appeared within the marking to match that ability. It is my understanding that camouflage – an Earth dragon trait – only appears once a child reaches five years of age." She looked over at Granite.

"Yes, that's correct. Otherwise we'd lose our babies and small children on a regular basis." He smiled, it was tense.

There were some laughs around the room but everyone quickly went back to looking at Meghan, waiting for her to continue. She sat right next to him this time. It was that, or not attend this meeting. Tide had been very fucking clear about that. They were right by the door as well. Just in case they needed to make a speedy exit. He was not putting his mate at risk. *Forget that!*

Meghan cleared her throat. "Another new development is with young Declan. He had green flecks appear in his chest marking, which is a sign that he is able to breathe underwater."

Granite nodded. "Yes, that's correct." This time the male's smile came easier. "Declan should be able to breathe underwater but my mate won't let me test the theory."

There were some chuckles and snickers. Tide had to smile as well. Meghan waited for things to quieten down before continuing. "That brings us to the Air prince and future heir to the crown. Your son, Thunder."

Thunder gave a deep nod.

"Young Bolt has developed the ability to produce lightning, as would be expected."

"No other abilities?" Coal piped up.

Meghan shook her head. "Nothing at this stage."

"So, the only normal child then," Volcano mumbled, folding his arms.

Meghan ignored the remark. "Fjord is seven weeks old." She beamed like the proud aunty she was. Oblivious to the potential fallout of what she was about to say. "The little one developed his green markings within the first two weeks, as is customary." Everyone hung on her every word. "However. He recently developed a new ability. He can…" She licked her lips smiling broadly, possibly a little too broadly. Okay, so she did have an understanding of how this could pan out. "He can breathe fire and has developed gold flecks within his outline."

Blaze frowned. "So, your son is able to breathe fire?" he asked Torrent.

"Yes." Tide could see that Torrent was working hard at looking relaxed. His hands were folded on his lap and he leaned back in his chair. The truth was, ever since little Fjord first breathed fire, Torrent had been on edge. Tide couldn't blame him one bit.

Granite seemed to relax, the male even huffed out a breath. It was as if he took solace in the fact that now at least he wasn't alone.

Meghan cleared her throat. "That brings us to the Fire youngsters. Firstly, Coal's son, Carmine, can both breathe fire and make lightening. He has the relevant markings. Blaze's son, Burn, can breathe fire."

"Finally," Granite mumbled. It was true, they had all been on eggshells waiting and praying the heir to the Fire throne would develop the ability. They could all breathe just a little easier now.

Meghan waited for the murmurs to die down. "He also has green markings to show that he can breathe underwater."

Blaze smiled. "I am happy to report that he can, in fact, breathe underwater. Since Burn is a now a little boy rather than a baby or toddler, we were able to test the ability, relatively risk-free."

"Wonderful news." Torrent looked like he meant it.

"So," Blaze clapped his hands together, "what does this all mean, Doctor Roberts?"

"I could delve deeply into DNA sequencing and even more deeply into… never mind…" She could already see their eyes haze over and their minds wander to other things. "I won't go into that kind of detail. What I can do is state categorically that there is definitely a fifth species of dragon. A species that is capable of all five abilities."

"I knew it!" Granite shouted. The others talked over each other. Meghan waited for the noise to die down. "All of the abilities are dominant traits in all of the children."

Tide could scarcely believe how relaxed Blaze looked. They had been expecting something along these lines though. The evidence certainly had pointed in this direction. Maybe that was it.

"Also," Meghan went on, her smile was wide and bright. His heart clenched just looking at her. "I'm happy to report that Fjord was born immune to silver."

The whole room rose to their feet. Thunder roared with excitement. Blaze clapped Coal on the back. Tide hugged Meghan and she hugged him back. It took long minutes before everyone was reasonably under control. "Creating a vaccine such as this won't be an overnight affair," Meghan cautioned.

"But in the meantime, we can keep up with the immunotherapy treatments in pregnant females," Blaze said, his chest expanding and contracting rapidly. Excitement was etched into his every feature.

"Yes, the programs will continue in each of the kingdoms. I am expecting more cases like Fjord." Meghan smiled.

"How long until the vaccine is ready?" Coal asked, also smiling. They all were.

"I can't say for sure. It could be months," she pulled in a deep breath, "but it could be years. The next step is to develop a trial vaccine and to begin testing it."

"How far are we away from that?" Blaze's brows were raised, his eyes were lit.

"If we can begin testing on grown shifter males, very soon, on account of your ability to heal so quickly."

"Done. Get started, Doctor Roberts. Inform me… us…" he looked around the room, "as soon as you have anything to report."

For the first time, ever, Tide felt a calm settle over the room. Could it be that their truce had now evolved into something more? Actual peace maybe? That they could finally call themselves united? Tide prayed it was true.

CHAPTER 32

Three and a half months later . . .

Her skirt was bunched up around her hips. Meghan moaned louder as he thrust into her warm, welcoming heat. Her lab coat hung open. Her blouse was unbuttoned and her glorious tits spilled over the tops of her bra cups. Her nipples were tight and dark. Her heavy mounds wobbled with each hard shove. *Fucking perfection.* Her mouth hung open. Her fingers dug into his shoulders.

They'd barely made it back to their chamber. He was fucking her up against the door. As hard as he tried, Tide still couldn't get enough of her. He needed to concentrate on the job at hand because there wasn't much time. His mate was on a half-hour break. Thirty short minutes and that included travel time.

Tide grinned at his female, even though his skin felt too tight, even though his balls were getting ready to shoot off. "Come for me, gorgeous," he growled. "I want to hear my name on those fuckable lips, Doctor Roberts." His voice sounded strained. Who could blame him? His female was tight and hot.

She somehow choked out a laugh between her cries of pleasure. "Stop… calling me… that." Another heavy moan.

"What?" he grunted, clenching his teeth for a moment. "Doctor…" *Thrust.* "Roberts?" *Harder thrust.* He didn't wait for a reply. "You…" *Thrust.* "like it." *Thrust.* "Doctor…" *More thrusting and much more grunting.* "Roberts."

She clutched his shoulders tighter, her eyes grew wider. Her moans and whimpers became more urgent.

"Makes you…" *Thrust, thrust.* "come." *Thrust.* "Every time." He bent his knees a little. Her ankles were locked at his back. Her lush as fuck thighs were around his waist. Those tits were bouncing now, despite the support. He jackknifed in and out, bouncing her on his dick. Even her cheeks bounced a little with each hard thrust. Her eyes were hazy. So fucking sexy, and all his. Every delectable curve. "Doc…tor… Rob…erts." Her eyes rolled back and she cried out as her pussy squeezed the fuck out of his dick.

Tide roared, he buried his head in her neck and bit down. *Not too hard! Not too…*

Meghan screamed his name, her whole body shook with the intensity of her orgasm. His shook just as hard. Tide fell to his knees. Sure to keep his hold on her. While she was much stronger than she used to be, she was still his to protect. He kept bouncing her, slowing down, his thrusts a little less urgent.

She was panting, working hard to catch her breath. Tide sat on his haunches, cradling her to his chest. Still deep inside her.

"You're good at that," she moaned, her head against his shoulder. "Very good."

"It's the reason you mated me." Tide chuckled. He knew that a statement like that would piss her off.

"It is not." She pulled back so that she could look him in his eyes. "I mated you because I love you."

"You love my dick." He grinned. "Admit it. That's why you kept my shirt after our first night together and why you shouted my name every time you used that purple, rubber cock."

Her eyes widened and she gasped. He loved messing with her. Loved! "I still can't believe you heard me that day when I... you know..." Her already flushed cheeks reddened up. "Even worse, I can't believe that Bay... heard me..." She groaned, covering her eyes with her hand.

"What?" He grinned. She was so cute when she was embarrassed. "Easing yourself?"

She groaned again, dropping her head back onto his chest. "I told you not to talk about it ever again. To pretend it never happened." Her words were muffled against him.

"Do you have any idea how many times I have replayed that moment in my mind? How many times I fisted my own cock thinking about you, my sweet little doctor?"

"Still..." Her face remained firmly planted in his chest.

"Still nothing. It's perfectly normal behavior." He smiled. "So I take it that you loved my gift?" Otherwise they wouldn't be here during a quick break.

She lifted her head. "So much. Thank you again. It's so thoughtful. You must have gone to so much trouble."

"It was nothing." It had only taken him three months to organize. He'd had to sneak measurements of her undergarments because the sets he bought were all custom-made.

She looked at him like he was mad. "I know it wasn't nothing. I've had these boobs since I was about sixteen years old. I know how hard it is to find a bra in my size. Especially ones like that." She looked at the large gift bag on the floor next to them. "They're so pretty. So lacey and silky. So colorful and beautiful."

"I'm glad you are happy."

"I am, I'm thrilled." She hugged him tightly. "I love you," she whispered in his ear.

"I love you too and as much as I'm enjoying being close to you, inside you…" He circled his hips, loving the feel of her around him. Hot and wet. So very wet. "We have to go soon. Our break is almost over."

She didn't react as he expected. There was no jumping up to her feet, or running for the shower. It wasn't like this was their first break-time sexcapade. "There was something I wanted to talk to you about." Her cheeks turned distinctly pinker.

"Oh yeah?" There was a questioning edge to his voice.

"Um… you know it looks like we've had a breakthrough with the vaccine?"

Tide grinned. "Yes. You are one hell of a scientist, doc."

"Lucky break. Besides, I wouldn't be able to push so

hard if my subjects were human."

"Please, you're brilliant. That's why we now have a vaccine."

"Not quite yet." She raised her brows.

"Soon then."

She grinned. "Yes, soon."

"Have I ever mentioned how your sheer brilliance is such a damned turn on?"

She smiled. "Yes, often."

"Good! Now, what is it you have on your mind?"

She chewed on her lip for a second or two. "Well, I was thinking that it might be time to start trying for a baby."

"You do?" he asked. Excitement coursed through him.

Meghan giggled, she nodded her head. "Yes. I do. I know how you really want to be a father and well, I feel the same." She laughed. "About being a mother that is."

"What about your asthma research?" he had to ask. "I know you planned on picking that up again." He frowned.

"I could start working on my asthma research during my maternity leave."

"What?" he growled. "You'll be busy, with the baby. You'll need your rest and…" He stopped himself from talking.

"You didn't think I would stop working entirely did you?"

He pushed out a breath and shook his head. "I guess not. You might be brilliant but you're also a workaholic. You have to agree to take the first few weeks off."

"Okay." Her smile grew wider.

"And, you start out half days for the first few months."

He narrowed his eyes at her.

She gasped. "Months? Months… that sounds long. I'll take the baby with me. I'm sure he'll sleep a ton in the early days anyway."

Tide could barely breathe. "You promise not to overdo it?"

"I promise to do my best and to always put our baby first."

"Are you sure you're ready?"

Meghan nodded, her eyes were both wide with excitement and hazy with emotions.

"It's a deal then." Tide pulled her close, hugging her tight. He was unable to get the goofy smile off of his face. It was the same one that he had seen on other males. Ones that were totally in love and willing to do crazy things for their females. He never thought he would like it on himself but he was wrong.

AUTHOR'S NOTE

A big and heartfelt thank you to you… my readers. For reading my work and for all your messages and emails. Also, to those of you that take the time to review my books. It means the world to me. You are what keeps me writing on days that I might not feel like it so much.

If you want to be kept updated on new releases please sign up to my Latest Release Newsletter to ensure that you don't miss out www.mad.ly/signups/96708/join. I promise not to spam you or divulge your email address to a third party. I send my mailing list an exclusive sneak peek prior to release. I would love to hear from you so please feel free to drop me a line charlene.hartnady@gmail.com.

Find me on Facebook—

www.facebook.com/authorhartnady

I live on an acre in the country with my gorgeous husband and three sons and an array of pets.

You can usually find me on the computer completely lost in worlds of my making. I believe that it is the small things that truly matter like that feeling you get when you start a new book or a particularly beautiful sunset.

BOOKS BY THIS AUTHOR

The Chosen Series:

Book 1 ~ Chosen by the Vampire Kings
Book 2 ~ Stolen by the Alpha Wolf
Book 3 ~ Unlikely Mates
Book 4 ~ Awakened by the Vampire Prince
Book 5 ~ Mated to the Vampire Kings (Short Novel)
Book 6 ~ Wolf Whisperer (Novella)

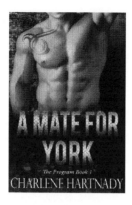

The Program Series (Vampire Novels):
Book 1 ~ A Mate for York
Book 2 ~ A Mate for Gideon
Book 3 ~ A Mate for Lazarus
Book 4 ~ A Mate for Griffin
Book 5 ~ A Mate for Lance
Book 6 ~ A Mate for Kai

Shifter Night:
Book 1 ~ Untethered
Book 2 ~ Unbound

Demon Chaser Series (No cliffhangers):
Book 1 ~ Omega
Book 2 ~ Alpha
Book 3 ~ Hybrid
Book 4 ~ Skin
Demon Chaser Boxed Set Book 1–3

UNTETHERED

SHIFTER NIGHT

CHARLENE HARTNADY

Shifter Night ~ Book 1

CHAPTER 1

Ana should never have agreed to coming to a place like this. The restaurant was a hive of activity. Every single table was taken. It was the best place to go to in town, so it wasn't that big of a surprise that even the waiting area and the bar were full. Crystal glasses, linen serviettes, the whole nine yards. It wasn't easy to get a table in here. The Red Mole was normally booked at least two weeks in advance. She'd only ever eaten here once for her best friend Edith's thirtieth birthday a couple of months ago.

Ana's heart beat faster. Her hands felt a little clammy and a knot formed in her stomach. Who was she kidding? The knot had been there the whole day. It had just grown and tightened since walking in. She stopped for a second to catch her breath. Then stayed there, hand resting on the wall, for another five just to be sure.

Was this normal nervousness or... something else?

Was she about to...?

She put a hand to her belly. Her breathing remained a little elevated, but nothing out of the ordinary. *I have this. I do!* Doctor Brenner had given her the go-ahead. It was just a stupid little date. Ana sucked in a deep breath and kept walking in the direction the hostess had pointed her. The table in the corner... to the left and...

There.

Right! Okay!

She could breathe a little easier since he looked just like his online picture. A suit, dark styled hair and a megawatt smile. Her date stood up... good god, he was tall too. In short, he was really good-looking in a neat, professional kind of way. His profile said he was an accountant, he looked like an accountant. It was a positive start. She willed her hands to stop shaking.

He stepped around the table and took a few steps towards her. "Hi, I'm Brett. You must be... Ana."

She said her name simultaneously, a nervous giggle escaped. Brett put his hand out and she shook it. His hand was soft, as was his skin. *Please don't let my hand feel sweaty. Please don't let me embarrass myself.*

Brett let go almost immediately, a smile still on his face. "It's so good to meet you. You look exactly like your picture." He gave her the once over and she could tell he liked what he saw. She had decided to go with a plain black figure-hugging dress. It came to just above the knee. Ana had taken the time to do her hair and to put on a little make-up. In short, she'd gone to a lot of trouble.

"So do you." Her voice was a little high-pitched.

"For a few minutes there, I thought you were going to stand me up." He arched a brow.

Ana smiled and shook her head. "I might be ten minutes late, but I would never not show." At least, not without telling him first. The thought of canceling had crossed her mind once or twice today.

"Here, allow me." Brett pulled a chair out for her.

"Thank you." She smiled at him as she sat down and he smiled back, taking his own seat opposite of her. So far so good. The knot in her stomach eased its hold just a smidgen and she could breathe a little easier.

The waitress came around to the table and took her order. A glass of white wine. Something light and easy, just like she hoped the evening would go.

Ana saw a tumbler of whiskey on the rocks already on the table. It was dripping with condensation. It looked like Brett had not only arrived on time but most likely, he'd arrived early. Another server came to the table with a basket of breads and a plate of different kinds of butter. "Truffle, herb and regular." He pointed at each of the creamy mounds before walking away.

"So, do you do this kind of thing regularly?" Brett asked as soon as they were alone, he leaned forward slightly in his chair.

Talk about hitting her with a difficult question right off the bat. "Um… are you talking about dating, or…?"

Brett chuckled. "Of course not, a woman like you must get asked out all the time. I'm sure you go on plenty of dates?"

Yeah… no! She smiled, hoping he wasn't expecting a reply. She couldn't tell him that this was her first date in one and a half years. She certainly couldn't tell him what a disaster her last date had been. She hadn't even made it to the one before that. *Not thinking about it!*

"I'm talking about online dating," Brett answered, not picking up on her discomfort. "Do you do this a lot?"

"This was the first time I tried online dating," she answered simply.

The waitress arrived with her chardonnay. "Would you

like some ice with that?"

Ana shook her head. "This is perfect, thanks."

"Are you ready to order your appetizers?" She held her pen poised over a pad. "The oysters are…"

"Give us a couple of minutes, please. We haven't even looked at the menus yet," Brett said, pointing at the leather-bound menus in front of them.

The waitress gave a nod. "No problem, take your time."

Ana picked up her menu. It would give her something to do with her hands which – thank god – had stopped shaking.

Brett drew her attention before she could open it. "Yeah, this is my first date where I had to swipe right." He smiled. "I must say, I'm glad it's not something you do all the time. I was a little worried about the kind of women I might meet through this type of service."

Ana wasn't sure what to say to that so she picked up her wine and took a sip. She gave a small nod to show that she was listening.

"Didn't you find it weird having to sift through all the profiles?"

"It *was* a little strange."

Brett picked up his menu but didn't open it. "I guess we live in a world where it's becoming more and more difficult to meet people in the regular fashion. I work twelve-hour days so…"

"I can understand how that must make it difficult."

"Yeah well, one must work hard to get ahead." He opened his menu but didn't look down. "I recently made partner at my firm." He took a sip of his whiskey.

"Oh, that's great. Congratulations!"

"Just last month and four years early."

Ana frowned. "Four years?"

"Yup, I had planned to make partner by forty. I'm only thirty-six so that's sooner than I'd anticipated."

"It certainly is. That's wonderful. You must be thrilled."

"I am." He looked serious for a moment, his brow creased and his lips pursed. "I have a four-bedroom home, with a pool and a big landscaped garden."

"Oh!" If he thought to impress her with money, he was sadly mistaken. "That's great!"

"Complete with a white picket fence." He swirled his glass. "Granite tops in the kitchen and marble finishes in all the bathrooms. It's quite lovely."

She nodded, taking another sip of her wine. "That's wonderful."

"All that's missing is a family." He was looking at her strangely, almost like he was judging her reaction. Maybe a guy like him had women coming onto him for his money.

Ana put down her glass, giving another nod. Maybe he just liked the attention that money brought him. Well, he was barking up the wrong tree. She scanned through the appetizers, a couple of things catching her eye.

"What do you do?" Brett picked up his own menu and opened it, he kept his eyes on her.

"I'm a nurse at the Sweetwater Hospital."

"Oh!" He smiled. "How nice!" The way he said it was kind of patronizing.

"I really enjoy my work, I've—"

"I guess being a medical worker is something that could come in handy." He rubbed his chin.

Ana frowned. "What do you mean?"

"In the home, that is. I'm sure you want to become a mother... have kids one day. Maybe even sooner rather than later?" He raised both brows.

"Yes." Her heart beat a little faster. "I would love to be a mom... one day that is." Her chest tightened. Ana picked up her glass and took a big glug of wine, not sure where this conversation was going. Not liking the direction.

"Shall I order some water?" He frowned, glancing at the

wine glass still in her hand. He had a look of disapproval but she knew she must be reading him wrong.

"Yes, that would be nice," she answered, trying to be polite. Ana put the wine glass back down.

He settled back in his chair and smiled at her. "It's good to know."

"What is?" she asked, as Brett flagged down one of the waiters and ordered water.

"Good to know that you want to be a mom." He turned back to her. "It's important to establish these things early."

What was he on about? He must have seen her confused look because he elaborated. "I'm looking for marriage and a family."

Ana took another big sip of her wine, her heart all a-flutter. Her stomach knotting back up. "This... um... this is our first date. It's too soon to —"

"It's never too soon to make your intentions known," he interrupted. "I'm looking for a wife... there, it's out. I know that most women want marriage and security so I doubt I'll have much trouble. I just don't want to waste my time, is all. I realize that not everyone is looking for the same thing. Not everyone wants kids." He paused. It was like he was waiting for her to interject if she had something to say. "That's why I was a bit worried about using a dating app. I'd heard that the people you meet... the type of person... some of them are just out for a good time..." He pulled a face. "Hey, are you okay? You look a little flustered."

"I'm fine." She tried to control her breathing. *I can handle this. I can!*

Brett gave a small nod. "So, you're not just here for sex, are you?"

"No," she blurted. "Not at all." *It's fine! It's all good.*

"Well, then we can relax and enjoy our date." He narrowed his eyes, leaning forward in his seat. "Are you sure you're okay?"

Ana gasped for air, her throat closing quickly. *Please no! No!*

"Can I pour you some water?"

Ana nodded. She was way beyond water. Way beyond trying to talk. *Shit! This isn't happening. It isn't!* The room was hot... that's why she felt flushed. That's why she couldn't breathe. *Damn! Dammit all to hell!*

Brett hurriedly poured water, some of it sloshed over the rim of the glass, his eyes were filled with concern. "You're sweating."

Gee, I hadn't noticed.

She grabbed the glass and tried to drink some but it gushed over her lips and down her neck. *Cold!* Ana swallowed the little bit she could. It felt like a rock trying to go down a straw. Her throat was officially closed. The room was both spinning and crystal clear, all at the same time.

Around them, waiters carried beautifully prepared meals and expensive bottles of wine. Diners chatted, drank and ate their meals, oblivious to the turmoil in the far corner of the room.

"What can I do?" Brett was out of his seat. "Are you having an allergic reaction? Do you have medication in your purse?" He lifted her purse from the chair next to her. "Is it in here? Try to breathe slower."

Gee, why hadn't I thought of that?

Ana realized that she was being a bitch but couldn't help it. She needed to get the hell out of there. She pushed her chair back, eliciting a hard scraping noise on the gleaming wooden floor. *Oh shit!* Now the people from the table next to them were gaping at her and one of the servers was making her way over, eyes wide.

Out!

Now!

She had to leave. If she made it outside and to the safety of her car she would be okay. It was a pity, but she didn't feel like that was going to happen. She was beginning to feel light-headed. Her stomach seemed to clamp and unclamp. Stars were beginning to flicker in and out of her vision. She felt dizzy… no, she felt… ill. Her legs might not work anymore but she needed to try.

"Out," she managed to somehow moan the word. She planted her hands on the table and used it to leverage herself up into a standing position. Well sort of. She was hunched over the table. Her glass of water tipped over, clanging as it hit, water soaked into the beautifully crisp white tablecloth.

"Ana," Brett kept calling her name. He clasped her elbow tightly. "Sit. You shouldn't be—"

Ana twisted around, trying to push past him… trying hard not to… her stomach gave a heave and out it came. The apple she'd munched on before coming here and the wine, her vomit was sour… it was disgusting and it was all over Brett's shoes, all over his left leg. He let go of her, taking a frantic step back. Then everything went black as she passed out.

Untethered—available now

21450058R00197

Printed in Poland
by Amazon Fulfillment
Poland Sp. z o.o., Wrocław